1/21

THAT
DARK
INFINITY

THAT DARK INFINITY

KATE PENTECOST

Ⓛ Ⓑ

LITTLE, BROWN AND COMPANY

New York Boston

Image credits: Page ii: skull © Jolygon/Shutterstock.com; flowers © mamita/Shutterstock.com; hourglass ornament throughout: © Yeroma/Shutterstock.com

Cover art copyright © 2021 by Ali Gulec. Cover design by Jenny Kimura. Cover copyright © 2021 by Hachette Book Group, Inc.

Little, Brown and Company
Hachette Book Group
1290 Avenue of the Americas, New York, NY 10104
Visit us at LBYR.com

First Edition: October 2021

Little, Brown and Company is a division of Hachette Book Group, Inc. The Little, Brown name and logo are trademarks of Hachette Book Group, Inc.

The publisher is not responsible for websites (or their content) that are not owned by the publisher.

Library of Congress Cataloging-in-Publication Data
Names: Pentecost, Kate, author.
Title: That dark infinity / by Kate Pentecost.
Description: First edition. | New York, NY: Little, Brown and Company, 2021. | Audience: Ages 14 & up. | Summary: Cursed with immortality, the Ankou has become a monster-hunter but when he meets Flora, the handmaiden who is prophesied to finally end his torment, he finds she has other priorities.
Identifiers: LCCN 2020047132 | ISBN 9780759557833 (hardcover) | ISBN 9780759557529 (ebook)
Subjects: CYAC: Immortality—Fiction. | Blessing and cursing—Fiction. | Fantasy.
Classification: LCC PZ7.1.P447375 Th 2021 | DDC [Fic]—dc23
LC record available at https://lccn.loc.gov/2020047132

ISBNs: 978-0-7595-5783-3 (hardcover), 978-0-7595-5752-9 (ebook)

Printed in the United States of America

LSC-C

Printing 1, 2021

"I am a forest and a night of dark trees: but he who is not afraid of my darkness will find rose-bowers too under my cypresses."

—FRIEDRICH NIETZSCHE, *Thus Spoke Zarathustra*

CHAPTER ONE

T WO MILES FROM THE VILLAGE OF IVO, IN A FOREST full of shifting shadows, a caravan stood alone in a shaft of moonlight. It was solid black, including the walls and the shutters and the curlicues of wood that ornamented the sides. The spokes of the wheels were black, the trimmings on the window and roof were black, and even the horses who pulled it were as black as the night they blended almost seamlessly into. This caravan was one of the greatest mysteries of Valacia, not because of anything about the caravan itself, but because of the one who drove it.

There was a stirring, and one of the two black draft horses lifted his head. A moment later, the door opened. A tall, angular young man stepped out onto the grass and yawned.

"Nik, Tal," he said, nodding to the horses. The young

man seemed like any other in Valacia: lanky and sharp-nosed, dark of hair and eye, with a smattering of patchy stubble on his chin. But his sleek black clothes, his broad black hat, and the tiny silver hourglass that hung around his neck marked this particular young man as the Ankou, the most fearsome and mysterious monster-slayer in all of the Five Lands—and the most abiding mystery.

He glanced upward, where the sky above the trees was just beginning to blacken. *Plenty of time until dawn,* he thought, and tossed a bundle of white sage into the fire. The sage began to smoke and billow, and the Ankou stood in its path, letting it permeate his hair and clothes. Soon, he began to cough. "I hate this stuff," he said to no one as he tried to wave it away from his face.

When he had cleared enough of it out of his eyes and nose, he reached into his pocket and pulled out the latest of several small black notebooks and opened the page he'd marked with a piece of charcoal. "Where was I? Oh yes..."

The word *possession* seemed to leap out at him from the page, and, following it, a brief description written in his own hand:

> Town healer bargained for greater power
> after failing to save child from sickness.
> Date of possession: unknown.

It was a classic story. A well-meaning healer had wanted to do something beyond her power and had paid ghastly consequences for it. This healer, unsurprisingly, had been a natural witch. Witches were very rare and had a subtle magic that was innate and touched everything, unlike mages whose big, flashy magic was limited to fire or water or whatever element they'd been born into. However, witches often resorted to more *drastic* means of getting what they wanted when things didn't go their way, and so once every few decades, he found himself on one of these cases. He heaved a world-weary sigh. Possession cases were always troublesome.

. *Animal victims:* _____.

He recalled his conversation with the town elder the previous evening. "When the animals began to disappear, were there any pieces left behind?"

"Whole," she'd said. "Save for a leg here, or a head there. But she always left the tongues."

Dismembered, he wrote in the blank. A bad sign. He went to the next line, and his hand hovered over the blank after *Human victims:* _____.

"Has she killed any people?" he'd asked next, hoping fervently for a no.

But the elder's wrinkles had deepened, and she said, in a voice so tired it rivaled his own, "We have no children anymore, thanks to her. They went missing, one by

3

one, starting about three months ago. And we began to find parts of them...wrapped in broad leaves, waiting on doorsteps..."

He shuddered. After *human victims*, the Ankou wrote, *Dismembered, eaten.*

The Ankou strongly preferred monsters to demons. When a demon possession case was so far gone that the victim resorted to killing humans, there was no saving them. He could only destroy whatever was left.

He shut his book and put it away. Then he strapped a silver greathammer to his back, cocked his broad black hat at his usual rakish angle, and headed out into the forest to find the demon.

The night was full of calls and cries and the fluttering of wings. The shadows seemed to deepen and grow, to flit and shift. Everything had a smell of frost and earth and cold, and the darkness was thick as velvet. Anyone else might have overlooked or misinterpreted the signs, but the Ankou found the demon's trail quickly. Disturbed ground made by human feet rather than deer hooves. A piece of cloth, torn from a shirt or tunic, resting in the leaves. And, most obviously, a smear of dried blood, stark against the silver of a birch tree trunk.

He followed these signs until the woods ended and he entered a clearing so misty he couldn't see the ground. In the back of the clearing were the remains of what once had been a cottage, short and squat, crouching in the mist. Inside, someone was standing there, still, watching him. A cold trickle ran up his spine.

In the lopsided black mouth that had once been the cottage door, the demon stood within the possessed witch's body, holding it so unnaturally still that the Ankou shuddered. The witch's dress hung in dirty shreds, and her nails made her hands appear long and clawlike. She took a step out onto the grass and sniffed the air like an animal.

"All that sage," the witch said, voice only vaguely human. "But still the stink of death beneath it... strange."

"Do you know who I am?" the Ankou asked. His voice cracked a little on *am*, but he hoped the demon wouldn't notice.

"Some young mercenary trying to make his name." The healer shrugged. "It doesn't matter to me as long as you're still tender."

As the Ankou stepped nearer, he could see something hanging around the demon's neck: a necklace made of white beads. He squinted. No, not beads. Children's milk teeth.

"Do you like my bauble, mercenary?" The witch grinned, pushing the teeth one by one along the string. "Perhaps when we're done I'll add a few of yours."

Something moved beneath the skin of the healer's cheek—crawled and disappeared again. So there really was nothing left of the victim, the Ankou thought, only the husk of her body. Having no one left to rescue made things easier.

"How long has it been since she came to you for power?" he asked.

"Eight years," said the witch, no . . . the *demon*. "Eight years of her blood in a teaspoon, and now there is only me."

So long, the Ankou thought. *No wonder. She must have fought against these urges for years without anyone knowing. And all for nothing.* But the Ankou could not spend too much time feeling sorry for her. The challenge came next. No one could defeat a demon without knowing the right name to banish it with.

The demon smiled, stretching the witch's mouth so wide that the corners of her dead flesh slowly tore. "And now I will taste new blood, mercenary. Yours."

The Ankou badly wanted to respond with something clever but couldn't think up anything like that on the spot—he never could, and it was one of his secret shames— so he just shrugged out of his black cloak and hung it on a nearby tree branch. Then he slid his falx—an ancient sickle-like blade—out of its sheath and faced the demon.

"Astaroth?" he asked.

"Ha! Trying to guess my name?" Jerky in its borrowed body, it stepped onto the dark leaves. "Good luck. I haven't been seen on this plane of existence in two hundred years."

Well, the Ankou thought, that narrowed it down quite a bit.

The demon's fists clenched and unclenched. It blinked its dead eyes, and its tongue flickered out between its lips like a snake's. A ball of pulsing darkness appeared in its hand, darker than the night around them. Then the demon slowly rose from the ground, floating in the healer's body, dirty bare feet just touching the leaves.

"Anamalech?" the Ankou asked. "Sabnok?"

The demon hurled the ball of darkness, its arm stretching farther than it should have been able to stretch, and the Ankou leapt out of the way as it hit a tree behind him.

"Vox?" he guessed as the leaves fell from the tree and went to dust. "Namtar?"

The dust began to whirl around the clearing. It thickened to an opaque blackness, and the demon disappeared completely. The Ankou saw shapes twisting in the black barrier around him like sculptures of smoke: faces with fangs, hands with claws, shadowy, twisted bodies that writhed and lunged out at him, but he knew it was all theatrics. Then the darkness drew back. It rose like a thunderhead before him, huge and ominous. He felt something behind him, but before he could lash his sword backward, the demon flashed into existence, one long claw sharp against his throat.

"My name," the demon hissed in his ear, "is Moloch!"

With a savage wrench, the demon slashed through the layers of bandages, deep into the Ankou's throat. His jugular severed. Blood burst, red and steaming, into the night air. He felt the heat and wetness of it running down his neck and closed his eyes tight, hoping against everything, praying for a miracle...

But the blood stopped.

Changed directions.

Climbed back up the Ankou's neck, back into his veins, like it always did. And as the Ankou's skin knitted itself back together, the demon glanced down and saw its claws clean of blood.

"This cannot be," it muttered.

But it could be, and it was, and it always would be.

"Moloch, was that it?" the Ankou said when his vocal cords were whole again.

"Wait!" the demon said.

But the Ankou drove his falx into the demon's stomach and pushed hard, holding the demon there on the curve of the blade. The demon lurched forward, clutching the blade, and gagged. Then its eyes went dark with recognition.

"I *know* you," it spluttered. "I have seen you in the Between!" It grinned, its too-wide mouth stretching into a bloody, toothy line. "You are the one who stands still at the place where all the worlds meet . . . waking and dying . . . waking and dying forever. The unholiest curse. And all for the love of a witch like this one."

Blood dribbled from the demon's mouth, and it began to change. Everything about it shifted until it was not the middle-aged healer, but a young woman impaled on the Ankou's sword, her olive skin paling with blood loss, her dark hair falling to her waist. The demon looked up at him with her eyes, Ana's eyes.

"Why, my love?" it said through bloody lips.

The Ankou gritted his teeth and pushed his falx all the way in to the hilt. "By your name I bind you, Moloch. Return to the place between worlds." He reached into his pocket and tossed a handful of black salt onto the demon.

There was a terrible sizzling sound, and the demon yowled. It writhed and sank to the ground, pulling his falx with it. But there was still the body to get rid of. The Ankou took the silver hammer from his back. Then, putting all his will into it, he brought it down on the demon with one great blow.

The demon's husk shattered like porcelain. Everything stopped. The swirling dust slowed and fell into a black circle around the Ankou; then the woods were still again.

"Well, that could've gone better," the Ankou said to himself when the fight was over. He was a bit embarrassed, really. The demon never should have gotten a hit in. But at least he'd gotten to see the shock on its face when his wound had closed.

Now I will taste new blood, mercenary. Yours.

The Ankou sighed. "*Too bad I don't bleed*," he said. "That's what I could have said. It would have been perfect."

He strapped the hammer back onto his back and rebandaged his neck, muttering to himself about creating a book of comebacks if he ever had to take another demon job.

It struck him, the silence of the clearing, the peace without the demon there in it. The sadness. Then, just for a moment, he pulled the small hourglass necklace from his shirt: the last reminder of his life before the curse. He held the hourglass in his palm like an amulet as he searched the bloody, ramshackle hut. He held it as he studied the slashes of blood on the walls, held it as he tore up the floorboards and found children's skulls, small and delicate.

Too late tugged around his ankles like a sad dog. Then

he let the hourglass rest outside his shirt and did not touch it again.

Invincibility had been interesting at first, and it was true that the curse had allowed him to do things that no other mercenary in history had done. But three centuries had passed, and still he was no closer to the end of his true mission: finding the cure for his curse. The Five Lands, which had once seemed so vast, now seemed as small and claustrophobic as a closet. There was nothing he had not seen, nothing new to explore. He had even begun to recognize the Black Caravan's tracks on most of the dirt roads in Valacia. That was when he had realized that, for all his travels, for all the generations of people he had watched born and grow old and die, he had only ever been going in circles. He shut the door to the healer's hut and pulled his cloak back over his shoulders.

He felt a cold prickle under his skin and then, from everywhere and nowhere, the demon's voice wound sinuously around him, getting one last taunt in before it had to leave this world. "You've heard what they say about you in the Between, haven't you?" it purred. "The way you can escape her power?"

"I know the prophecy," said the Ankou. "And so does everyone else in the Between, so spare me."

But the demon carried on in a singsong voice.

"Lightning from the very earth,
a hidden golden key,
and one whose palm is starry
as the sky above the sea.
If the bound one gathers them,
these destined items three,
he can walk the Fates unfettered,
and come back whole and free.
But if he cannot find them,
though faithful he may be,
then by her love she'll bind him,
and hers he'll ever be!"

"There's no use in being a sore loser, Moloch," said the Ankou. "I've already tried all of that nonsense. Now back to the Between."

"*Oh, I'm not the one who has lost,*" the demon said. "*I wouldn't have your fate for all the souls in ten worlds, Ankou.*"

Then, cackling, the demon leaked out of the plane of the living, back to the shadowy world where it belonged.

CHAPTER TWO

LESSONS WERE OVER, AND FLORELLE TANNETT LAY in the grass by the cliff, eyes closed, her long red-blond hair streaming out around her head like flames. Beside her, with straight brown hair intermingling with Flora's curls, lay Princess Betheara Ilurosa, future queen of the island city-state of Kaer-Ise. It was a warm day, and the two of them had stripped to their underdresses, feeling the cool ocean breeze, as they had so often done since their friendship began. Lying there in the grass, they could have been any two girls in the world. Except, of course, for the ornate white gold circlet Beth spun on her finger. That braided circle of gold and pearls, however small, marked them as inhabitants of two different, yet interconnected worlds. And as much as she was tempted to on occasion, Flora never let herself forget that.

"I just don't know," Beth was saying. "I know it's traditional, but I'm going to miss my hair. Do you think I can just give a royal decree that the hair-cutting part of the Calling ritual can be declared obsolete? I'm not going to look good with my head shaved."

"It won't be that bad," Flora said. "And think of what will happen if you don't. All the priestesses will be clutching their collars and saying what a rebellious princess you are—then somehow they'll blame me for being a bad influence as a handmaiden."

"Please," Beth said. "You're practically the Virtuous Goddess Emir yourself. You never bat your eyelashes at the guards or talk back to the tutors. You're the one who really should be princess of Kaer-Ise."

"You are kind of horrible at it," Flora said, not opening her eyes.

"Hey!" Beth hit her in the shoulder.

"I'm joking," Flora said. She sighed. "And you can complain all you want, but I'm kind of looking forward to my Calling. It's just so important, you know? So... ancient and sacred. Holding that golden bridle in your hands, sitting in the forest—"

"Waiting for an extinct creature to come and lay its head on your lap and let the world know you're a pure and virtuous maiden ready to go out and officially be a woman," Beth said. "I know, I know."

"It's our culture, Beth," Flora said, turning her head to look at her. And it was. The Calling of the Unicorn was a sacred part of Kaer-Isian life and had been even before the unicorn maidens of Kaer-Ise had ended the Necromancer's War three hundred years ago by calling the unicorns from the sea to slay the dead. They lost all the unicorns as a result, but after the war, Kaer-Ise finally gained the respect it was due from Valacia, directly south, Skaard to the north, and even Parth, far to the west. A Kaer-Isian maiden's Calling was a ceremony that invoked the goddess Emir, the maiden of eternal virtue, and even if unicorns were gone now, there was no more sacred ritual in all of Kaer-Ise.

"I know," said the princess. "I just think it's a little... outdated. The war was three hundred years ago. You don't see Valacians still hanging on to it like we do." She huffed. "You know, I'd love to see Valacia. Maybe when I'm queen. You'll go with me, of course, no matter what my husband will say."

Her husband. Beth hadn't chosen a suitor. She had recently refused an engagement to the prince of Skaard, and for a moment it had looked like it might get ugly between the two nations, but nothing had come of it. Still, the thought of Beth being married, about it not being just the two of them anymore, always made Flora's heart catch in her chest. It would be a husband for

Princess Betheara, of course, and not a wife, though women marrying women and men marrying men wasn't uncommon in Kaer-Ise. Beth only had eyes for handsome young men, and Flora...well...A beautiful girl could fluster her just as much as a handsome young man could. Not that she had told Beth this. Not yet. She would one day soon, but right now things were so good and uncomplicated that she hated to run the risk of anything changing. Still, she didn't want to think about Beth being married, so she said, "Where would you want to go if we went to Valacia?"

"Davasca," Beth said decidedly. "That water mage who does the tricks told me that the bazaar there is the best in the world, that it goes on and on and on forever and you can find anything you've ever dreamed of. Imagine all the interesting things we could find! All the people we could meet. Who knows?" She put a playfully eerie tone in her voice. "Maybe we could even meet the Ankou!"

"Beth!"

"Maybe he'd spirit us away in that Black Caravan!" Beth said, grabbing Flora's shoulder.

"Ugh, you know I hate those stories!"

"I wonder what he looks like under all that black?" Beth said. "I hear he's handsome."

"Gods, you're hopeless." Flora rolled over in the

grass. The sky had begun to change colors. Soon they'd have to go back to the palace. Flora peered into the forest that separated their cliff from the rest of Kaer-Ise. Sometimes, when she was little, she had imagined that a unicorn had survived somehow and was waiting for her there. Sometimes she almost thought she caught a glimpse of one through the trees. Absently, she pulled something from her pocket: a red pincushion stuck through with pins and needles. Her mother's. It was the only thing she'd had with her when she'd been taken in by the priestesses at the temple, after her mother died and before Betheara had chosen her out of all the orphans to be her handmaiden. Her prized possession. She held it up, letting the orange light of the sunset dance on the pins.

"Do you think Emir is really watching us, Flora?" Beth said. "Do you think there's really anybody or anything up there that cares?"

Flora thought about this. But before she could answer, a high, metallic peal broke the serene evening air. The alarm bells. And that could only mean one thing. For the first time in over three hundred years, Kaer-Ise was under attack. A sound of shouting rose all around them. A smell of smoke. And out beyond the cliffs, she could see the black silhouettes of dragon-headed ships. Skaardmen.

"Come on!" Flora shouted.

"But our dresses!" Beth cried, reaching for her gown.

"We don't have time for that!" Flora grabbed her hand. "Come on!" They left their dresses on the bush and rushed into the forest. Smoke was rising from beyond the trees and in the distance, Flora could hear shouting and the clash of steel. Then came the war drums. They seemed to shake the whole island, beating almost as loud as Flora's heart as she and Beth ran back toward the palace, hitching up their underdresses.

Back to the castle! The thought beat in Flora's brain. *To the castle!*

Beth's hand was in her own. Flora wished for her sword, to protect the princess as a handmaiden should. But she had left it back at the castle, because what cause would anyone have to attack Kaer-Ise?

Three horned shadows stepped into the path in front of them, eclipsing the light. Soldiers. Their swords were drawn, and in a moment, they would see Beth and Flora even in the shadows. *I must protect her,* Flora thought. *At all costs, I must protect her.* Before the Skaardmen could see them clearly, she took Beth's crown and put it on her own head.

"Run!" she whispered.

"But what will you—" Beth started.

"Just go! To the escape ships, through the forest! I'll hold them off! I'll lead them away."

"Flora!" Beth grabbed for Flora's hand, but Flora pulled it free.

"You are more important than I am!" Flora whisper-shouted. "Now go!"

And she threw the rock. The Skaardmen turned. They saw her, with her circlet shining in the light of battle fire.

"The princess!" one of them said. "There, with the red hair!"

She began to run, crossing their path, leading them away, so Beth could go onward. A final glance backward confirmed that, behind them, Beth was running, running toward the castle. To safety.

And Flora ran, too, clutching her mother's pincushion in her hand. The other way, through the forest, back toward the cliff, the only place she knew, far enough to give Beth time to escape.

But they were soldiers, fast and used to running, and as Flora's long red-blond hair streamed out behind her, she felt one of them grab it and yank hard, pulling her backward into their arms.

"Such pretty hair, Your Highness," one of them said, winding his fist into her curls to better hold her down. The nearest one began to unbuckle his belt.

"I thought she belonged to the prince?" another of them said.

"What the prince don't know won't hurt him." He wrenched the circlet from her head and threw it into the weeds. "Besides, you heard him: Leave no one alive."

Everything about her was screaming. She struggled, fought against them as well as she could, but they hit her, kicked her in the stomach, in the chest, in the ribs until she couldn't breathe. *I'm going to die*, she thought, a strange, faraway sort of thought removed from the agony of the moment. *I'm going to die now.*

As they pulled her into the darkness, as she clutched her mother's pincushion so hard that the pins pierced her hand, she saw the escape ships set sail. *Beth*, she thought. Then the sound of the ocean, the sound of the drums, rose and swallowed all.

CHAPTER THREE

T HE ANKOU DROVE THE CARAVAN ONTO THE NORTH-
ern road, following the smell of fire. He leaned
forward, craning his neck to see as far into the horizon
as he could, hoping that he was mistaken, that his senses
had gotten jumbled in his fight with the demon. But as
the Black Caravan drew farther northward, toward the
sea cliffs, the Ankou saw the source of the smoke.

Out in the sea, Kaer-Ise, the tiny island city-state
between Valacia and Skaard, was burning. He rum-
maged until he found his spyglass and squinted through
it, holding his breath. The mountains, the forests, the
palace, the castle town that spanned most of the island—
all was blooming into the sky like a great, angry flower.
A tremendous cloud of smoke hid half the stars. Corpses
of Kaer-Isian soldiers and citizens alike floated in the
ocean, littered the shore, washed in and out on bloody

waves, their bodies stuck through with arrows. This hadn't been a battle; it had been a massacre.

The Ankou dismounted and walked to the edge of the cliff. He could not imagine what could motivate such annihilation. Kaer-Ise was a peaceful place. The Kaer-Isians had not gloated or demanded recompense after their unicorn maidens had won the Necromancer's War for the Five Lands, even though their unicorns had been what finally defeated the dead. They had simply sailed back to their island, forever neutral throughout all the centuries of bickering between Skaard and Valacia.

In the light of the flames, he saw the remains of a dragon-headed longship smashed against the reef. So it had been the Skaardmen. It had been a harsh year in the north. There were stories of the Skaardmen running out of food, something about a failure of trade between the nations, but the Ankou had never understood economics. Perhaps snowbound struggle had driven them to take Kaer-Ise for their own. *Or perhaps*, a tired, cynical part of him thought, *Kaer-Ise's new prince is as truculent as the villagers said. Perhaps Kaer-Ise had merely been in the way.*

The Ankou scanned the beach, looking out over the bodies. At the water's edge was a pale white thing lying limp beside a piece of driftwood. The Ankou wasn't sure why he felt compelled to go and investigate it. Perhaps it was its starkness, its bright contrast against the dark stones and bloodied bodies. Perhaps he recognized it for what it was before his mind let him realize it. But none-theless, the Ankou found himself climbing down the cliffside, weaving through the silent bodies, toward the white thing on the beach.

It was a girl, he saw as he moved closer. A girl in a white underdress, lying faceup on the stony beach. Unlike the corpses that surrounded her, this girl was not shot through with arrows or maimed with blades. He couldn't tell much about her face due to the purple bruises that covered it. She was not yet twenty, though, because her long hair had not been shorn to her scalp, as was the custom when a Kaer-Isian maiden came of age. Instead, it lay lank around her body like seaweed. In the places where she was not black and blue, her skin had been paled nearly to transparency by the water. The ruined silk underdress, once plainly fine and luminous, had been ripped at the bodice. On her legs and thighs and ankles were five-fingered bruises. He did not have to look closer to understand what had happened to her, and it turned his stomach.

The Ankou removed his black gloves and put two fingers on her neck. There, beneath the transparent skin, he felt her pulse, slow but present. Working quickly, the

Ankou pushed down on her chest. *One, two, three, one, two, three.* He put his mouth on hers and breathed into her lungs, then pushed her chest again.

One, two, three, one, two, three.

Just when it seemed impossible, she began to cough and gasp. He tilted her head to the side, and she vomited seawater over the stones, wheezed, then fell back, unconscious but alive.

"Gods, that was close!" the Ankou breathed, sinking down beside her on the beach. *Now what?* he thought, looking down at her on the stones. He couldn't just leave her there. He supposed he could take her to the nearest city. Yes, that was a good idea. He would leave her at an inn. He would give her some money, of course. He would also leave instructions that no one was to touch her or he'd come in his caravan and . . . suck out their souls, or whatever it was that people thought he did in this part of the country.

As he wrapped her up in his cloak, he saw that she was clutching something in her hand. Gently, he pried open her fist, finger by finger, and a red pincushion fell to the stones. Her hand was marked with wounds. She had squeezed it until the pins had punctured her palm, and the wounds, washed free of blood, looked like . . . stars. Like stars in the night sky.

A tingle of recognition ran over the Ankou's skin. *One whose palm is starry as the sky above the sea.* He took a final look out at the remains of Kaer-Ise, the high black cloud of smoke. Then he gently lifted her in his arms and carried her up the ridge to where the Black Caravan waited.

CHAPTER FOUR

FLORELLE TANNETT LAY IN THE DARKNESS OF A room she did not know. She tried to move, to reach for her sword, but it wasn't there. Of course it wasn't there. Then came the pain, rushing to fill the emptiness that had come before. It pulsated through her head, her limbs, between her legs. She breathed in as deeply as her cracked ribs would allow. But instead of the sea, she smelled incense, spices, leather, and beneath it all, the smell of decay. When she tried to move her hand, she found that it was bandaged, as was her torso.

Princess Betheara's eyes in the dark. Flames. Screams. The sounds of the bells and the war drums. The princess shouting, "Flora!" Three Skaardmen holding her down. Her hand clasped around her mother's pincushion. Focusing on that pain instead until everything stopped. Then she was being carried... carried to the edge of the cliff. Suddenly, she was in the air, falling down, down, into the arms of the ocean.

She screwed her eyes shut and shuddered. It had been nightmarish. But it was no dream; it was real, every horrible part of it. And so was this, and so was she, wherever she was.

There was a sound. Someone was nearby in the dark, muttering to himself and rummaging through a cupboard. Her body tensed and fear woke inside her, humming in her bones. She lay as still as she could and prayed that the voice wasn't one of the Skaardmen's. One of Theirs.

"Silphium," the voice said. "Where is it?" Someone knocked things over and did not pick them up again, clattering and clanging. "Ugh! Of course I'm out of silphium. Just wonderful. Hmm. What was the other recipe? Blue cohosh . . . but where is the tansy?"

The high screech of the kettle sent a red flare of pain through her head. She opened her eyes just a crack. He was not a Skaardman. He was not pale and blue-eyed, with the curly blond hair all Skaardmen had. He was Valacian, lean and angular, olive-skinned and dark-eyed, with thick, black eyebrows. His shoulder-length hair was black, and when he tucked it behind his ear, Flora saw that his cartilage was pierced by three small silver hoops. (*An archaic style*, she thought.) He looked one, maybe two years older than herself.

But as he worked with his mortar and pestle,

something about him didn't seem young. He moved in the assured, world-weary, familiar way of someone much older. He spooned whatever he had been grinding into a steaming cup and stirred it vigorously. Then he bent over her and she froze, screwing her eyes shut.

"Um . . . I know you're awake," he said, his voice gentle but awkward. "And I know what has . . ." He paused, as though he were searching for the right words but was unable to find them. "What's happened to you. But I made you something, and it could help you if you want it."

Slowly, she opened her eyes. He was so close she could see the hollows of his cheeks. In his hand was the cup into which he had mixed the herbs and who knew what else. Her heart was pounding so loudly she was sure he could hear it.

"What is it?" she managed, her voice feeling like fire in her throat.

"This potion is for women who don't want to become mothers."

Oh.

This would keep her from being pregnant. Shame, guilt, revulsion swelled within her like a wave.

"I know how Kaer-Isians feel about this kind of thing. I know," he said. "And I won't lie to you: It'll make you very ill for a while. But it's early enough now to use it."

Flora shut her eyes tight again, wishing fervently that

she could go back to that place on the cliff with Beth and that the day could have just ended normally. That she could have gone back to the castle, gone to bed, woken up to a new day, anything rather than have to make a decision like this. She had always been so good, always done what she had been told, always honored Emir. Why had this happened? Why had this happened to *her*?

"Look," the young man was saying. "This has to be your choice. I'm not going to make it for you."

In Kaer-Ise, this was illegal. Against Emir. Against her culture. But she thought of her womb full with one of Their children and shuddered. She tried to speak, but her throat hurt too much. Instead, she nodded. Yes.

The young man tipped the cup into her mouth. The potion was bitter, even with the honey, but she drank it to the dregs. Then she drifted into unconsciousness and slept.

There wasn't much time left until dawn, but the potion he'd made was strong, and he doubted the girl would wake for the next few days. He had done what he could for her, and he was thankful that he'd happened to have most of the herbs on hand, and that the ones he hadn't had been easy to find. He had dressed her wounds and bandaged her ribs. He'd even brushed her hair as clean as he could without waking her again (quite a task with as much hair as she had). All that was left was to wait for her to bleed.

A fever came eventually, as he expected. In the long black tunic he had dressed her in, she seemed somehow even paler than ever. Her forehead glistened, and she winced as she fought through her nightmares. Of course, for her, the real nightmare would come when she woke.

Her people were gone. Her culture was gone. And after what had happened to her, even her "virtue," as Kaer-Isians called it, was gone. This girl, whoever she was, had nothing. If she were in Kaer-Ise, she would be punished for what had happened to her, held chin-deep in water for three days, then shunned until the next new moon. He didn't agree with that punishment, or many Kaer-Isian laws, for that matter. Then he had a thought: What if she turned to *him* for comfort? What would he say? He, of all people, could not simply tell her to be grateful to be alive.

He looked at her, asleep on the sofa. She had plainly been accustomed to some sort of luxury; this was no peasant girl. But her hands were not the soft hands of a lady of the court. And when she had woken, just for a moment, hadn't he seen her reach to her waist for a weapon? What had this girl been back on Kaer-Ise?

Outside, the horizon had begun to lighten. Dawn was coming.

The Ankou put the girl out of his mind and began his predawn routine. He bolted down all the windows, locked the caravan doors. Checked once, twice, three times. Then he went to the back of the caravan and shut his chamber door behind him. He took a deep breath, then lay in bed, waiting, counting down the seconds.

Three.

Two.

One.

His blood began to warm. Pain grew in his belly and vibrated through him, his ribs, his skull, his spine. His blood began to dry in his veins. Pain lit up every part of him, and his senses began to weaken and vanish. He shut his eyes so that he would not know the difference when his eyeballs were gone. Slowly, his flesh disappeared— tongue, liver, lungs—and he was simply there in the marrow of his bones, holding on for the last few seconds. Then he was wrenched away from his body, through a long, dark tunnel, and into the Between.

The Between was the night sky, far above and beyond Valacia, where the stars blazed in the cold, colorful silence. The Between was dark colors that shifted like a still life ruined by water and left to bleed. Some of the colors did not exist in the world of life, and in it he hung, his soul stuck, immovable.

Somewhere inside the Between, the Ankou could feel that familiar power, great and nameless, silent but present. The God of the Unknown. The Ankou had appealed to Her countless times in the past, but always She was silent.

The God and he were not the only ones in the Between. Souls streaked by, leaving phosphorescent trails like comets behind them. They shot from every angle, from every world—the Ankou had discovered long ago that there must be countless other worlds—and shot toward what lay beyond the Between: death and whatever came with it.

"*Teacht liom*," a soul said to him as it went past in a blur, coming from another world nearby.

"*Ven conmigo!*" said another, and though the Ankou did not know their language, he knew they were telling him to come on, to join them in death.

It was one of these spirits who had given him his title, the Ankou. Two men, presumably slain in battle, had seen him standing still as the others moved forward. "*Vous êtes l'Ankou! La mort sans mort!*" one had cried, and though the Ankou did not know which language they spoke, he understood it plainly in the Between.

You are the Ankou: the deathless death.

When his first client, centuries ago, asked what he should be called, he gave them that title (it didn't feel right to give them his name, after all) and the name had stuck. And now the Ankou was the name by which he was known in his world, and probably in a few others, too.

The deathless death. That was what he was. His soul was stuck, unable to move onward into death. And he could only hang there in the Between as the demons, dark blots of black against the color, darted among the worlds, beckoning to the occasional soul and striking their nefarious bargains. They had stopped trying to bargain with the Ankou long ago. Too many of them bore him a grudge.

"*Well, if it isn't the Ankou,*" a dark shape hissed. "*I'd say you're here more than I am these days.*"

"Moloch!" the Ankou said.

"*Tsk, tsk. You poor thing. Just like that man Lazarus, a thousand worlds away, wrenched from death back into life he never asked for. Except that eventually, even Lazarus got to die.*"

And the demon Moloch zoomed away to one of the other worlds, cackling as it went.

CHAPTER FIVE

THERE WAS A BUZZING IN THE NIGHT. A FLY. FLORA woke, groggy, her head spinning as the potion slowly faded. Then she smelled an odd combination of leather and incense and decay and remembered where she was: in a caravan with a young Valacian man she didn't know. Though she knew these things, they were...somehow unreal, sleepy and quiet and far away from Flora.

She felt strange. Not right somehow. It was because of the medicine the young man had given her, she was sure of it. Her senses seemed to open and expand, blurring, slurring, dreamlike. Her body still hurt, especially her ribs. Her womb felt as though it had been scraped hollow, her throat hurt horribly, and her head pounded.

Where was the boy who had saved her? And who was he?

Whoever he was, he didn't seem to be home at the

moment, so Flora rose to examine her surroundings. The fire was dying in the small iron stove across from her, but coals still glowed in its belly. She took a nearby candlestick from the little table near her cot and lit the wick on the coals. Then she saw that the soft thing she felt underfoot was a rug made of some sort of animal hide. White fur and scales. She stood on it and steadied herself, breathing in. The interior of the caravan was more spacious than she'd have thought a caravan would be—its ceilings were higher, more comfortable. She searched the room for an exit. There was a full-size door in the front room, just beyond her cot, locked with seven deadbolts. On the other side was a window, shuttered, which mirrored the window behind her cot. There was a small slit of a window at the very front, and when Flora slid it open she could see the horses' tails swishing in the cool air. There did not appear to be another exit.

It was a sad, strange home, Flora thought. But plainly well-loved.

Next to the locked door there was a small fireplace and chimney. The woods were dark and gray and soft beyond. There were more windows, one on each side and tightly shuttered, above built-in, cushioned seats, like the long one on which she had lain for who knows how long.

Flora opened a wardrobe. Inside hung all manner

of black clothing, made of fine material: black shirts, breeches, tunics, cloaks, capes. Flora reached in and touched one of the cloaks, feeling the fluidity of its fabric. There were patches, she noticed, here and there, only subtly different in texture. She ran her hands over the other clothes, over the black tunic she now was wearing. All had been mended at some point or another, all patched meticulously. Toward the back of the wardrobe, sitting atop a pile of ripped and torn black clothing, there was a needle, a thimble, and a spool of black thread.

Something prickled in her mind, a sense of familiarity. A tingle of fear. But the medicine had softened everything, dulled it, and as Flora closed the wardrobe and moved onward, the prickling in her mind left as quickly as it had come.

The next thing she noticed were the books. They were everywhere. On the seats, on the cupboards between colored glass bottles, stacked on the floor beside her makeshift bed. One row of small black leather-bound books that looked like hundreds of journals sat by themselves on the shelves. *He must like to read, and he must have a bit of money to be able to buy all of these.* It made sense, she supposed. Valacia was a wealthy country.

But there were other things that were less expected. In another cabinet, she found one large box of what looked like golden keys gathering dust. *Strange.* Then, in a barrel of coarse Kaer-Isian salt, she saw an arrangement of weapons, resting points down. The weapons were varied in purpose and origin (indeed, she had studied many of them as a handmaiden), but all must have been either galvanized steel or silver to not have corroded in the salt. All were honed and sharp, ready to be used at any moment. These, she saw, had no dust on them at all, as though they were used frequently. One was particularly interesting, a falx, an obscure weapon somewhere between a sickle and a machete, sharp, but ancient and well-worn. *Is he dangerous?* Nervousness grew inside her. But he had clearly meant her no harm. He'd saved her, hadn't he?

Suddenly, Flora felt someone watching her. On a small piece of parchment behind the weapons barrel, yellowed with age, was a portrait of a young woman. *Just a portrait.* Flora heaved a painful sigh of relief, then clutched her ribs. The girl in the portrait was exceedingly beautiful, with long, wavy black hair; dark eyes; thick, arched eyebrows; and a necklace that disappeared into her blouse. Something about her reminded Flora of her rescuer. A relative? A past lover? Whoever she was, she had been drawn with great care and love. Those eyes, especially . . . Her gaze was soft but intense. Uncomfortable.

The world seemed to spin just then, and weakness surged through her. The textures of the caravan seemed to blur, to melt together, then right themselves again.

Flora rubbed her temples and steadied her legs. She left the drawing behind, bracing herself against the built-in furniture, and in the corner, she saw a worn violin and bow leaning against the farthest barrel. At the very back of the caravan, there was a tapestry—an ancient tapestry that, to her surprise, was Kaer-Isian. It had the traditional curling, white-capped wave design over the body, with familiar stylized unicorns leaping over the waves. She reached out to touch it, to run her fingers down it—and felt something through the thin tapestry. A doorknob?

Flora pushed aside the tapestry. Behind it, there was a hidden door made of dark wood, somehow forbidding. She knocked timidly and waited. No response. Finally, she turned the knob and quietly pushed the door open.

For a moment, she could not see anything at all. But when her eyes adjusted to the darkness, she saw simple furniture, dark and plush, a worn rug on the floor beside a bed, in which lay—

Flora's breath went whooshing from her body. All haziness and dreaminess were gone and she was utterly, terrifyingly awake.

There, on a plain, broad bed covered in white linen, lay a skeleton.

It was wearing black breeches draped over the sharp blades of its hips. Its bony hands were grasping the coverlet, its eye sockets staring upward, its mouth hung open. And resting on its sternum was an hourglass necklace.

Flora knew him then. The Ankou. The thief of souls, the night-traveler of Valacia. She remembered the stories she'd heard from Beth and the other handmaidens, how if anyone climbed into the Black Caravan, the Ankou would ruin her, take her straight to Hell. Maybe he was already doing just that.

The fly buzzed over her shoulder and landed on the skeleton's jaw, then climbed into its open mouth and disappeared. Flora gagged and groped for the doorknob. But as she reached the door, she heard a sound that froze her blood in her veins and turned: The skeleton was regrowing its flesh. Spidery layers of muscle latched onto raw bone, veins crept over the muscle and filled with blood. Organs swelled like wineskins. The heart began to beat and lungs whooshed as they filled and released, filled and released. Eyeballs grew in the gaping sockets of the skull, and a tongue appeared between the jaws. Skin slithered over everything, and hair regrew itself, falling to the skeleton's shoulders. At last, the eyeballs hid themselves under new eyelids.

The Ankou didn't see her at first when he woke. He groaned and reached for a nearby clay pot and bent over it, coughing until black soil fell from his mouth. Then, when his coughing and retching was done, his eyes flickered open and locked with Flora's.

The Ankou looked just as shocked as she was for a moment, blinking as though he couldn't quite believe what was happening. When he spoke, his voice was rusty and inhuman-sounding.

"What . . . Why are you here?" he said.

"I'm sorry, Ankou, I . . ." Flora stumbled backward, reaching for the doorknob. "I didn't mean to . . . I—I just wondered . . ."

"Well, is this enough?" he snapped. "Am I as terrifying as the stories? Am I?"

Flora found the doorknob. A rush of fear-strength roared through her body, and she ran out of the Ankou's chamber, across the caravan, and to the door. She could hear the Ankou's footfalls behind her and she fumbled with the locks.

"Wait—" he said.

Flora pulled a dagger from the salt barrel. She slashed at him, slicing his hand open.

He cursed and drew back. Flora unlocked the door and fell onto the cold, damp leaves. The Ankou's big black horses stamped, startled, as Flora picked herself up and ran out into the misty darkness.

Ignoring the pain, she plunged into the forest,

darting between the trees, searching for a path. Vines and branches tore at her, but she struggled through them. She ran until she couldn't feel her feet and her broken ribs screamed in her chest. She turned, expecting to see the Ankou right behind her, his black horse rearing, a scythe in his hand.

But there was nothing. Only trees, vines, and dead leaves just curling with frost. Somewhere close by, a night bird called, and the sound echoed through the forest. Then there was silence.

Flora bent and clutched her knees, tried to catch her breath. She had gotten far, but the fear-strength was fading fast. She was growing dizzy again. Her legs were weak. When she reached out to steady herself, her hands touched something cold—a long, sharp rib. A jolt of horror rang through her, but it was only the skeleton of a deer whose antlers had gotten stuck in the branches of a small tree.

"Well, that was embarrassing," said a voice.

The Ankou came out of the darkness, whole and, from what she could tell, entirely human. She backed up and stumbled over a branch. Her heart was speeding. Her mouth was dry. She could only hope that whatever he planned to do to her, he would do it quickly. She squeezed her eyes shut and curled in upon herself.

"Sorry about that," he said. "For scaring you, I mean. I . . . don't usually have visitors."

"You're out for my soul," Flora said. "Or my blood or my—"

"I don't *do* that, I promise," said the Ankou, putting his hands up to show that he had nothing in them.

"But I saw—"

"What you saw was part of my curse, and I suppose I was taken aback since no one has ever walked in on me while it was happening before." He sighed. "Anyway . . . what is your name?"

"Florelle Tannett," she said, her heartbeat slowing just a bit. "Handmaiden to the princess Betheara Ilurosa of Kaer-Ise. So please let me go! My princess needs me, and—"

"Listen to me," the Ankou said, his eyes dark and grim. "Kaer-Ise has fallen. There is nothing left. No one left."

Flora's heart fell like a stone. "But . . . but surely there were survivors?"

The Ankou shook his head. "Not that I saw," he said. "On the northern beach, there were hundreds of bodies. You were the only one of them who was still alive."

"It was the Skaardmen," Flora said. "But why would they attack us? Because of the marriage proposal?" She pulled her sleeves down over her hands.

"Marriage proposal?"

"Beth—the princess. She received a marriage proposal from the prince of Skaard. She rejected it and he was angry. Very angry, according to the queen, but . . . all that for a rejection?" Then her chest constricted. *Princess Betheara.* Her voice grew frantic. "The royal family. Did they make it out?"

"I don't know," said the Ankou. "I wish I did. But I don't have answers for you, and we are twenty miles from the nearest town." He looked at her as though he wanted to say something else, then said, "Oh! I forgot." He reached into his pocket and pulled out her mother's pincushion. "This is yours," he said, and set it on the ground between them, as though she were a cornered animal he were trying to tame.

When she reached to take it, she saw the five-fingered bruises They had left on her wrists. She held the pincushion in her hand, feeling its warmth, remembering the pain. "Why did you save me?"

"I need your help to break my curse," he said, almost sheepishly.

Flora blinked. "What?"

"For three hundred years, I've been like this, alive at night, dead during the day. I can't be killed. I can't change or grow old. I've been between nineteen and twenty for three hundred years. I'll see kingdoms rise and fall and I can't even grow a mustache." He rubbed the little stubble he had ruefully.

Flora was silent. She wasn't sure what she had been expecting, but helping the Ankou break a curse of life and death wasn't it.

"I can't continue like this," he said. "With the curse unbroken, I'll remain this way until the end of the world. *Past* the end of the world, maybe, since nothing I've seen yet can kill me. It's the very worst thing that there can be. And I want . . . I just want *peace*. I just want *death*."

"But what do I know about curse breaking or killing anyone?" she said. "Why does it have to be me?"

"Gods," the Ankou said, rubbing his temples in frustration. "I suppose there's really no way around it, so here we go: There is a prophecy. About me. And it states that the only way I can be rid of the curse is to gather three things: lightning from the earth, a key, and . . . someone with stars on her palm. And when I saw your hand, I thought . . ."

She covered her bandaged hand with her other, unmarked one. "So you think I'm part of your prophecy."

He heaved the heaviest of sighs. "I *know* that it sounds ridiculous. But you're the only hope I have left. And I'll help you however I can in return. We're both pretty poor off right now, I'd say."

It was only then that Flora realized how dire her

situation was. She was alive, yes, but she didn't know how to hunt, nor to identify plants. She had no shoes for walking, and she would freeze in what she assumed were his thin black clothes—that is, if she ever found her way to a town. She was the only Kaer-Isian left in the world, as far as she knew, and she was shamed. She had no money, nothing to sell, not even anything to trade, except the gold in the pincushion's pins, but she could not sell or trade those, not in a million years.

Being in the princess's service had made her untouchable back on Kaer-Ise, but what was she now? What had she ever been but a glorified playmate? Now she had less value than the dirt she stood on, especially to the goddess Emir. Especially after what They had taken from her.

She looked at the Ankou shivering slightly in the cold night air, his face an open book. He needed her. He wouldn't harm her. And with him, she would be safe. Who would threaten the Ankou?

"I'll do it," she said finally. "I'll stay with you."

"Really?" the Ankou said, taking a step back in surprise. "You...you'd do that for me?"

"I'm doing it for me," she said. "And I do have a condition. You have to teach me to be a monster-slayer, like you are. Because my training didn't prepare me for what happened. It wasn't enough, and...and if I can do what you do, I'll never have to be afraid again."

The Ankou's face fell. "What I do is extremely dangerous. It would be ridiculous to—"

"More ridiculous than picking a girl up from the beach and asking her to help you die?"

"*I* have nothing to lose slaying monsters," he said. "That's why I do it: Because what else is invincibility good for? *You*, on the other hand—"

"What have I got to lose, exactly?" she asked bitterly.

She had him there. The Ankou considered this. "We have a deal," he said. "Though I hope, for your sake, you know what you're getting into."

CHAPTER SIX

THE ANKOU CLEARED HIS THROAT AND MADE ROOM for her at the small fold-out table in the caravan. "Would you like some tea?" That was what people said when they had guests.

"Um . . . yes," Flora said. "Please."

The Ankou put the kettle on the stove and filled it with water. He reached into the back of the pantry and pulled out two tiny teacups, which he discreetly dusted out with a rag. "I don't have anything to eat right now," he said. "But I can make a batch of scones, if you'd like."

"No, that's all right, I . . ." She paused. "You can bake scones? I just never thought of the Ankou baking."

"The Ankou can do whatever keeps him occupied for three hundred years," he said, a little offended. "Besides, it's not as though they're difficult."

"Oh . . . I'm sorry," she said.

"Forget it. You don't want scones. That's fine. Just . . . relax, I suppose. As well as you can in the circumstances." As if on cue, the kettle began to wail. He poured the tea into the two tiny cups. Flora took a sip of hers and, though she tried not to show it, she gagged before she swallowed. Valacian tea was quite bitter and smoky. Perhaps it was more of an acquired taste than he thought.

But she did not complain. She merely put the cup down with a delicate little clink on the saucer. "Where are we going?"

"Korwez first," he said. "To a small night market. I need to buy some supplies. It's been a long time since I've had a guest, and if I'm going to train you, you'll need clothes, boots, equipment. Then we can go from there. As for you, anything here is free for you to do with as you'd like, so . . ." He summed up the caravan's main room with a flap of his hand. Suddenly, all his possessions seemed shabbier than before, the caravan itself more cluttered. "Make yourself at home, Florelle."

"Flora is fine," she said.

Flora looked for a moment as though everything would be all right. Then he saw her face fall as she saw her reflection in the mirror that hung on the inside of his chamber's open door.

"What have They done to me?" she muttered, and

the Ankou could tell that the *they* had a capital letter in front of it. He didn't wonder who she meant.

She rose and stood in front of the mirror, taking in her appearance. Leaning forward, she touched her face, feeling its sharpness, maybe, its sunkenness, looking at her dry lips or the bruises that yellowed and greened along her cheekbone, eye, and jaw. Then her hands went to her hair, that beautiful, knee-length hair, now matted and full of leaves. "Do you have scissors? I can't keep my hair like this."

"I'm sorry," he said. "I did my best to get the salt and mats out, but all I had was—"

"It's not that," she said flatly. "I can't keep it long anymore. It's a symbol of virtue and . . . well." She looked away from her reflection. "I can't shave my head either, because that would mean I'd had my Calling. I have to do something else."

"Of course." He retrieved his sewing kit and handed Flora the scissors. She stood in front of the mirror for a moment more; then she took a deep breath and began to cut. He looked away as she cut off each spiral, each curl. It didn't feel right to watch. He focused on the white scales of the rug as the soft *snip, snip* of the scissors rose over the silence. Then the snipping stopped.

"That's it, I suppose," she said dully.

He turned back to her. Reflected in the mirror was a girl with short, wild, red-blond hair only a little longer than her chin. It didn't look bad, in all honesty. But see-ing her there, staring at herself with those sunken gray eyes, it felt like watching a one-girl funeral march. He didn't know her, but his heart hurt for her nonetheless.

He glanced at the halo of hair on the floor around her. After a Calling it was customary for the hair to be placed in trees so birds could use it for nesting, or so he'd heard. "What do you want done with—"

"It doesn't matter," she said. Then she turned to him and asked, "What should I call you? If we're going to be traveling together, I have to call you something besides Ankou."

"My name is . . ." He stopped. Nothing came to his mind. He tried again. "My *name* is . . ."

But there was simply nothing. "I'm sorry. I must have forgotten." He smoothed his hair and tried to act as though this didn't worry him. "I've spent too many years being called only the Ankou, I expect."

She was looking at him, waiting. Desperately, he tried to think of a name, any name. And the first that came to him was the one he had heard most recently, the name of another man who had come back from the dead, one who had gotten to die in the end.

"Lazarus," he said, the name rolling off his tongue easier than he'd thought. "Call me Lazarus for now."

CHAPTER SEVEN

THE ANKOU—LAZARUS, NOW—STOPPED THE BLACK Caravan in a copse of trees near the walls of Korwez. As he was fitting Nik and Tal with their feed bags, Flora wrapped a cloak around herself, shoved her feet into another set of his boots (comically large on her), and went to join him.

"Are you sure you feel ready to come to the market?" Lazarus asked. "You're not healed yet."

"If it's about me looking terrible, I'll keep my hood up," Flora said. "But if you're buying equipment for me, I need to be there. Besides, what if we hear about Kaer-Ise?"

"Fair enough," said Lazarus. "But I'll warn you right now: It's awful. Come now, stay close to me. We'll try to be quick." He took off toward the glow of the nearby market, and she jogged to keep pace with his long stride, following just behind: a black-clad shadow of a black-clad shadow.

When the gate opened for them and the market shone brilliantly beyond, Flora couldn't see anything awful about it. With its spiral of tents and booths, the night market of Korwez was a brightly colored, never-ending whirl of sights and sounds and smells. Blown-glass lanterns threw multicolored light down on the tent roofs and cobbled streets, turning them every color of the spectrum. Even their own black clothes took on the shifting, dark rainbow of a raven's wing. Everything smelled of spices and incense and fish and fruit, and a variety of oils and perfumes. All was hustle and bustle and movement and noise.

"Ugh," said Lazarus. "People. Just...well...stay close, so you don't get pickpocketed or anything." He pulled a square of folded paper from his pocket (a shopping list, she guessed) and opened it. "Don't worry. We'll be out of here soon. If everyone will just get out of the way."

Though the market was crowded, the townspeople parted on either side of them, wondering, probably, what the Ankou could need from their night market and who the cloaked figure following him could be. Flora was reminded of once when she and Beth had watched a school of fish avoiding a seal that had swum into their midst.

Then the whispers began.

"Is that the Ankou? It must be!" said a voice to her left.

"He doesn't look no older than my boy," Flora heard one man say to another.

"I didn't think the Ankou would look like that," one girl said to another, their eyes slipping appreciatively over him. Then they saw her. "Who's that with him?"

"Look away, Doro, look away, or he'll take your soul," said a mother to her son. "See? He's already got somebody!"

She looked up at Lazarus. It was plain that he was pretending not to notice. "Come," he said, eyes forward. "Don't let it get to you."

They stopped at a vegetable stand and bought two cabbages, a bundle of carrots, and a bag of potatoes, and moved on to a nearby tent with tunics and breeches and cloaks hanging on lines just outside. The saleswoman's face paled when she saw Lazarus, then grew quizzical when she saw Flora behind him.

"I need several items, please," Lazarus said, showing the list to the woman. "To fit her."

The woman glanced at Flora. "I'll need to do a fitting," she said.

"I'm sorry, but that won't be possible," said Lazarus. "I need these items in the nearest estimation of her size. Quickly."

The woman nodded, gave Flora a long look, then disappeared into the back. She returned with a large bundle of clothing. Lazarus paid several silver coins, and they left with three tunics, a pair of thick leggings, and a dark green woolen cloak.

At a cobbler's he bought her a pair of boots that were both stylish and sturdy, and two cakes of soap (one plain and one that smelled vaguely of violets).

"That's it," he said, heavily laden with packages. "The whole list. Unless you can think of anything else you need?"

But before Flora could respond, she heard someone say, "Kaer-Ise? Completely ransacked." Her heart thudded in her chest. She found herself drifting toward the voice.

Lazarus grabbed her hand. "Wait," he said. "If they see us, they'll scatter and stop talking. Better to keep out of sight." He pulled her behind a stack of apple crates close to the speakers.

A textile merchant said to the man at the thread

booth next door, "We won't be getting any more ship-
ments of dye from them, and neither will anybody else,
for that matter. Expect the prices to go up."

"You can only be neutral for so long before you make
enemies of everyone," said the thread man. "At least
with an island the size of Kaer-Ise. Better them than us,
though, when it comes down to it. Three pints of indigo,
correct?"

His words sent a cold wind across her heart. She
leaned closer to listen.

"Three pints, yes," said the textile merchant. He
continued. "But come now, man. The Kaer-Isians
didn't deserve that, no matter what they did. They were
slaughtered. Just rounded up and executed. The Skaardmen burned everything, then destroyed the dikes and
flooded the city, just for spite. Showed them no mercy
whatsoever."

Lazarus said something to her then, but she could not
hear it. Everything was gone. Kaer-Ise truly destroyed.
Gone forever. She could barely fathom it. Grief and
shame hit her like a wave. Grief for her people; shame
for what had happened to her. Suddenly, she knew how
fish must feel when they are pulled from the water to
gasp in the air.

But the conversation wasn't over.

"The princess should have just cut her losses and married him is all I can say."

Flora's hands clenched into fists. Her heart roared like the sea, so loud it seemed it would burst her eardrums.

"That was just an excuse for Skaard, I think," the man said. "What it came down to in the end is that the Skaardmen wanted Kaer-Ise and made up their mind to take it one way or the other."

Tears began to leave hot trails down her cheeks.

"We can leave if—" Lazarus started, but Flora paid him no mind.

"I think if Kaer-Ise'd just had some backbone, none of this would have happened," said the thread man, measuring out three pints of indigo dye. "If they'd just been like Parth a hundred years ago and closed their doors—to us, too, mind you, I'm a fair man—it wouldn't ever have happened. They'd be well-off."

"We don't know how Parth is faring, do we? And besides, for Kaer-Ise, that would have been like building a knee-high fence to keep out a pack of wolves."

"Didn't any of them get away?" asked a woman nearby, examining a skein of yarn. "What about the royal family?"

Flora stopped breathing. Everything else in the world went quiet but the conversation she was straining to hear.

"Word is, the royal family of Kaer-Ise got out in an escape ship, all three of them," said the textile merchant as he took his bottles of indigo and put them gently in his satchel. "But no one knows what happened next. Some say the sea swallowed them. Some say the Skaardmen caught them. Some say they landed in Valacia and are making their way inward."

So Beth did escape, Flora thought, relief washing over her like a warm breeze. *Beth and her parents. Thank Emir! Thank Emir!*

"Do you think there will be war?" the woman asked, her voice high and nervous. "Do you think the Skaardmen will come here looking for them?"

"Don't you worry, Mum. They've stood down. Those Skaardmen wanted to make a threat to us, but they're too afraid to come for us proper. They could have used Kaer-Ise as a fortress if they hadn't been so intent on flooding it and destroying everything. They've got no advantage. Besides, we have twice the people, twice the army."

"Twice the mouths to feed," muttered the thread man. "And half the goods we owe to Skaard after the war because of it. You'd think three hundred years of peace would have settled things."

"I can't imagine the fear they must have felt," said the woman. "Never have I heard of anything like that."

Something flashing and sharp caught Flora's eye. Something familiar. Without thinking, she darted from behind the apple crates and went to the booth.

"Flora!" Lazarus said, but she ignored him. "Flora!" he said again, and she heard him leave his place behind the crates and follow her. "What are you doing?"

The conversation came to an abrupt halt as they approached, as Lazarus had said it would. But Flora didn't care. In the back, hanging on the wall, gleaming, was a silver sword with a leaf-shaped blade.

"Ankou!" the textile merchant said, his voice shaking with nervousness. "I didn't know you had joined our market tonight. How may I be of service?"

"That's a handmaiden's sword," Flora whispered to Lazarus, her eyes never leaving it. "I think it might be mine. Please."

"That sword." Lazarus nodded to it. "Is it Kaer-Isian?"

"Yes," said the textile merchant. "Might be the last of its kind."

"Let me see it," Lazarus said.

Obediently, the man passed him the sword and the Ankou held it in his hands, checking its straightness, its balance. Then he gave it to Flora. As she gripped it, she felt like she'd gotten a part of herself back. The textile merchant eyed her with interest and just a tiny bit of fear.

"How much for it?" asked Lazarus.

"Uh . . . it's not . . . ," the man started. "I mean . . ."

"How much?" Lazarus said again, and she heard him put a little steel to the edge of his voice.

The textile man sweated. "Uh . . . three hundred silver?" he said. "I couldn't take less after the massacre. Scarcity, you know."

Lazarus laid down three hundred-pieces as though it were nothing. "Thank you," he said. "No need to wrap it up. We'll carry it out."

And with that, they left the textile merchant blinking in surprise—already aching, no doubt, to tell someone the story of the Ankou and the strange cloaked girl who had bought a Kaer-Isian sword from him.

"Thank you," Flora said to Lazarus as they left the market and headed back to the caravan. "Thank you so much."

"Don't thank me," Lazarus said. "It was your property to begin with. But now that you've heard that dreadful conversation, what do you plan to do?"

"Go to Davasca," she said. "If Beth and her family did make it out on an escape ship, I know that's where she would go. How far away is it?"

"Far," said Lazarus. "But don't worry. As we travel, just focus on what we might find there. Maybe we will find your princess."

"And maybe we will find your death," she said.

"One can only hope," said Lazarus.

CHAPTER EIGHT

THE WHEELS OF THE CARAVAN TURNED EVER onward through the nights, their steady rhythm lulling Flora into ease as she healed from her wounds and her nightmares faded. She felt like a stranger at first, an intruder into the Ankou's private life, but gradually her own life in the caravan grew from a shadowy half-existence into its own strange sort of routine. Day became night for her as she began to sleep during the day and wake when the Ankou rebuilt himself.

Lazarus, as it turned out, was not so much frightening as he was peculiar. He spent a good deal of time dressing and making sure that his hat sat at just the right angle, and he never spoke to anyone unless he had to—even to Flora. The caravan was cluttered, but he often said, "Everything is just where I need it. It's efficient."

And he was absolutely nonverbal for about two hours after he rebuilt himself in the evenings.

Yet for all his strangeness, he was trying to make things easier. He frequently cooked for her: pork and mutton, custard-like cakes with plums and apples, crêpes with meat fillings flavored with juniper and cardamom. But she never had an appetite. She was too numb for that still and instead spent time reading Lazarus's small black notebooks, which he used to catalog his various missions, as he called them. The stories in the books were often full of pain and death, and if she wasn't careful, the real horror of her own situation would drift into her mind like smoke and stay there, obscuring everything. When this happened, she put Lazarus's books down and instead let herself get lost in the memory of the smell of the castle, the color of Beth's eyes, the roar of the sea.

"I've read everything," she said to Lazarus one night. "I'm ready to train."

"How do you banish a ghost?" Lazarus asked, not taking his eyes from the road.

"Oh, come on!" said Flora.

"This is serious business!" Lazarus said, blowing hair out of his eyes. "You said you wanted to learn to do what I do. And what I do is more than simply *fighting things*."

"Fine. You tell them their names, weaken them with water, and bid them gone three times."

"How do you *keep* them out?" Lazarus asked.

"Four sprinkles of black salt and pine tar painted in the corners of the house."

"Five," said Lazarus.

"*Five*, then. I was close."

"Close can get you killed. How do you tell if a baby is human or a changeling?"

"Please, Lazarus," she said. "I need to do something besides read and...and think. And you promised, remember? We made a deal."

"All right," groaned Lazarus. "But there's a lot to do before you even think of going into battle, do you understand?"

Flora nodded.

As it turned out, what Lazarus meant was that she needed to undergo what he called physical conditioning. This began with learning three types of punches, three types of kicks, and three types of blocks, then practicing them over and over and over again. When these were easy, Lazarus added in throwing knives at several targets (bags of salt that Lazarus had helpfully written things like *wyvern* and *striga* on), then picking them up and trying over and over again until her muscles ached and her chest burned. The idea was to make her more physically fit (and, Flora suspected, to persuade her not to go through with fighting monsters herself). But Flora was seized by a sense of nearly otherworldly determination and threw herself into physical conditioning with all the strength she possessed.

The one thing that Lazarus seemed to be avoiding was swordplay—the one thing that she already had experience in. So one night, after he rebuilt himself and came out into the main room of the caravan, she asked him about it.

"You're not ready," he said bluntly.

"I already know swordplay," she said. "I just need to learn to . . . specialize."

Lazarus cocked a skeptical eyebrow at her.

"Princess Betheara and I studied it since we were five years old. Handmaidens have to, you know."

"Were you taught anything about fighting honorably?" he asked.

"Don't strike when your opponent is down," Flora recited. "Don't hit the . . . um . . . below the belt. Only attack if you're attacked."

Lazarus drew the caravan to a halt and dismounted. "Well, tonight, I want you to forget all of that. Tonight, if you are truly ready, we can begin in earnest."

Finally, Flora thought. *We're getting somewhere.* And she grabbed her sword from the salt barrel and followed him.

"All right, here's what you've got to do," Lazarus said as they stood in the clearing. "Always aim for the most vulnerable parts. Eyes, throat, neck, ribs, knees, groin—all the things an honorable fighter should never attack. Most creatures have those parts in one way or another. You have to make every strike count. But first, three hundred thrusts followed by three hundred parries, then we can think about sparring."

"I thought we were going straight into it!" Flora said. "I don't need a foundation in this. I already have one!" She groaned. "I feel like I'm standing still. How will this help me when I'm on my own?"

"Have you ever even drawn blood?" Lazarus asked.

Flora bit her lip and said nothing.

"And you think you're ready to fight the things I fight with a few quick swordplay techniques. I see. Well, let's look at what you've got. Run me through."

"Run you through?"

"What's the use of practicing with someone who can't die unless you use the situation to its full advantage?" He paused for dramatic effect, opening his arms wide in a T pose. "Unless you'd like to call the whole thing off. In which case, I understand and completely support your decision."

"Oh, I get it now," Flora said. "You're afraid I'll get killed and your curse will never be broken, so you're trying to scare me. Very noble of you."

"Look, if you are squeamish at the sight of blood, you'll never make it as a mercenary," said Lazarus. "So why not find out now, instead of in battle?"

Flora pursed her lips. He had a point and she knew it. "Fine," she said eventually. "I'll do it." She planted her feet and held her sword in the classic upper-class fencing stance. "But you have to pretend to fight me or something. Just . . . *do* something so I can react to it."

"All right," Lazarus said. "When I come forward, try to hit me. And if you get the chance, run me through."

He came toward her, and she swung out at him, once, twice. Their swords clanged together, flashing in the moonlight. She was far better than he anticipated, quick and sure. But the things he fought would not play by the rules of fencing. He spun and pivoted behind her, then grabbed a handful of her hair. "They may try to attack you like this, especially striga," he said. "So if this happens, I want you to take the sword in your hand, and thrust backward with it like—Flora?"

Something was wrong. Flora had gone stiff and her breath was coming in gasps. He could see her pulse ticking in her neck.

"No . . . no . . . ," she whimpered, the sword dropping from shaking hands.

"Flora, it's just me," Lazarus started. But Flora didn't hear him. Instead, she fell to her knees, shaking. And suddenly he knew. She was not there in the clearing with him any longer. She was back on Kaer-Ise, reliving it all. And he had caused it. "Oh gods. Oh no..."

A small animal noise came out of her throat, and she crumpled into the leaves. Lazarus got on his knees in front of her. "Flora," he said as calmly and steadily as he could. "Flora, listen to my voice. What happened to you is over. You're safe. It's all right. You're safe."

Flora shuddered and sobbed. Then she rose and vomited into the leaves. She turned back to him, still shaking, but her eyes had lost some of that unfocused, terrified look. Slowly, she was coming back to herself.

"Are you all right?" he asked, being careful not to move too quickly, careful not to frighten her again. "Gods, Flora, are you all right?"

"One of Them grabbed me by the hair like that," she said finally. "He thought I was the princess. Told me I had...such pretty hair." She sobbed again.

Lazarus had never felt so low in his life. "I'm so sorry, Flora. I should've known. I shouldn't have—"

"It's all right," she said, taking a handkerchief from her pocket and wiping her face. "It's all right...You're right. I've got to master this."

"No. *I* can't do this," he said. "Not if this is going to happen every time. I think we're better off—"

"I can do it."

"This is not the time for stubbornness!" he said. "You can't train for what I do without close contact! It's crucial. I don't think you can—"

There was a sharp, excruciating pain and a sickening *squish*. Lazarus looked down and saw her sword buried deep between his ribs.

"I *said* I can do it!" she said, her teeth gritted, her hands shaking. "Now you keep your promise, and I'll keep mine."

"All right," Lazarus gasped. "I'll keep my promise."

Flora nodded. Then she pulled her sword out of his chest.

"Doesn't that hurt?" she asked as the wound healed itself.

"I'm used to it," Lazarus groaned as the blood drained out of his clothes and the wound knitted itself back together.

"Don't ever underestimate me again," she said.

"Don't worry," he said, smoothing the skin where the wound had been. "I won't."

The nights went on. They passed down white stone roads, rode alongside rivers whose bends had narrowed over the hundreds of years Lazarus had known them. And as they traveled, peace grew between them. No, not quite a peace. That wasn't the right word. A respect.

After the night that Flora stabbed him, something seemed to have changed between them. Lazarus could not tell exactly what it was. She had gone in his mind from being something to be taken care of to someone who took care of herself. It began to feel almost normal having her around, if *normal* was a word that could be applied to a relationship in which he was stabbed, sliced, and run through multiple times every night. The silences that fell between them began to feel somehow comfortable.

Twenty miles from Davasca, they sat by the fire, Lazarus mending some shirts and Flora doing something very peculiar. One by one, she was taking certain weapons and tying little strips of cloth around the pommels.

"They don't need decoration," Lazarus said.

"I'm marking the ones I prefer so I can remember them. And you're wrong." She held a beribboned dirk up into the light. "They're much better this way."

"If you say so," said Lazarus. "But leave my things plain."

"Of course." She regarded him over the fire, watching him sew.

"What are you looking at?" he said, his eyes narrowed.

"Nothing," she said, tying up another bow. "You're just . . . not what the stories made me think you'd be."

"Which stories?" Lazarus asked. "The ones where I can disappear into thin air, or the ones where I prophesy the deaths of everyone in whatever region I'm in? Or maybe the ones where I turn into all sorts of animals?"

"The one I heard the most was that you were a demonic rake," she said. "That you seduced young ladies and carried them away to a life of sin in your Black Caravan. Then you discarded them by the side of the road, used and stripped of virtue, old women before their time."

"Pfff!" Lazarus snorted. "Surely not."

"Those were the stories!" Flora said. "Why do you think I was so afraid when I knew that you were the Ankou?"

"It's just so ridiculous." Lazarus laughed. "Of all the things to become through folklore, a rake was one I hadn't expected."

"Why?" said Flora. "Look at you with your hat and your hair. And I've seen the way people look at you every time we pass through a village. Afraid but *intrigued*."

"The *Life of Sin in the Black Caravan* business is particularly funny. I haven't lain with anyone in three hundred years."

"That seems like a long time," said Flora.

"Well, think about it. What if, after a dalliance with

a girl in a village or something, I passed my curse on to her? Or worse, what if I fathered a child with my curse?" Lazarus shook his head. "It's not worth it. So I've been . . . alone." He blinked in realization. "You're the first person I've spoken to for longer than maybe a paragraph in over a hundred years."

They were quiet for a moment, letting the fire crackle between them. He could feel her pity for him heavying the air.

"I'm sorry," she said.

"Eh, what can you do?" Lazarus sighed. "Life goes on, as they say, even if none of it means anything. So I keep busy. I've taught myself drawing, painting, the violin, the viola, the guitar, baking, sewing, mapmaking, weaving, haberdashery—I made this hat—and so many other things. I have many talents now. Thank you, immortality."

"Maybe in three hundred years I can learn to be useful again, too," Flora said, her eyes on the fire. "It all just feels so far away. Where am I now? Who am I now? I feel so . . . stuck."

"But you can grow and change," Lazarus said. "I will always be the same, but you improve every day. You already have done so—you are doing very well. Maybe you can even make a career out of demon hunting when I am gone. Be the next Ankou or something."

"If only I could learn to turn into different animals," she joked but he could tell that she was pleased. Still, there were things that worried him. He looked at her, at the shadows beneath her eyes, the hollows under her cheekbones.

"Have you eaten today?" Lazarus asked, trying to sound casual.

"I ate some soup," she said. "After the first time you asked me."

"Sorry," he said. "I'm just trying to help."

"I know," she said. "It's all right."

Flora lined up the sharpened, ribbon-marked weapons in a row on the ground. "Who is the girl in the picture, back in the caravan?"

"Ana," Lazarus said, her name a dull weight on his tongue. "She was a girl in my village, far to the east. We fell deeply into a love that consumed both of us body and soul." He took a deep breath. It had been a long time since he'd spoken of Ana to anyone. "We planned to leave our village together, to move to a city somewhere. But then the dead came walking, and our village was one of the first that was hit. After that I got the curse. I stayed away as long as I could. And when I returned, seventy-five years later, I was the Ankou, and my people had gone."

"What happened to Ana?" Flora asked. "And how did you get your curse?"

But Lazarus was tired, and as Flora sat across from him, with her scarred hand and her long Kaer-Isian hair cut short, he knew that he could not tell her. Not yet. "We will save that for another time," he said. "Suffice it to say that it was all born from a love so intense that it will never have an equal."

A silence fell over them, and Flora finished the last of her ribboned weapons.

"There is another story of the Ankou in Kaer-Ise," Flora said. "I never liked the other ones, but I liked this one. In it, you were a hunter. The best in the land, and the most arrogant. One day Death challenged you to hunt a mysterious black stag. You tried and tried, but when you couldn't kill it, Death punished you for your hubris by making you roam the forests at night hunting whatever it is that needs to die, until Death finally takes pity on you." She smiled to herself. "It's more poetic than real life, I think."

"Stories always are," said Lazarus, looking into the fire.

CHAPTER NINE

IT WAS JUST BEFORE DAWN WHEN THE CARAVAN crossed the drawbridge into Davasca, and as the sky began to lighten at the edges and simmer with the promise of the coming sun, Flora was growing impatient and Lazarus was growing nervous.

"Wait for me, Flora," Lazarus said loudly, tying the horses and securing their feed bags before he climbed back into the caravan and went about his routine for his daily death. "Don't go by yourself, please."

Flora, itching to find out more about Beth and her family, didn't bother to disguise her irritation. "I can manage alone. Otherwise, what has all this training been for?" She secured a cloak around her shoulders and pulled on her boots.

"It only takes one time for something to happen and

you to be killed or worse," Lazarus said. "I'd really prefer to be with you. You don't know what it's like here."

Flora rolled her eyes. "Kaer-Ise was smaller, sure, but I know what cities are like, Lazarus. I'm not a child." She pulled her sword and three beribboned dirks from the salt barrel and made a show of securing them on her person. "Besides, if I find out everything I need to know, we can leave without you having to even get out of the caravan."

"But—" Lazarus started. Then, from a tower somewhere in Davasca, a bell chimed a mechanical song. Dawn was coming.

"I'll be back before nightfall," Flora said, climbing out of the caravan. "I promise!"

Lazarus shut the door behind her, and she heard the locks click. He gave her a disapproving look through the window, then closed the curtains.

He'll get over it, Flora said to herself. Pushing Lazarus and his paranoia to the back of her mind, she turned to get her first good look at the morning in weeks. The sun rose over the arches and gabled roofs of Davasca, bright and brilliant, and after becoming basically nocturnal as of late, Flora's heart ached at the sight. Tired but invigorated, she was glad to have this moment to herself.

All around her, Davasca was awakening. Windows

were opening, shutters were being thrown wide, people were coming out of their houses, and smoke rose from chimneys. She heard horses' hooves on cobblestone, the hustle and bustle of people going to and fro, the chatter of women on their way to market.

She did not have to look for very long before she saw red flags tied high up on the lampposts, leading toward the bazaar, no doubt. Flora followed the flags, holding her nose at the smell of the tanners' shops and passing a particularly colorful sign (NEW PRINTING PRESS! FIVE COLORS!). The crowd thickened as she traveled, and when she removed her hand from her nose, she smelled roasting nuts and fresh fruits and incense.

Flora realized she missed the day. She missed people. Not people cowering in fear or giving her and Lazarus a wide berth, but people laughing, running, smiling, living their lives. She was fascinated with all the different types of Valacian people. Pale skinned, dark skinned; fair-haired, black-haired; short, tall, and everything in between. Flora had never seen such a variety of people in one place before. She was puzzled, however, that the couples she saw greeting each other in the streets were only boy-with-girl or girl-with-boy. Never two boys or two girls, as had been very common in Kaer-Ise. The mages had never mentioned this, nor had Princess Betheara, who had been to Valacia twice with her parents. Of course, Beth had preferred men to women, so she may not have even noticed. Flora wondered what Beth would say if she were with her now.

She would think Lazarus is handsome, Flora thought. *Just like all the girls do.* Then she had another thought. *Would Lazarus think Beth is beautiful if they met?* The princess had long, dark hair and eyelashes like Ana had in Lazarus's drawing. Beth was delicate and shapely, with an alluring laugh and eyes the color of the shifting sea. A jolt of something like jealousy ran through Flora, and she suddenly felt very uncomfortable.

Fortunately, she didn't have long to ponder the feeling. She turned the final corner, and the bazaar spread before her, an endless tapestry of color and motion, an enormous maze of booths that stretched out under the banners and multicolored smoke as far as she could see. Excitement and nervousness flickered through her, and with a deep breath, she dove into the crowd.

In Kaer-Ise, crowds had parted for her and the princess when they went to the market. People had genuflected, lowered their voices, taken off their hats, and smiled as the girls passed. People had offered her white roses and called her Daughter of Emir. But here, there were no images of Beth's family staring down from sea-colored stained-glass windows, no waving poplars, no sound of the sea. All of that was gone. Now she was just a fair-haired girl in black, milling around the bazaar, asking odd questions and not buying anything.

Twelve hours later, Flora sat by a fountain near the center of the bazaar, her head pounding and her heart sinking so low she could almost feel it in the soles of her aching feet. She had asked every shopkeeper, every booth man, every likely looking bazaar-goer, even the women selling cream-filled "unicorn horn" pastries from a cart by the apothecary, and no one had heard anything about the royal family of Kaer-Ise. For the life of her, she couldn't think of who else to ask, where else to look.

Is this it? Flora asked herself. *Is this the end of it?* She thought of Princess Betheara, of the pincushion in her pocket. She thought of Lazarus and his prophecy, how the star-palmed person would give him direction. What would she tell him when she went back to the caravan?

Flora looked at the rows of booths she had already visited. The old woman at the used book booth was pulling a cloth down from a painting set up on an easel in her booth. When she saw it, Flora felt a sharp, unexplainable tug in her heart. It was a temple carved into a cliffside, with columns and arches, and steps leading up into a rectangle of mysterious blackness. Flora *knew* this place, knew it beyond knowing.

Flora headed to the booth again. "Excuse me."

"I already told you, dear, I don't know anything about the Kaer-Isian royals, and neither does anybody else," the old woman said.

"I'm not here for that," Flora said. "I'm here for—"

"And I don't sell anything Anky-related," the old woman said, her eyes flickering over Flora's clothes. "No scarves, no skulls, no rings for your nose, or any of that nonsense. So unless you're here to buy a book, you'd best be on your way."

"I am not an Anky, whatever that is," Flora said. "I just want to know—where is that?" She pointed to the painting of the temple built into the cliffside. "What is that place?"

The old woman took in Flora's messy hair, her plain black clothes, green cloak, and boots. "You're the girl who came from the Black Caravan earlier, aren't you?" she said, as though this new information made her regret sending her away before. "I'm afraid the place in that painting doesn't exist, dear. The Temple of Fates is what it's called. It's just a story. Though some would say your lover was just a story if they hadn't seen him driving that caravan through the gates this morning."

"Laza—I mean, the Ankou—is *not* my lover!" Flora said, blushing deeply at the very thought. "We're traveling together right now. I'm looking for the Kaer-Isian royal family. And...and this place feels..." She struggled to find the words. "It feels significant somehow."

"I'm surprised you don't know the stories." The old woman smiled. "But I can't vouch for everyone's grandmothers and the stories they choose to pass down." She leaned forward. "No one knows where it is, or how it works, but the story is that if somebody goes into the Temple of Fates and completes three tasks, they will be granted anything they want, no matter how impossible."

"Anything?" Flora said. She thought of Princess Betheara laughing with her back on Kaer-Ise. She thought of their Callings, just a month apart, of unicorns—real, living ones—coming out of the forest to lay their heads down in their laps like they did with the maidens of old. She thought of Kaer-Ise resurrected, full, repaired, untouched. Herself untouched.

"So if someone found it, they could undo something horrible?" she heard herself ask. "Make everything all right again?"

"But of course it's only a story," the old woman said. "Long ago, before the Necromancer's War, bands of knights set out looking for it. Lots and lots of them.

No one ever found anything. It's been mainly forgotten these days."

"Do you have any books about it?" Flora asked. "I have money."

"Not in a long time," said the old woman. "Sorry, dear."

Flora's heart sank again. It must have shown on her face, because the old woman said, "I can tell you where you can find someone who's as good as a hundred books. He lives here in this very town. A lightning mage. Name's Dr. Kell, and if I remember correctly, he's studying the temple and old myths like that."

It was better than nothing. The sun had already begun to sink over the city's labyrinth of roofs and chimneys. Soon Lazarus would be alive again, and she wanted to have something to tell him, some direction to give him. And, sure, this Temple of Fates business might amount to nothing, but it *felt* different when she thought about it. Destined. And, at the very least, what could it hurt?

"Where does Dr. Kell live?" Flora asked.

"Just down that street there," said the old woman. "The tall yellow house at the very end. Name's on the door."

"Thank you!" said Flora, giving the old woman five silver coins.

"I will warn you, dearie!" the old woman shouted. "He's a bit of a strange one!"

"Then we should get along just fine!" said Flora. And she headed off toward the big yellow house, as the sun was setting, hoping that Lazarus would forgive her for being a little late.

Lazarus rebuilt himself as usual when the last bit of orange disappeared over the horizon. He coughed the dirt from his lungs into the pot beside his bed, then rose and dressed. Flora had not returned.

I knew it, he thought. *Something awful has happened, and now I have to go find her.*

He went to the washbasin and freshened up, ready to rush out and track her down. But as he glanced into the mirror while buttoning his shirt, he saw something that made the new blood stop in his veins.

A black mark on his side, stretching under his rib cage.

A mark that he'd never had before.

He rebuilt exactly the same way every day, with no exceptions, not even a pimple or a gray hair. This mark...this was something else. Something sinister. It was shaped almost like a hand reaching across his torso.

A sensation of blanching dread and recognition flashed over him. But how was this possible? And what would this mark do to him?

He buttoned his shirt quickly, hiding the mark under black fabric. But he had seen the fear in his own eyes when he glanced into the mirror. He turned to Ana's portrait. From her place on the wall, Ana's beautiful face gave no answers.

For the first time in longer than he could remember, Lazarus felt the urge to talk to someone. He needed to confide in someone. He needed to find Flora, not just for her sake, but for his own. Quickly, Lazarus threw on his cloak and his broad black hat. Then he climbed out of the caravan and went into the city of Davasca to look for her.

CHAPTER TEN

THE HOUSE WAS BRIGHT YELLOW, WITH A NEEDLE-like spindle that reminded Flora of a wasp's stinger. An alarming number of pigeons gathered on the windowsills of this house. Tall and teetering and covered with birds, the house was definitely strange. Flora could easily see how the old woman had thought the house's owner a little odd. But maybe he, out of everyone in Davasca, would have something useful for her, something to go on. A sign painted onto the frosted glass door of the yellow house read:

DR. ATONAIS KELL,
PHYSICIAN OF MAGIC:
ORDER OF LIGHTNING, 2ND CLASS
SCHOLAR AND INVENTOR

Flora took a deep breath, then she rapped on the door and waited.

She rapped again. When there was still no answer, she lifted the brass lid on what a nearby sign called a "voice pipe" and shouted into the tube. "Doctor, please! I just want to talk to you!"

Still, nothing stirred inside the house.

Flora jumped as the nearest streetlamp flared with strange, cool white light. Against that unnatural light, the sky was fading from blue to black. Lazarus was definitely alive by now. She had to get back to the caravan. Flora scrambled down the street, and as she turned around a corner, she collided with the largest of three men.

"Watch where you're going!" the man shouted from behind a thick black mustache.

"Pardon me," she said. "I'm just heading back to..."

She tried to push past, but the men didn't move. Instead, they came closer, towering over her, smelling of ale and sweat. In the light of the streetlamps, she could see their broad grins. Their eyes crawled over her, up and down.

"Look at this little red fox, wearing men's clothes, with her hair cut short," the biggest man said. "Not a clever fox, though, to approach a pack of hounds."

The second man, tall and thin, nudged the big man and gave him a wide smile. The third man gave a lascivious howl and laughed. "Wonder what she's hiding under them breeches? Smile, girl, let's see how many good teeth you got left."

Flora did not smile.

"No," she said. "Get away from me."

They came forward, began circling her, and without thinking, she moved into the stance that Lazarus had taught her.

"Well, well, look at Foxy," the man with the mustache said.

"You weren't what we were hunting for tonight," the thin man sneered, eyes crawling up and down her body once more. "But you'll do."

"I said no," Flora growled.

"No?" The big man laughed. "No don't mean anything anymore. Look what happened to Kaer-Ise when the princess said no."

She felt the swell of an ocean rising within her.

The dark waves crashed.

Crack! Her elbow connected with the big man's nose. His friend lunged forward, but she blocked his attack. He staggered back, and she slammed her elbow into the third man's stomach. They stumbled and fell, but the waves were crashing inside Flora. She wanted to destroy them all with her bare hands. She wanted to destroy everything about them.

When the big man, blinded by blood, threw a punch, she dodged it easily and felled him with a kick. He was on his back, the wind knocked out of him. She fought savagely. *Making it count.*

"Oh gods!" the thin man shouted. "Run!"

Flora kept punching, stomping, pounding with her fists and feet. Blood began to redden the ground. A tooth skittered onto the pavement. The big man whimpered, tried to raise his hands to shield his face, but she put her knees on his arms and held him down, his back against the cold cobblestones.

"Stop . . . ," he croaked, "please . . ."

Inside, the dark waves leapt, crashed again, and Flora kept hitting him, even though tears rolled down her face. Even though a small pitiful voice in the back of her mind told her that she had heard those words before. The stormy ocean inside her was bigger than herself, big enough to swallow fleets of ships.

The sounds of fighting were unmistakable, and as Lazarus turned the corner, he stopped midstride. Flora had a man pinned down and was beating him to a pulp as the man's friends retreated into the shadows. Blood spattered and beaded on her hands. She was in a trance, like the trances he'd seen berserkers go into during the Necromancer's War.

"FLORA!" he shouted. "FLORA, STOP!"

Flora's fists stopped in midair. She shook herself as though waking from a dream. Then she looked down at the man on the ground. The man's face was already swelling. Three of his teeth lay in puddles of blood on the pavement. But he was alive.

Lazarus rolled the man onto his stomach with his boot. The man groaned. He would be fine, Lazarus knew. His nose was broken, as was his right cheekbone. But he would live. It was Flora he was worried about. "Are you all right? What happened?"

Flora clutched her shirt over her heart, her gray eyes wide and staring. Her breath came in short, sharp gasps. "There were three of them!" she said. "They were going to...they were going to hurt me like...just like the Skaardmen. And I...I..." She shuddered all over, her bloody fist clenched over the fabric of her tunic.

The bastards. They deserved what Flora had given them and more. But he saw how Flora was shaking, how she stared at the blood she had spilled, and worry rose and doused everything else. "Here, step back," Lazarus said gently. "Come."

He pulled Flora behind him. The man pushed himself onto all fours and rose, shaking, to his feet. He took one look at Lazarus and paled beneath the blood.

"Go," Lazarus said, knowing full well the terrifying picture he presented in the dark alleyway. "And if you or your men ever touch anyone like that again, you'll find me on your doorstep one dark night, ready to take your soul." He pulled out the hourglass from under his shirt and held it up for the man to see. "Or should I take it now?"

The man cried out and ran, limping, leaving a trail of blood on the pavement behind him.

"Filth," Lazarus said.

Flora was staring down at the teeth she had knocked from him, lying in their pool of blood. "He said stop," Flora said softly. "He said *stop* just like I did...a-and I..."

"No. No, no, no, no, no, this isn't like that." Lazarus reached out to touch her shoulder, but she jerked away.

"It's the same. It's the same." Her whole body shook all over. "I need to be alone," she said. Without another word, she disappeared into the dark streets.

High on top of the wall that fortified Davasca, Flora sat, staring into the filthy moat below. After she had cried out all her tears, she felt empty and shaky, drained and angry, sad and ashamed and righteous at once. Her fists were red and torn, and her knuckles hurt. She imagined herself again and again, beating the man in the alley. Inside her, the roaring ocean echoed, and she shuddered. Then, from the ground below, she heard a very familiar set of footsteps.

"Are you all right, Flora?" came Lazarus's voice.

"No," she said.

"May I come up?"

Flora shrugged and kept looking out at the moat. She heard the boxes creak as Lazarus climbed onto the wall. He sat down beside her, long legs dangling.

"Are you going to say it?" Flora asked, not looking at him.

"Say what?" he asked.

" 'I told you so.' Or 'See, Flora? All it takes is one time.' "

"No," he said. "There's no point in it now." He held out his hand. "Let me see."

She gingerly put her hand in his, and gently he inspected her knuckles.

"Not too bad," he said. "Good thing you'd already built up some calluses."

She didn't say anything. She just sat there, quiet, and

he did the same. In the silence, the high tide inside her began to ebb, and her breathing came easier.

"The water down there is filthy," Flora said finally, without knowing why. She shivered and shut her eyes tight.

Lazarus took off his cloak and put it over her shoulders, a second layer over her own. She clenched her fists and pain radiated through them. She began to sob again, deep and racking, like she hadn't since the day she'd found out about Kaer-Ise.

"I hate Them," she heard herself say suddenly. "I hate how They've made me become like Them."

Lazarus hesitated for a moment, then he put his arm around her and pulled her into a surprisingly gentle embrace. "You could never be like Them."

A tear slipped down her cheek and disappeared into the folds of his shirt. No, she couldn't, she thought. But to hear someone say it took a weight off her shoulders, made her seem like a person again instead of a monster. She closed her eyes and breathed. Spices, leather, earth, decay. It was a calming smell, one that grounded her in the here, the now. She pressed her ear against his chest. Beneath his breastbone, Lazarus's heartbeat, quick, steady, alive.

She sat up again, remembering herself, and pulled

away, glad that it was too dark for him to see her blush. Beth *would* have found him handsome. Flora was sure of it. Lazarus *was* handsome, she realized. But there was more to him than most people saw. Others saw a brooding young rake, as she had at first, but they didn't get close enough to see through the artifice to what lay beneath. Certainly Beth, with all her flirtatiousness, wouldn't look close enough to see how tired he was beneath his youthful exterior. For all her beauty, she wouldn't see how the very act of being alive seemed to draw his whole body downward, draining him of color. His young face looked exhausted, more tired than she'd ever seen him.

"You really do want to die, don't you?"

"Yes," Lazarus said, not looking at her. "I really do. *You* don't want to die, though, do you?" He was trying to sound casual, but she could tell that her question had worried him.

"No," Flora said, her voice heavy. "I don't want to die."

"Good," he said, sounding relieved. He was quiet for a few moments, then he said, "Why are you looking for the royal family? If you don't mind, I mean."

"They're the closest thing to a family I've ever had. And Princess Betheara . . . she was—*is*—the closest person in the world to me." She tried to think of a way to put her complicated feelings for Beth into words. "I loved her," Flora said finally, and even though she had thought before she spoke, using the past tense about Beth felt quietly shocking.

"Ah," said Lazarus.

"It's unethical, of course," Flora went on, her face growing hot. "I mean, I was her handmaiden and she was my ruler. Besides, she wasn't in love with me. Princess Betheara only liked men, and I...I like men and women."

"Ah," Lazarus said again. It was different from the first *ah*.

"But, still, I..." She trailed off, unsure what to say.

"Don't worry," he said. "We'll find out what happened to her. I promise."

They sat in silence for a moment. Flora wasn't sure why she had bothered to clarify her preferences. But Lazarus was a Valacian, and for some reason she felt like she had to explain, so he wouldn't get the wrong idea. But a tiny part of her mind wondered why she wanted him to know.

"Did you find anything today?" he asked.

"I didn't," she said. "I'm sorry."

"Don't worry," said Lazarus. "We'll find something. I'm sure of it."

"What are the words of your prophecy again?" she asked. "You told me once, but I've forgotten."

Lazarus recited, *"Lightning from the very earth, a hidden golden key, and one whose palm is starry as the sky above the sea. If the bound one gathers them, these destined items three, he can walk the Fates unfettered, and come back whole and free."*

"That sounds promising," Flora said, looking down at the scars on her hand, the stars. "If I'm really the star-palmed person."

"There's more," Lazarus said. "There's always more with these kinds of things." He cleared his throat and continued. *"But if he cannot find them, though faithful he may be, then by her love she'll bind him, and hers he'll ever be."*

"Hers?" Flora asked.

"Ana's," Lazarus said. "She was a witch. She had the best of intentions when she cast the spell, as people often do, but . . . it's complicated, and only growing more complicated."

Ana. Of course. Everything with Lazarus went back to Ana, that beautiful woman who died three hundred years ago. *It's a good thing Beth isn't here to develop an infatuation with Lazarus,* Flora thought. *No one could ever compete with Ana, even though she was the one who cursed him.*

Flora started to ask what he meant by it growing more complicated, but Lazarus turned to her and asked,

"What were you doing in that alley in the first place? It's not close to the bazaar."

Feeling more foolish by the minute, she told him about the painting and the mage in the yellow house. "I wanted answers," Flora said. "And I didn't want to bother you, so I went looking for them. It was stupid. I'm sorry."

"No," Lazarus said. There was a spark in his eye that she hadn't seen before. "Even I don't know much about the Temple of Fates beyond the old wives' tales, but if there's anything I've learned over the centuries, it's to trust my intuition. What did the mage have to say?"

"He wasn't there," Flora said.

"Well, let's go find him. If he's still not there, we'll head back to the caravan and start over. How does that sound?"

"As good as anything else we have right now," Flora said as Lazarus helped her down from the wall. "Thank you."

"Of course," he said. "Now let's go."

They walked quietly through the dark city, and Flora marveled at its emptiness, its silence in the places outside the bazaar. In the misty evening, it was easy to imagine that there were two Davascas, one a brilliant, never-ending circus, and the other a city of ghosts. "Are we the only ones out in this part of town?"

"I wouldn't say we're the *only* ones," Lazarus said as they passed the fountain.

Flora saw a group of teenagers lounging on the other side of the fountain. They were all dressed in a very particular manner. Like Lazarus.

"Ohhhh," Flora said. "You're going to hate this, Lazarus. They call them Ankies. Like *Ankou*. Look."

"What?" Lazarus said, spinning around to get a better look at them.

They wore black, with broad hats and leather gloves, and tall boots over slim-fitting pants. But where Lazarus's black layers were sleek and unpretentious, the Anky motto seemed to be "More is more." Their black clothes were ornate and often embroidered with skulls or hourglasses or roses. Their eyes were lined heavily with black, and they were draped with all manner of darkly printed scarves and sashes. There were peacock feathers in their broad black hats, and they all wore hands and ears and noses full of silver jewelry. A few of them wore thin, looping chains or dark, iridescent beads piled around their necks, tiny skull charms dangling here and there, glittering against their black layers.

Their jaws dropped at the sight of the Ankou, but they did not approach. They sat stock-still with all their chains and their scarves and their tiny metal skulls, watching as Lazarus and Flora walked by.

After they had passed, Flora heard one of them say, "Did you see that?"

"Young people these days," Lazarus muttered.

She couldn't help laughing. But as Flora led Lazarus around the corner, her heart sank. A man was chaining the door shut on the yellow house. Another was hammering a sign over the door.

FOR SALE PENDING CLEANING.

"For sale?" Flora breathed. "But I don't understand. I was just here and—"

"I'll handle this," Lazarus said. "Excuse me!"

The men turned, and when they saw him, all the color left their faces.

"The mage who lived here, where is he?" Lazarus asked. "We have business with him."

"Um, I don't rightly know, Ankou, sir," the first man said. "We're just here to close it up for cleaning. But... er... word is he ran afoul of the Council of Mages, and they kicked him out of the city effective immediately."

"What did he do?" asked Flora.

"Probably invented something dangerous," the second man said. "I didn't know Dr. Kell, but I saw him all the time, running around with pieces of scrap metal and strange contraptions, then shooting lightning into 'em.

The council would always be by later to scold him. Guess he finally made one weird metal thing too many."

"But why would they care?" Flora asked. "Were his inventions dangerous?"

"We're just here to clean, Miss...er...Miss Ankou," the first man said. "All I can tell you is that he left about two hours ago and caught a ride with a bunch of traders. Where they were headed, I can't say."

"Thank you, gentlemen," said Lazarus. He left the men to their work and turned to Flora. "Do you feel like this Dr. Kell is worth trying to find?"

Flora thought about the painting, about the Temple of Fates and how it had made her feel. So resonant in her mind. True. "Yes," she said. "I'm sure of it."

Lazarus nodded. "In that case, back to the caravan before—"

"Ankou!" said a voice.

They turned to see a man running toward them through the dark streets. Huffing and puffing, he stopped in front of them. "Ankou, I'm so glad I found you," he said. "I have been searching for a mercenary, and when I heard you were in Davasca, I knew you were the only one for the job." He gulped to catch his breath and continued. "A monster has destroyed our temple and killed twenty of the villagers. It keeps coming back, but none of us know what to do. Please help us. Throth is just ten miles northeast of Davasca, under the Lone Mountain. We will pay you whatever you ask, but please help us!"

Lazarus looked at Flora for a moment, then he said, "I'm sorry, sir, but we have urgent business elsewhere. There is a mage we must find and—"

"No," Flora interrupted. "We'd be happy to help you."

Lazarus looked at her, confused.

"We can't just leave them to fend for themselves," Flora said. "Not when there's a monster on the loose."

"Flora, this is a real mission," Lazarus said. "With a real *monster*."

"I want to use my training," Flora said. "I want to use it on the things I'm supposed to use it on. As it's supposed to be used." She glanced back at the yellow house, now completely boarded up. "Besides, maybe we can find Dr. Kell along the way. A lightning mage who invents strange machines shouldn't be too hard to find."

Lazarus rubbed his temples. "All right," he said to the man. "Go ahead of us and tell the elders that we're coming."

"Yes, Ankou! Right away!" said the man, and he set off running again, back the way he came.

"I hope you understand what you're getting yourself into, Flora," Lazarus said. "Because this is going to be nothing like fighting people."

"Good," Flora said, glancing back in the direction of the alley. "I hope it's not."

CHAPTER ELEVEN

THEY ARRIVED AT THROTH THE FOLLOWING NIGHT. It was a small village sequestered a little way up in the pines and elms of the Lone Mountain, and though Lazarus was familiar with it, he hadn't paid it a visit in over a hundred years. The townspeople waited outside their log cabins. An old man and a long, low dog with drooping ears stood in the road with an official sort of air that marked the old man the town elder—and the dog was the elder dog, perhaps.

"We are happy to see you, Ankou," the old man said, stepping forward.

Lazarus tipped his hat. A few village men ran to unhitch the horses and take them to a nearby watering trough. Two women came with steaming mugs of coffee and a small basket of fresh rolls.

"It's just as they say," said a red-bearded man to

someone in the crowd. "He doesn't even have a full beard yet."

Lazarus stroked his chin and turned his attention to the town elder, glad that Flora was still in the caravan, in case the townspeople needed more to gossip about. Maybe if he was lucky, Flora would forget about the whole monster-fighting business and stay inside where she couldn't get killed. But knowing Flora, that was only the smallest of possibilities.

He took out his book and charcoal. "Good evening. A pleasure, I'm sure. Let's get to work immediately. Tell me about the day the monster came. Tell me in detail."

"It was about a week ago, the evening after we finished building the temple. The first ceremony. The bells were ringing out, and we heard something yowling, like the earth was splitting in two! Then the sound of great feet thudding toward the temple. People ran every which way. The monster was enormous. Seemed nearly as big as the mountain."

"What did it look like?"

"Like a man in some ways, made out of rock or earth, but bigger than any man in the world. It began pounding at the temple's walls. Everybody ran out of the temple, breaking windows and trying to escape. The screams... the blood..."

Oof! thought Lazarus. *This might not be as quick or easy as*

I thought it would be. "Have you been back to the temple?" Lazarus asked, scribbling into his book.

Monster: Big, manlike. Bloodthirsty. Sensitive to noise?

"No," said the elder. "We are too afraid. But our grazing grounds are near the temple. We didn't have time to let the sheep out."

Eats sheep? Lazarus wrote.

"Wool is our life here. That monster might as well be killing us with every sheep it takes."

Lazarus crossed out the question mark. "Don't worry," he said. "I'll take care of it."

"Who's this?" asked Red Beard. Flora had climbed out of the caravan and was standing beside it, wrapped in her cloak. Lazarus saw Flora draw herself up taller.

"She's my...assistant," he said, and though Red Beard looked at Flora dubiously and a small wave of whispers rippled through the crowd, no one questioned him further.

"The temple is just up that path there," said Red Beard, pointing at a ragged-looking little trail, the start of which could barely be seen in the light of the torches that lined the street. "Come with us, Ankou."

They followed Red Beard and the elder up the path through the forest until it turned into nothing more than a sheep trail in the leaves. The night was full of cries and rustlings and movements, and the air grew colder as they ascended the mountain. Flora pulled her cloak tighter and drew closer to Lazarus.

They stopped at a clearing where a few thin sheep were confined by high fences, rustling nervously on weeds and brown grass. "So few of them," the elder said.

The sheep began to bleat and crowd the fence as if to say, *Oh, thank goodness, you've returned!*

Red Beard and the elder started to move toward the sheep, but Lazarus cautioned them against making too much noise, and, with grave expressions, they kept moving. Flora crept along the tree line and followed.

They continued to a gray stone temple with a high, pointed bell tower. It would have been beautiful had it not been marked with great cracked craters where the monster had beaten at it. The oaken doors had been pounded until they had caved in and the hinges had bent. One of the doors was ajar, revealing rows and rows of velvet-cushioned benches, toppled this way and that. The dog whimpered and would go no closer.

They stepped into the temple's dark, open mouth. The smell of blood was strong and foul. The elder lifted his lantern, and it illuminated a circle of bloody clarity so gruesome Lazarus was glad Flora couldn't see all of it at once. Dried blood covered everything—the floor, the walls, the pews.

Looking up in the sanctuary, Lazarus could see the stained-glass images of gods he did not know. He was surprised by how much gold could be stuffed into a temple. Gold on benches, gold on censers and scepters and bowls. "Was *anything* taken?" Lazarus asked the elder. "Any gold? Jewels?"

"No," he said. "Nothing."

"Hmmm," said Lazarus. "Not hoarding. Sometimes ancient monsters can be awakened by the presence of gold, but they usually sleep for eons. I wonder what woke it?"

"What about these?" Flora asked, peering up into the bell tower. The bells inside were solid copper, the kind of bells that would make an enormous, booming ring. But sound alone wouldn't be enough to wake a monster like that.

"The copper for those bells, was it mined from this mountain?" Lazarus asked.

"Yes," said the elder. "Hewn from the very mountain's core and molded here in the village. Nearly as fine as Parthan copper."

"Were the stone blocks carved from the mountain as well?"

"My brother cut them right out of it," said Red Beard. "Took seven years to make them. There weren't nothing more beautiful in the whole of Valacia or Skaard, for that matter."

"Why do you ask?" The elder looked worriedly up at Lazarus.

"Because many monsters are bound to the earth or the water or, in this case, the mountain," said Lazarus. "When you made your temple out of the mountain, you woke it. Who knows how long it would have slept if you hadn't made those bells. Now it's awake, and it's angry, and it's hungry."

Red Beard seemed annoyed.

"We . . . we didn't know! I swear it!" the elder said.

"I suppose I would've had to come up here sooner or later," Lazarus said.

"So you can take care of it?"

"Yes," Lazarus said. "Now leave us be, and the monster will be dead by morning."

The elder and Red Beard went back down the mountain. As soon as they were out of sight, Lazarus, torch still lit, went back into the temple and rang the bells three times as though to say, *Come. Come. Come.*

"What do we do now?" asked Flora.

"Wait," said Lazarus.

"Feel free to watch this time," Lazarus said as they sat across the fire from each other, breathing in curls of sage smoke. "This monster will be a challenge, even for me."

Flora said nothing. Her palms were slick with sweat, but she held her sword tight in her grip. The night turned blacker and colder, and the sheep in the meadow made their shaky little noises in the darkness.

Lazarus took off his hat and fanned the smoke toward her. "Let the smoke cover you. We can't have the monster catching your scent and coming for you instead of me."

She tried to think of peaceful things as the smoke wafted over her. Sunny days, a warm bed, the smell of almond trees, the sound of the ocean. None of it helped.

The ruined temple disturbed her. Why hadn't the gods saved them? The gods who were carved into the walls, who shone down with divine light from the windows? The people had been there to worship them, after all. Perhaps those horned, muscular gods were not the true ones. Emir certainly hadn't been. If She had, Flora wouldn't be shivering in front of a sage fire with the Ankou. She would be at home telling stories with other ladies and handmaidens, or laughing with Beth, or simply breathing in the sea air. But Emir was not real, and neither were the gods of Throth, and there was no one to keep the monsters from coming whenever they decided to. Only someone to kill them after they'd done their damage.

Flora closed her eyes and took a deep breath. Then she asked Lazarus a question that even she did not expect to ask. "How is it when you come back to life every evening?"

"Disappointing," said Lazarus, blowing a strand of hair out of his face.

"No, really," Flora persisted. "I'd like to know. What happens when you die and when you come back?"

Lazarus furrowed his brows and thought for a while. "I know only what happens to *me*," he said. "I know that *I* go to bones every dawn, and that when *I* leave my body, *I* go into the Between. It's not death, though. Just a temporary place. A place for souls to go on the way to death, and . . . and over all of it, She watches."

"She?" Flora asked.

"The God of the Unknown. That is what I call Her. I feel that She is a She, anyway," said Lazarus. "Maybe She's Emir. Maybe She's one of the old gods of my people. Maybe She's a Skaardan god. Maybe She's every god that has ever been and all the gods that will be. I don't know." He paused. "But there is a god of some sort, and there is something after death. Some kind of afterlife. I just haven't gotten to it yet."

The afterlife is real, she thought. It was an enormous, mind-expanding thing. Her chest felt tight, and she wasn't sure if she was relieved or disturbed. Flora turned away from the temple. She could not look at it. But old songs about the purity of Emir, the maiden who had first called a unicorn, rang in her memory. God of the Unknown or not, Emir was part of her. Unicorns were part of her. Kaer-Ise was part of her. Even if none of them existed anymore. Even if she would no longer be welcome among them if they did. "Have you ever seen a unicorn?"

Lazarus, who had spoken so candidly of what lay beyond the bounds of life and death, was quiet. Finally, he said, "Yes. Long ago.

"It was in the forest, close to my village," he continued. "About a week before I was sent to fight. Ana and I were beside a clear pool in the forest, one that we'd never seen before. And it stepped right onto the path. It shone so brightly everything around it seemed dim—made *us* seem dim. As though it were the only true thing and we were the stories."

"Then what happened?" Flora whispered.

"Then it was gone. And the night seemed darker and . . . *lesser* somehow than it was before."

"Do you think they still exist?" Flora asked. "I know they're supposed to be extinct after the war, but do you think any of them lived?"

Lazarus opened his mouth to respond, but as he did, the sheep in the meadow began to bleat and panic. The copper kettle over the fire began swinging back and forth. The bells in the tower began to sway, to ring of their own accord. Then they heard it: a piteous wailing that seemed to come from the mountain itself. It was a ragged, angry sound and soon the thud of great feet joined it.

Flora could see the tops of the trees moving in the wake of something large and full of rage lumbering down the mountain, toward them.

"There!" Lazarus said, pointing. "Across from me, in the brush! And when I tell you, do what I say!"

Flora did as she was told and crouched behind a bush, pulse drumming in her neck, watching the tops of the trees close to her dance like waves on the sea.

She saw Lazarus draw his sword. He was alert but not frightened. His demeanor was calm, cool, focused. *Professional*, Flora thought. He tucked the hourglass into his shirt.

The creature burst through the trees, its swinging arms longer than its legs and ending in great balled fists. It was darkly colored, but which color, she couldn't tell in the low light. It was covered with all manner of scales and small, horny growths. Its body was manlike, but twisted, deformed—uncanny. It stomped through the trees, straight toward them.

Lazarus motioned to her, and she crouched lower to hide herself better, and, though she did not know why,

she reached into her pocket and clutched the pincushion with her scarred hand. The creature took stride after
huge, loping stride and stepped right over her. As it drew
itself up to its full height before Lazarus, it eclipsed the
stars.

All she could smell was the scent of blood and fear.
No, she thought. *This is nothing like fighting people.* She steeled
herself, her hand on her sword. The monster lurched
forward and its arm shot out to grab Lazarus.

Lazarus leapt to the side and brought his falx down
on the creature's claw; it merely bounced off, leaving the
creature without a scratch. The monster raised its fists
over its head and brought them down, hard, right where
Lazarus had been standing. The ground underfoot
cracked and buckled, but Lazarus dodged again, leaping
backward this time.

Lazarus didn't seem fazed. He slashed out with his
blade, catching the monster's wrist, and it reared back in
pain. Lazarus backed up toward the temple. The monster followed until it had its rough back to Flora.

Then it turned. Its nose—or what she thought was its
nose—was in the air. Sniffing something. It turned completely around and began to come toward her.

Behind it, Lazarus cried out and threw dagger after
dagger, but the monster did not seem to care. It just kept
coming. Flora froze like a rabbit until it was right over

her. Then, in sheer desperation, she ran between its legs, her blade out, and she slashed and slashed at the tendons just above the monster's heel.

"Flora, what are you doing?" Lazarus shouted. "Run! Go!"

The monster shrieked and began to topple. It teetered once, twice, then caught its balance, leaning on its other foot. And as Flora backed away, it fixed its fiery eyes on her.

The last thing she saw was the huge dark hand coming toward her to swat the little bug that had bitten it.

Lazarus's stomach felt as though it had dropped out of his body. The monster swatted at Flora and connected. She flew several feet into the bushes and did not rise.

The monster bent to pick her up. As it turned its back to him, Lazarus ran toward it.

The monster threw its arm back and hit Lazarus with the force of a landslide. Lazarus flew through the air and he hit the trunk of a tree. His sight went red as he felt his spine bend and shatter. Bone fragments rocketed into his tissues. He fell to the ground like a broken puppet, arms and legs askew, paralyzed and dying, but only for a moment. His spine repaired itself quickly and painfully, but with the pain came movement. He twisted himself into place, pulling his shoulders and knees into their sockets. He gritted his teeth as his shattered bones pieced themselves together, sniffed the blood back up his nose, and rose to his feet.

The monster picked Flora up and dangled her above the ground, one of her arms in each hand, preparing to pull her apart.

Legs still wobbly, Lazarus stumbled forward and leapt onto the monster's back. The monster didn't seem to notice as he clambered up its spine. He had to make it quick—but the monster's head was too close to its neck when it stood upright. He'd never be able to get a clean blow inward.

The monster raised Flora higher. Lazarus swung his falx down and forward, slicing into the tender place beneath its arm. The monster roared and dropped Flora. Her body rolled twice before laying still. Lazarus dug in harder to keep from toppling off. The monster rotated its shoulder and reached its other arm behind it and raked at him with its claws, sending deep, painful lacerations down Lazarus's back.

But Lazarus did not budge. He pulled his blade upward, gritting his teeth as the inky blood flowed, as the muscles beneath the skin began to give way and his blade connected with the joint at the shoulder. The monster roared. Lazarus strained, pulling the blade until he ripped through the last sinew and the monster's arm fell from its body, spraying more blood as it went.

A wound like that will surely kill it, Lazarus thought.

The monster howled its death howl, and Lazarus dropped from its shoulder. It turned and limped into the forest, leaving a trail of dark blood behind it. Lazarus could follow it later. He ran to where Flora's body had fallen.

"Oh no," Lazarus breathed. "Oh no, no, no."

She lay, arms spread on the forest floor, head against a stone.

There were high walls all around them.

They were indoors, in a vast cave . . . no . . . there were oil lamps glowing with strangely colored fires. Behind them were seemingly endless eaves and stairways, and beneath their feet was an intricately woven rug. The place was enormous, stretching onward and onward into darkness, a great temple, empty of people save Flora herself, Lazarus beside her, and one other person, who she could not see clearly. Lazarus was wearing strange clothes. Black, but in a strange, foreign-looking style that she could not place.

And a voice echoed through them, the voice of something great and powerful, humming their bones, deep and resonant as a cello.

"Why have you come to the Temple of Fates?"

"Please, Flora...come on..."

She woke to a face covered in dark, drying blood, and for a moment it was terrifying. But her eyes focused through the blur, and she saw that it was only Lazarus. He had leaned her against a boulder, and his cold, bloody fingers were on her neck, feeling for her pulse. Her head felt as though someone had hit it with a battering ram. She brushed his hand away.

Lazarus sat back and let out a deep sigh of relief that fogged and disappeared into the night air. "Oh gods! I thought it had killed you!"

Flora shook her head, bringing on a sudden flare of pain. Her stomach lurched. "Where did it go?"

"Let me see your eyes," he said. "Turn toward the fire so I can see your eyes."

While Flora focused on calming her stomach, Lazarus put his hand on her face, opening first one eye, then the other. "You aren't concussed, miraculously," he said. "And there's no blood. How badly does your head hurt?"

"Where is it?" she asked again. "Did you kill it?" She tried to turn her head to look for the monster, but her head hurt too much.

"Wait," Lazarus said. He set off into the darkness.

When he came back, he had three broad green leaves and one yellow flower shaped like a thin cup. He handed them to her. "Chew these together and hold the pulp in your mouth until your head stops hurting."

She put the bitter plants in her mouth and chewed. First her mouth tingled, then her jaw, and then the pain dimmed miraculously to nothing.

"It'll only last for a few hours," said Lazarus. "We've got to hurry if we want to finish the mission before daylight."

"You didn't kill it?" Flora said through a mouthful of pulp.

Lazarus nodded. "Mortally wounded it, I think. All that's left is to make sure."

Behind him, she could see its great dark arm stretched out on the ground. She saw the bloody footprints trailing into the forest. "I'm sorry—"

Lazarus helped her to her feet. "It's okay," he said. "You're alive."

He looked up the mountain after the trail of blood. "Now we just have to bring back proof we killed it. Are you all right to continue or do you want to go back to the caravan?"

Flora flexed her arms and legs. Her head spun but didn't hurt, and she remained standing. "I'm fine."

Lazarus nodded. He fashioned a torch out of rags from his ripped shirt and one of the branches from the fire. They followed the bloody footprints up the dark mountain and into a yawning cave whose cold, close darkness hung on their shoulders like a wet cloak.

Flora kept seeing the monster in her mind's eye, rising up, its head among the trees—its fist coming toward her. Could there be more of them? Flora peered into the throat of the cave, but she could see nothing beyond the halo of light that danced around Lazarus's torch. A feeling of heaviness, of anger, grew around them.

"Be prepared," Lazarus said. "We're not alone in here."

Farther in, the moon shone down through an opening in the ceiling and they saw an expanse of black water stretching out before them. It was marbled with blood, still roiling, and there was a sort of island at the center. And on it, lying bleeding and crumpled, was the monster, plainly dead.

Lazarus waded into the water, holding the torch and his blade up. As he moved, the blood washed off him and spread over the water's surface like a black web before disappearing. Flora took off her boots and cloak and followed.

"There's a drop-off here, so be—" Before he could finish, a scaly, monstrous hand grabbed Lazarus's entire leg and pulled him under, dousing his torch.

"Lazarus!" she shouted. She splashed forward until she could see him below the water's surface, fighting what looked like an enormous, stony, scaly woman. He was too close to use his sword but pulled a dagger and slashed the woman in the shoulder. She slashed back at him with her claws, and when his wounds healed, she held him under the water.

Flora stood still, horrified as he thrashed and fought, his movements eerily silent beneath the water. Then his body went still and began to sink. Fear and shock rang like a cold bell through her, and though she knew he couldn't die, she fell back gasping. Then she saw the monster leave Lazarus's corpse and float back to the surface. Twice Flora's size, the monster rose, dripping, from the bloody water, claws bared, legs bent. She opened her mouth and roared. Shuddering, Flora held her sword up.

The monster lunged at her, nearly knocking her to the ground, but Flora held firm. She dodged swipe after swipe of the monster's long black claws. She thrust with her sword, aiming for the monster's neck; she took a swing and missed.

The monster rushed her again, tearing a swath from her tunic and slicing into her side. The wound hurt, but it wasn't deep, and Flora returned one of her own, slicing outward with her sword and catching the monster in the face. It shrieked, and when it turned back to face her, one of its yellow eyes was a bloody slurry, dripping down the stony scales.

The monster drew itself up for another swipe of those deadly claws. Flora took a step back and felt the stone wall of the cave against her. There was nowhere to go. She steeled herself and stood, ready to strike.

Suddenly, there was a sickening *thwack!*: Blade through bone, and the monster's head fell from its body. The body toppled to the ground, and behind it, Lazarus stood, dripping wet and holding his falx.

"*Anyway*," he said, flinging his wet hair back, "I was going to say be careful, but it looks like you handled things well." He glanced down at the head on the ground. "Sorry it took a while. It takes more time when I drown."

Flora sank down against the wall, breathing in huge, relieved gulps. "See?" she said. "I...told you I could do it."

"Good job," said Lazarus. He bent and grabbed the monster's head by its weedy hair. "It looks like the villagers will owe us twice our fee. And an explanation." He looked down at Flora. "I'll go and get the arm. With this head it'll be enough. Take a moment to breathe. You've earned it."

Flora sat with her eyes closed for a while, letting the fire die down inside her. The feeling of evil, of anger, in the cave was gone. Now, for a reason she did not understand completely, she felt somehow truly and thoroughly herself, hers alone. She was her own, a being with her own lungs, her own teeth, her own muscles aching. Only herself, and for the first time in a long time, she felt something like satisfaction.

CHAPTER TWELVE

T HEY SET OUT THE FOLLOWING NIGHT AFTER THEY had been paid their dues. As they rumbled down the mountain and back out onto the main road, watching as the shepherds ran back up the mountain to tend to their flocks, they were feeling pretty good about all they'd accomplished. Then Lazarus remembered Atonais Kell and his heart sank. They had no idea where he was or how to find him.

"We'll just have to search," Flora said as the days grew into weeks. "You have three hundred years' experience tracking things. Finding one man can't be that difficult."

Lazarus did have three hundred years' experience under his belt, but he had never met or even seen Atonais Kell. How could he be expected to find someone he knew nothing about?

Beneath his shirt, the black mark on his torso pained him, and he covered it with his hand. It had not gone away when he had unbuilt and rebuilt the first night after it appeared, nor had it the night after that, nor any other night. The hope that he'd had of the mark simply going away like that had been a small, vain hope to begin with. This was magic. This was Ana's magic. And he knew that it could not be escaped. She would have her way in death as she had in life, always, and at his expense, he realized.

He thought of Flora. There was no use telling her now, not when he didn't know what effect the mark would have yet. He would only worry her. And what was the point of that when she had so much to be concerned with already? No, it was better to keep quiet about it. To keep quiet and search.

But Lazarus couldn't lie to himself. For the first time in three hundred years, he was worried.

Flora was amazed that Lazarus never looked at a compass or a map or even the stars as he drove. Of course, Flora thought, he wouldn't *need* to after roaming Valacia and the neighboring countries for as long as he had. One night she felt he was uncharacteristically quiet. His hands gripped the reins a little too hard, and it seemed that they were going a bit faster than usual. The country-side was blowing past, so scenes like cows sleeping in the moonlight were not as serene as they should have been. But Flora understood having bad days, and she sat beside him in silence as he drove the caravan ever onward.

Ahead, in the shadows, a stone bridge loomed over a great crack in the earth that spanned the length of the dim horizon. "Though no one uses this bridge anymore, even I don't remember a time when it did not span the ravine," Lazarus said.

But there was something stopped on the bridge. A dark smudge.

"What's that?" Flora asked, pointing. As they drew nearer, she could see that the smudge was a structure made of wood and fabric. There were odd items strewn all around, most of them gleaming metal in the full moon light. "It looks like a lean-to or a tent or some-thing. I wonder—"

"Hello!" came a voice. A dark figure appeared beside the lean-to, waving them down. "Please, can you help me? My party abandoned me and I don't know what to do!"

"Someone is stranded, Lazarus!" Flora said. "We have to help!" Flora moved to jump down from the cara-van, but Lazarus held her back. When she turned to look at him, his sight was turned to the sky.

Bats. A cloud of bats, hundreds of them. They didn't dip and dive and swoop like normal bats did. Instead, they hovered, hanging in front of the moon. Then they began to swarm together, to consolidate. Suddenly, there were only three large figures, perched on the bridge like giant vultures. And even in the darkness, their eyes gleamed yellow.

"Striga." Lazarus pulled his blade. "Your sword is silver, right?"

"Yes," Flora said, eyes on the three shapes advancing in the night.

"Seek shelter!" Lazarus shouted to the person on the bridge. "Striga!"

The person seemed to hear them, because the figure gave a frightened yelp, then dove back into the lean-to.

Lazarus and Flora leapt out of their seats and ran to meet the striga. The beasts flew higher into the night sky, taunting them. In the moonlight, Flora could see their fleshless faces, human and inhuman at the same time, with rows of stained teeth and eerie yellow eyes, too wide and glowing with their own light. These were not the striga of legend, with their wooden coffins and mostly human appearance. These things were what became of striga when they grew old. Their flesh had grown pale and mottled, stretched over visible ribs and sharp shoulder blades and hip bones. Their hair had fallen out. Their backs bent like animals', and their skin and wings were tattered in places. Unlike Lazarus, their curse hadn't made them invincible. It had only driven them mad with the lust for blood.

One of them screeched, a high, ear-rending sound, and the three striga pulled their wings in and dove. As they came down, Flora lashed out with her sword and felt the blade connect. The striga screamed and tumbled backward onto the ground and lay still.

Flora looked over to see Lazarus facing off against the other two. He slashed out at one, keeping it at bay, then Flora saw him uncork a small glass bottle of blessed water and throw it onto the other. It shrank and screamed as though the water were acid, and it flew at Lazarus, tackling him to the ground as the other swooped overhead. Lazarus rolled with it once, stabbing it through the chest, but it was blood-mad, and as Lazarus held it back, it snapped and lunged for his face.

The other striga wheeled in the air and swooped toward where Lazarus and the other striga struggled. Flora ran to meet it, her sword out. Then she heard a noise and turned just in time to see the striga she had knocked to the ground launch itself at her, mouth open, showing rows of fangs.

There was a blinding blast of light from behind them, throwing the darkness into relief. The striga shrieked and turned toward the east, looking for the sun as they sizzled and fell, writhing. But this brightness was coming from the lean-to on the bridge. As the striga crumbled to ash, Flora helped Lazarus to his feet. Shielding their eyes, they squinted back at the caravan.

"What on earth . . . ," Lazarus said.

The person—a man, Flora could see now, in yellow robes—was standing near the caravan with one large glass globe in each hand, each shining with light nearly as bright as the sun. He dimmed them, leaving dark spots floating in Flora's eyes.

"I wasn't sure that would work," he said as they approached. "But I read that many creatures are vulnerable to light, so . . ." He shrugged as though he were trying to seem nonchalant. "Never did I think I'd be helping the actual Ankou, though! Truly a landmark moment for me, even if it did come a bit late."

"And just who are you?" Lazarus asked.

"Atonais Kell, Order of Lightning, Second Class," the man said. His eyes were so light behind round spectacles that the irises were nearly colorless, and Flora noticed a yellow crystal winking between his dark brows. "Though that doesn't mean much these days. I'm pleased to meet you."

Flora and Lazarus exchanged looks of openmouthed

disbelief. "*The* Atonais Kell?" Flora asked. "From Davasca?"

"Well, recently expelled from Davasca to be more precise, but yes. Why? What are they blaming me for now? And who are you?"

"I'm Flora! We've been searching for you for weeks!" Flora said, barely able to contain her excitement. "You're . . . Oh, there's so much to explain!"

"Searching for me?" Atonais asked, bewildered. "What could the Ankou possibly want with me?"

"Gather your things," Lazarus said. "We have a lot to tell you. If you don't mind taking a ride in the Black Caravan to wherever you're going next."

"Mind?" Atonais Kell said. "I've been waiting all my professional career for something like this. But let's get off this bridge first?"

"Of course."

"Also, may I say something?" Atonais Kell said, grabbing a coil of metal from the ground.

"Sure."

"You really do look as young as they say."

"That's what I hear," grumbled Lazarus, and together they loaded Atonais Kell's things into the caravan.

They stopped in a copse of trees where they could conceal the caravan in case any more striga were in the area. Lazarus led the horses to a nearby pond to drink, and then headed back into the caravan. Inside, Flora had made tea and Atonais Kell was trying to find places to shove his belongings so that they were out of the way.

And what strange belongings they were. There were sacks of birdseed slouching in the corner; an extra set of yellow robes draped over a chair; a stack of large, difficult-looking books under the table. On the wall behind the table, a faded piece of cloth curtain sagged, covering something in a frame, probably a mirror. (Lazarus knew he'd cover his mirror if he looked as unkempt as Dr. Kell.) But most interesting was all the metal. There were coils and coils of wire—copper and silver, mostly—and many pieces of scrap metal lying about. There was also a strange device that looked a bit like a metal mushroom, which Lazarus could tell from a glance was nothing to trifle with.

"I can't thank you enough," Atonais said to Flora. "After the traders I was traveling with dropped me off so unceremoniously at that bridge, I didn't know what to do."

"Why did they leave you there?" Flora asked, handing Atonais a cup of tea.

"Oh, something about me talking too much or some such nonsense," Atonais said. His pale eyes were darting here, there, and everywhere in the caravan, taking everything in with an air of plain fascination that made Lazarus slightly nervous.

Lazarus reached to push a candlestick out of his way and felt the sting of leftover lightning magic. "Ouch!" he said.

"Oh, Lazarus!" Flora said, seeing him for the first time. "We were just finding a place for his things. Would you like some tea?"

"No, thank you," Lazarus said. "But we should ask Dr. Kell our questions before dawn so we can help him on his journey to . . . wherever you need to go. Now, we have a few questions about the Temple of Fates."

"Never mind about me for now," Dr. Kell said, taking a seat at the table with his tea. "That's not what I would have expected the Ankou to ask me but you've come to the right place. I have the beginning of a whole thesis on the thing if you'd care to—"

"Just give us a basic idea of the thing," said Lazarus. "What is it, where is it, how do you get in, things like that."

Dr. Kell nodded, then clapped his hands together, sending sparks flying from between his palms. "All right, so, first off, despite popular belief, the Temple of Fates is a real place, not a story. It's meant to test worthy heroes."

He created a small ball of lightning and began passing it from hand to hand while he spoke. "It's endlessly fascinating. The most interesting thing about it is what's in it: the Artifact. I call it that because it appears as different things to different people. But regardless of what it appears as, literally anything is possible with the Artifact. The sick become healthy. The weak become powerful. The foolish become wise."

"Could it cure a curse?" Lazarus heard himself ask. "A powerful one?"

"Oh, the Artifact could cure anything," Dr. Kell said airily. "The Artifact is the ultimate boon for those who have no hope."

Lazarus and Flora looked at each other, and he could tell that she was thinking what he was thinking: *This could really be it.*

For both of them, this could be it. A way for him to finally die. And for Flora, a way to find the family that she missed. The words of the prophecy said *walk the Fates unfettered.* Did that mean the Temple of Fates?

The mark on his side throbbed again, but Lazarus ignored it. "How does someone enter the Temple of Fates?"

"You have to have a party of three," Dr. Kell said. "And the group faces three challenges designed specifically for them."

"But how can that be?" Flora asked. "I thought the temple was supposed to be ancient?"

"The temple is . . . *alive*, for lack of a better word," said Dr. Kell, nearly quivering with excitement. "The temple thinks, moves, changes, speaks with its own voice. It challenges all who enter with trials specifically made for them. And it's *the temple itself* who chooses which people—if any—will receive the Artifact."

"Then it's just a matter of the three people being worthy," Lazarus said.

"Wait a moment," Flora said. "If this place exists, why haven't there been hundreds of people changing the world and working miracles every year?"

"Several reasons," Dr. Kell said. "First off, the challenges the temple throws people aren't just difficult; they're deadly." (*Deadly*. Lazarus almost smirked.) "There have been many attempts to enter it, and rarely has anyone been successful. Another reason is that someone has to *let* you in. There's a key, and no one knows where it is, or who might have it.

"But the biggest challenge is probably the location itself," Dr. Kell said. He snapped his fingers, and the tiny ball of lightning disappeared. "You see, after years and years of research, I've narrowed the location of the Temple of Fates down to one place: Parth."

"Oh no," Flora said.

"Exactly," said Dr. Kell.

Parth. The Desert Nation, the fifth of the Five Lands.

One of only three remaining now that the land beyond the mountains was uninhabited and Kaer-Ise had been sacked. After suffering heavy losses in the Necromancer's War, Parth cut itself off from Valacia, Skaard, Kaer-Ise, and of course, the now uninhabited fifth land, the Dead Land beyond the eastern mountains. Parth put up its famous wall to separate itself in case of another attack. Magic had been outlawed, but Parth had not suffered. There were rumors that it had become a nation of mechanization, of science. And Parth's borders were very, very closed.

"You see the problem," said Dr. Kell. "Until Parth decides to communicate with the rest of us, my thesis will remain unfinished. And that's a problem. All mages seeking first-class status must complete a thesis solving or at least offering a hypothesis for the solution of a great mystery of the magical world. I suppose I aimed too high. My unfinished thesis is one of the reasons they decided to expel me from the council. That and all the inventions. I was told I had to choose between magic and science. I told them I couldn't choose, that both had applications that could help the people of Valacia and all the Five Lands. Master Kandrigan, my adviser, didn't take kindly to it."

Dr. Kell looked into the distance for a moment, lost in an unpleasant memory. Then he shook himself back to reality. "And now that I have given my life's work on the temple to you, I suppose I should give you directions to the commune I've been sent to, to spend the remainder of my days in exile from the magical academic community."

"I'm sorry," said Lazarus. "At least you'll be among your own kind, I suppose."

"Ha!" Atonais laughed bitterly. "If only you knew." He pulled the cloth from the mirror and then Lazarus saw that it wasn't a mirror at all. It was a portrait. An imposing-looking family stared up at them. They looked very serious, stocky and dark-eyed, with black crystals between their brows and dark brown robes. Earth mages. And among them, standing thin and crooked as a lightning-bolt himself, was young Atonais Kell. Yellow-robed and pale-eyed, his dark hair puffy and askew. "Lightning mages are rare, born into families of other elements randomly. I will never be 'among my own kind' even back with my own horrible family."

"Lightning from the earth," Lazarus said softly.

"Pardon?" Atonais said.

"It all makes sense." Flora turned to Lazarus. "The vision, the parts of the prophecy... and if no one has heard of the royal family here, maybe that means their escape ship couldn't come to Valacia. The only other place they could have gone is Parth!"

"What's all this talk about prophecies?" Atonais sipped tea and then put his cup down on the saucer. "And surely you don't mean to actually *go* to Parth in search of the Temple of Fates?"

"We do," said Lazarus. "Both of us have reason to search for it. We are hopeless, as you say. Flora wants to find the Kaer-Isian royal family, and I want to *finally* die. If the temple can help us, then that's where we'll go. And we believe that you're meant to go with us."

Atonais Kell's mouth opened and closed. He was clearly trying to figure out which question to ask first. Then he shook his head in disbelief. "So am I your prisoner now? Is this a kidnapping?"

"What?! No!" Lazarus was bewildered. "We're not going to force you to do anything you don't want to do, but . . . it seemed like . . ." He struggled for the right word, but all he could come up with was "*Fate*."

"Look, I'm *flattered* that you want me to go, but getting into Parth is impossible, even for you. Every inch of that wall is patrolled, every day."

"Not *every* inch," Lazarus said. "There's one patch that the Parthans don't bother to patrol. Admittedly, going that route would be pretty stressful, but there is a way."

"You're serious about this?" Atonais's eyes flickered

from Lazarus to Flora and back to Lazarus. "You're really going? And you really want *me* to go with you?"

"Yes," Lazarus and Flora said together.

Atonais Kell rubbed his temples. "They're already expecting me back at the commune," Dr. Kell said, strings of nervous lightning crackling around him.

"If you came with us, you could invent whatever you wanted, to your heart's content," Flora said. "We love science, right, Lazarus?"

"Oh, yeah, definitely."

"And don't you want to actually see your thesis through?" she persisted. "Your life's work? This could be a chance for you to solve the mystery—to see all your work come to fruition!"

Atonais considered this for a moment, stroking his weak chin. "What am I thinking? This is ridiculous! I— I . . . I could be killed!"

Lazarus took a breath and made a desperate suggestion. "You can study me, too," he said, and everything went quiet. "I'm a mystery, just like the Temple of Fates. And if you went back to the council with information about the Temple of Fates *and* the Ankou, they'd have no right to expel you, even if you did invent things on occasion."

"So you're saying I can interview you?" Atonais said. "And document your answers for magical academia?"

"Yes. Whatever you want," said Lazarus. "So what do you say?"

The air seemed to thicken with anticipation. Then, finally, Atonais spoke.

"I say, when do we leave?"

CHAPTER THIRTEEN

L AZARUS HAD GROWN ACCUSTOMED TO FLORA—HER stealing his shirts, her cups leaving rings on the furniture, her arguing with him about this or that. It was comfortable. With Ana, things had always been intense. There had always been some sort of a crisis he'd had to solve for her, always a condition he had had to meet in order to keep her happy. He hoped that Atonais wouldn't disrupt his and Flora's easy partnership, especially since, for the first time in a long time, he felt something close to human.

But, as he was quickly learning, Atonais was quite disruptive indeed.

"So," Atonais said, plopping down next to him with a book, quill, and ink. "Let's begin the interview, shall we? Can I call you Laz?"

"No."

"All right, no, then," Atonais said, steadying his book as the caravan rocked into motion. "How long have you been immortal and how did you achieve your immortality?"

"*Immortality* isn't really the right word," Lazarus said. He flicked the crop across the horses' flanks, and the caravan picked up the pace.

"I second that opinion," Flora said from the roof of the caravan, where she had climbed to eavesdrop.

"So, what *is* the correct word?" Atonais asked. "Also, were you born immort—ahem . . . *how you are*—or did you become that way?"

"It's a curse," Lazarus said. "Placed on me inadvertently by a witch I loved long ago."

"The girl in the portrait?" Atonais asked.

"Yes," said Lazarus, enunciating the *s* with a sharpness that he hoped would cut that line of questioning short.

But Atonais was not interested in talking about Ana at the moment. "Could you describe the conditions of your curse?" he asked instead.

Lazarus sighed. Thinking about the curse made him feel his unnatural age—if *age* was the right word. No, he supposed *age* wasn't, since he stayed exactly the same. Forever stalled. But nevertheless, he had promised to answer Atonais's questions. He told him about being ripped apart by monsters only to come back together again, how nothing could kill him. He told him about waking up and hacking dirt from his lungs. About how his flesh fell away every morning as he hung suspended in the Between. He told him about the other worlds and the pain and the endless march of time, and when he was done, he looked over to see Atonais regarding him, openmouthed.

"Astounding," said Atonais. "Truly astounding. And what a terrible curse it must have been. I'll have to get more details on—" He regarded Lazarus for a moment. "Is Lazarus your real name?"

"No," said Lazarus. "I forgot my real name a long time ago. I overheard Lazarus in the Between and took it for my own, just like I took the title Ankou."

"You really don't remember?" Atonais asked. He stopped writing completely and looked at Lazarus with an expression of great confusion. "Not at all?"

"No," Lazarus said. "Whenever I try to think of it, it's . . . not there."

"Hmmm," said Atonais, scribbling something into his book. "Interesting. Very interesting."

Talking so much about himself was making Lazarus uncomfortable, so he changed the subject. "The quickest route to Parth is coming up soon," he said. "It'll take us over a great stone bridge. Very beautiful at night. It should cut two days from our time if we hurry."

"Excellent," said Flora. "Let's go."

"Hang on up there," said Lazarus, and he flicked the horses with his crop and the caravan lunged into motion, rumbling along faster than before.

"I have one more question for tonight," Atonais said, struggling to hold his book and pencil still. "Why all the black? Any other color would make you so much more approachable."

"For invisibility at night," Lazarus said.

"Don't let him fool you." Flora reached down, snatched Lazarus's hat, and put it on her own head. "It's just that he loves a theme. A theme and looking fashionable. You'll see."

"Hey, quiet!" Lazarus shouted, trying to keep himself from smiling. Then he turned to Atonais and said, "The Ankou is nothing if not practical. Write that down."

They traveled all through the night, until they stopped in a small forest whose branches bent and swayed in the wind and whose leaves smelled soft and fragrant. The sky began to lighten and Lazarus retired to his room to let the curse come and take him.

"I'd love to observe," Atonais said, but Flora grabbed his sleeve.

"Trust me," she said. "You really wouldn't."

As the two of them sat down in the main room of the caravan, a nervous silence fell. Having someone else alive in the caravan when the dawn came was strange for Flora.

They watched the sun rise through the curtains. Minutes seemed to elongate. Flora could tell that Atonais was being polite, that he wanted to ask her questions about Kaer-Ise. About the massacre. About Lazarus, probably. But he didn't.

"Those were your brothers in the portrait?" Flora said, the urge to fill the silence finally overtaking her. "What are their names?"

"The older two are Ignius and Ignair. The younger two are . . ." He furrowed his brow. "Ibron and . . . Izoyan. Yes, Izoyan."

"Wow," Flora said.

"What?" Atonais asked.

"I don't understand how someone can be unsure of his family's names," she said. "I could never forget anything about the royal family. Beth's favorite color, the queen's favorite embroidery stitch, the way the king fidgeted with his crown sometimes." As she recounted these memories, the hurt that had gone dull over the last month seemed to deepen.

"If you'd had my family, you'd understand," Atonais

said, and left it at that. "I hope this works. First class was—*is* everything to me. First-class mage status means that the council pays you to be out in the world simply to study magic. You don't have to do anything menial like being a—a lamplighter if you're a fire mage, or a water-purifier if you're a water mage. Or a glassmaker. That's all lightning mages have outside their communes. With first-class status, I could finally be free."

"Why didn't you keep quiet about your inventions, then?" Flora asked. "Or why not invent things at your commune?"

"Because it's not enough," Atonais said. "Lightning has so very much potential for use, not only for mages, but for everyone. Lightning is everywhere! In you, in me, even in the earth itself. And with it, I believe that even those who can't feel it can do fantastic things, like— I created a device. With it, I could light an entire city. No flames. No smoke. Just light. And that idea, progress for everyone, is what I want more than anything."

They sat in awkward silence for a few moments. Then Atonais said, "Well, I suppose I should try to get some sleep if we're going to be traveling by night and sleeping by day."

He closed the curtain and went to the chair by the kitchen table with a blanket and pillow he'd brought from Davasca. Flora was suddenly uncomfortable to be sleeping in the same room with a man she'd only recently met, but she refused to treat Atonais as a threat, and she began to make her own cot for the morning.

"He's done an excellent rendering," Atonais said suddenly. He was looking up at the picture of Ana, who gazed outward with dark, mysterious eyes. "He must have loved her very much."

"I suppose," Flora said dismissively.

"Do you think he still loves her?" Atonais asked.

"What does it matter?" Flora said, surprised at the bitterness in her own voice. "She cursed him."

"It probably doesn't matter," Atonais said. "I'm only wondering." He glanced one more time at Ana's picture, then at Flora, then he curled up as well as he could and was snoring in moments.

But silly questions were already rooting themselves in Flora's brain. *Ifs* and *maybes*. She shook them away and did her best to go to sleep. Because, as she had said, what did it matter?

Lazarus disrobed in front of the mirror in his room as he prepared for his daily death. The black splotch had spread until it was nearly double in size. It had stopped hurting, though, so even though his hands shook and a cold sweat rose on his brow, he decided to take that as a good sign.

"I'll be all right," he told himself as he stood in front of the mirror, unbuttoning his black shirt and looking away from the spreading darkness as well as he could. He closed his eyes, held the hourglass in his hand, and said, twice more, "I'll be all right. I'll be all right."

If you said something three times, that made it true. That's what Ana had told him the night before he went to war. He remembered how they had stood in the dim light of the kitchen as she had uttered the words that had doomed him. *If only you were like the unicorn in the woods. If only you never had to die.*

"*I will live,*" he had promised her. Three times he promised her, and it had come true, just as she had told him it would. He had lived. But he'd had to die first.

Lazarus unwrapped the bandages around his neck, revealing the deep, angry scar that ran the circumference of it, the one wound that would never completely heal. His young face, usually handsome, looked sunken. The dark circles that he had always had seemed darker than usual.

"Oh, Ana," he whispered as he lay down to die. "What have you done to me?"

CHAPTER FOURTEEN

T HEY SET OFF THE FOLLOWING NIGHT AT A FASTER
pace, with the understanding that Lazarus would
get them to Parth, and from there, Atonais would help
them find the temple. The nights seemed to blow by in a
blur of dark blue and silvering fields, and after Lazarus
showed Flora how to drive the caravan during the day
(given that the horses were capable) they found themselves ahead of schedule.

But a shadow seemed to have fallen over Lazarus.
He wasn't his usual self, and more than once, Flora had
caught him looking off into the distance with a mel-
ancholic expression. When she asked him about it, he
changed the subject, speeding on to the next leg of their
journey.

"Why don't we take some time for ourselves?" Flora
asked when they stopped to rest the horses. "We're making

good time. We've found the lightning from the earth. For the first time we've got a real destination. Why not take a moment and celebrate it?"

Lazarus thought about this for a while, then finally shrugged and said, "Why not?"

As ambivalent as Lazarus had seemed when she first suggested it, the act of cooking something special seemed to perk him up a bit, as she hoped it would. He'd gathered a few ingredients from the forest and hummed as he made a dish that he told her he hadn't made in a hundred years. Lazarus even decided to open a bottle of wine.

"To the first battle won, and to the first time in centuries with a hope of finally ending this curse," Lazarus said, pouring three glasses.

The three of them raised their glasses and drank. And as the warmth spread through their veins, the night turned to merry-making. They laughed and told stories, and at one point Lazarus even played the violin while Atonais made a tiny ball of lightning dance between his fingertips. When the evening began to wind down, Lazarus took out a map. Emboldened by the wine, Flora scooted closer and leaned against him.

The supposed location of the Temple of Fates had been marked with a blue ink star and a question mark. Lazarus spread the map across their knees. "This is the route we'll take," he said to her. He traced a thin line from Valacia all the way to Parth. And though he commented on the places they'd stop, the monsters they'd need to look out for, all Flora could focus on was the feeling of his fingertip on her leg through the map.

"What do you think?" Lazarus was asking her, his dark eyes golden in the firelight.

Before she could answer, a crackle of lightning zipped through the air and set everything sparking. Flora jerked away from Lazarus as though he had shocked her.

"What?" Atonais squeaked. "You didn't say we were going through the Weir!"

"It is the only route that has not been closed!" Lazarus said.

"Because no one in his right mind would go into the Weir! There are *monsters* in there!"

"Imagine that," Lazarus said dryly.

"What's the Weir?" Flora asked, edging closer to him.

"Nothing to worry about," Lazarus said.

"There's a werewolf colony in the Weir!" Atonais said.

"We won't be going through during a full moon, so what does it matter?" Lazarus said. He turned to Flora. "Anyway, the Weir is merely a deep forest swamp that borders the mountains." He pointed to the forest region on the map, where their knees met, a large mass of trees and swamp due south of the Alaran Mountain range.

There were very few names or labels within it. *Here there be monsters* was scrawled around the edges of the handprint forest. "People say it's dangerous, but most of it is only talk. We'll be fine."

"There *are* evil spirits, though!" Atonais's voice rose. "I've heard that they lure people there to *kill* them! I've heard that there are hundreds of evil spirits. Thousands! Waiting!"

"It's stupid not to take the straightest path." Lazarus rolled the map closed. "I've been through the Weir many times. Don't worry. And with your inventions, I'm sure it'll be even easier than I remember."

"I think I need to lie down," Atonais said, and he climbed back into the caravan and shut the door behind him.

"You're sure about this?" Flora asked when he was gone.

"We'll be fine," Lazarus said. "We always are. Kaer-Ise and Parth had a friendly relationship in recent years, correct?"

"Parth sent an emissary of goodwill about fifty years ago," Flora said. "But they have a new king now. One of the instructors at the castle told me that he was very strict for how young he is, but I don't know much about him."

"We might not even have to deal with the king if we're lucky," Lazarus said, tying a string around the map. "But even if we do, he won't kill us. Not if there's even a slight risk of war. Not after..." He didn't want to talk about the massacre of Kaer-Ise, she realized. "I think...no, I *feel*...that this quest is one with a happy ending. So much has happened since we met. Like it was meant to be."

And though she knew Lazarus was a little tipsy, it was true. It seemed to Flora that beneath all of it, everything that had happened since she had met Lazarus was destined. Unless that, too, was the wine.

"When we go to the temple, what will you wish for?" Lazarus asked.

"I'll make it so that the massacre never happened, and that Skaard will never come for us." The wanting of it rang through her every sinew. But that wasn't all she wanted. "What about you?" she asked. "Will you wish to die?"

"Of course," Lazarus said. "But I might not wish to die right away."

"Oh?" she said, leaning closer to him without realizing.

"I want to see a sunrise," Lazarus said wistfully. "And flowers blooming."

"That's a long time to go without beauty," Flora said.

"Oh, there is still beauty," Lazarus said. "It is just a matter of knowing where to find it."

She saw his eyes flicker down to her lips, and for one wild moment she thought he was tipsy enough to lean forward and kiss her, that she was tipsy enough to pull him close and kiss him back. Then Lazarus winced as though he'd been burned and put a hand to his side.

"What's wrong?" Flora asked.

"Nothing," Lazarus said. But he gripped his side again and gasped in pain.

"Are you wounded?" Flora asked, then she realized how ridiculous that was. Still, he was in pain, so what else could it be? "Let me see."

Lazarus hesitated.

"Lazarus, let me see right now!"

Reluctantly, Lazarus took off his shirt.

In the firelight a mark, corroded and dark, like a burn, stretched over his stomach and chest. "What is this?" Flora breathed. "Did the striga—"

"Magic," Lazarus said. "Ana's magic. It appeared back in Davasca."

"Why didn't you tell me?" Flora shouted.

"Because I knew you'd react like this!" Lazarus said, scooting away from her. "Whatever it is, as long as we get to the Temple of Fates and we get our wishes, I'll be fine!"

"You don't know that!" Flora snapped.

"You don't know what I don't know," Lazarus pointed out.

"Lazarus, you need help!"

"Help who? What doesn't somebody know?" Atonais stuck his head out of the caravan. Lazarus tried to pull his shirt back on, to cover the black splotch on his chest, but it was too late. "Good gods! Let me get a better look at it."

"What can you do?" Lazarus asked. "You're an inventor."

"Yes, well, I've studied a lot of magic in my day, and I'm the best you've got right now," Atonais said. "Now come inside and let me see."

They climbed back into the caravan, and Lazarus lay down on his cot, shirt off, the black mark in full view. Flora sat close by, her heart racing, all the warmth from before replaced by the cold rush of fear. How could something hurt Lazarus? How was it *possible*?

"Hold still," Atonais said. He poked the black mark with the tip of a knife. "Does that hurt?"

"I don't feel anything there," Lazarus said. "Nothing at all, except when it burns."

Atonais made a small, shallow cut in the blackness. No blood leaked from it, but the wound—the wound didn't heal.

"Lazarus . . . ," Flora said.

"It's all right," Lazarus said. "I'm sure it's nothing."

Atonais went to his bag of things and pulled out a dusty-looking book that he sat down with and began to thumb through.

"It seems to me that we're dealing with two curses here," said Atonais. "There is the first curse—the one that's made you *immortal-ish*. Then something set the second curse into motion."

"I know that," said Lazarus. "It's Ana's magic."

"Look, I'm not one hundred percent sure here, but if that tissue is what I think it is, the second curse is causing your soul to slip out of your body, despite the fact that you're not really dead. As more and more of it leaves you, this dark tissue—I think—is spreading. The more of this tissue, the less of your soul is left, and that means you'll become something else."

Something else.

"What do you mean?" Lazarus asked, his young face slack with shock. "I've been the same for three hundred years."

"This tissue is very similar to tissue of undead beings, which we've been studying for three centuries now. The Necromancer's dead. I think that, whatever this second curse is, it's causing you to become something like one of the dead. A drog, more specifically."

Lazarus went pale. He put his hand to the bandages around his throat. "I remember drogs," Lazarus said, his voice soft with horror. "I fought them three hundred years ago. I can't let this happen."

They began to smell the unmistakable scent of decay.

"Time is of the highest importance," Atonais said. "We've got to find out what caused the second curse and find a way to reverse it." His eyes were grave as he regarded Lazarus. "Or you must find a way to die. Once and for all."

"That's what I've been trying to do for centuries! Die!" Lazarus said, turning from them. "And now that I'm on the way to do so, I'm turning into a ... a ..."

"The second curse is recent, right?" Flora said, going to stand next to him. "Well, what's happened recently? What's changed about you?"

"I *can't* change!" said Lazarus.

"Your name," Atonais said suddenly, snapping his fingers. "Lazarus isn't your real name!"

"Yes, but I fail to see how—"

"Names are linked to our souls—so the council thinks, anyway. Maybe this curse is linked somehow to your name. Your true name. Maybe you have to remember it in order to get rid of the curse."

"But how?" Lazarus asked. "Whenever I think of my name, there's nothing there!"

"It'll come to you," Atonais said. "You can't just forget your name. Not permanently."

Lazarus didn't answer. He simply looked over at the portrait of Ana hanging on the wall, but, as always, she was silent.

CHAPTER FIFTEEN

FLORA COULDN'T SLEEP. NOT AFTER SEEING THE drog tissue reaching its way across Lazarus's torso. His soul was leaving him, Atonais had said. A second curse was making his soul leave him, only to turn him into something horrible, something inhuman. She looked at Ana's picture, hanging on the wall, a ray of sunlight thrown across her face.

By her love she'll bind him and hers he'll ever be, Lazarus's prophecy had said.

Why would you do it? she wanted to ask. *Why would you make someone you loved suffer like that? Hasn't he suffered enough?* Ana hung there on the wall, almost smug in her silence. Flora turned away in disgust, then she heard a clinking of metal on glass. Atonais was sitting in the middle of the floor with an assortment of glass globes and small metal parts, fitting one thing to another, shaking his head. The air was thick with lightning.

"What are you doing?" Flora asked.

"Inventing," he said dully.

"Yes, but inventing what?" Flora bent to get a better look.

"Something to help Lazarus," said Atonais, shooing her away. "I'll know what it is when I'm finished."

He continued fiddling with the metal and glass bits around him, clinking and clacking. Every sound grated on Flora's nerves. She had to get out of the caravan. So she dressed and went out into the daylight.

She walked all day in the forest, bone-tired, trying not to think of Lazarus's drog tissue or Betheara or the Weir or the many, many things that could go wrong on their journey. Instead, she hunted, not knowing what she was after. The entire day slipped by, and when Flora started trudging back to the caravan, the sun had just begun to set. Lazarus would be alive again soon, and she wanted to be there in case he needed anything.

Flora brushed a long swath of vines out of the way with her gauntlet as she turned the corner into the clearing where the caravan sat, and though her eyes were bleary, something caught her attention. Flowers. Delicate white flowers spreading from the base of a tree up into its branches. Moonvines. They were the flowers of

Emir, of Kaer-Ise and its unicorns, and they had grown on the walls of the courtyard back at the castle. Flowers that bloomed at night, rare outside of Kaer-Ise.

It was odd. Flora had never really thought much about moonvines before, preferring the small, vibrant pink roses that grew in the princess's garden. She had even considered them pointless once or twice. After all, who wanted a flower that could only be seen at night? But now Flora knew better. Carefully, she sought out their roots, and she scooped the whole vine into her hands and carried it back to the caravan.

She emptied a small pot that Atonais had left on the caravan's back steps "to measure rainfall," filled it with earth, and planted the moonvines in it. She wouldn't tell Lazarus right away. She'd let it be a surprise. And with a final look at the moonvines, she went inside to check on Lazarus.

The door to Lazarus's room was open, and Flora could see him sitting on the bed with his eyes closed, one of Atonais's inventions in his hands, as Atonais hovered nearby. The air was still thick with lightning.

"What's all this?" Flora asked.

"Desperation," said Lazarus, with an odd tone to his voice.

"It's a memory-catching device," Atonais explained. "I'm hoping that if we go through some of Lazarus's memories and catch them in these globes, maybe they'll lead to the memory of his name."

Lazarus did seem nervous and fidgety, as though he would rather be doing anything but this. Flora imagined that, like her own, Lazarus's mind was full of things that were not fun to remember. "Well, it seems worth a try, at the least," Flora said. "Do you . . . want me to leave?"

"No," said Lazarus. "Please. Stay."

So Flora stayed. She sat down on the rug opposite Lazarus and did her best to look comforting and supportive instead of nervous and frightened.

"No, don't open your eyes," Atonais said to Lazarus in a strange, soothing voice. "I want you to remember long, long ago . . . imagine yourself after you left your village. I want you to imagine yourself as you were when something important happened. You can choose what it is. But you must tell me everything that is happening as you are seeing it, feeling it, experiencing it. You may begin whenever you're ready."

Lazarus's eyes closed. After a few minutes, his brows furrowed.

"Have you chosen a memory?" Atonais asked.

"Yes," Lazarus said. There was a deep thrum, and all the glass globes on the invention in Lazarus's hands lit up.

"What do you hear?" Atonais whispered.

"Drums," Lazarus said, his voice far away, sleepy-sounding. "Drums. All around. The ground shakes."

"What do you see?"

"The sky...it's orange—there's a fire behind the dead army...from the forests and cities they've burned. It's summer, but I can't hear the cicadas, only...the drums. Our drums. They're supposed to give us hope."

"Are they working?" Atonais asked.

"No."

Flora watched Lazarus's face. It was as though he were having a terrible dream. His eyes moved beneath his eyelids, his mouth tightened. His chest rose and fell as his breaths grew shallow.

"Our faces are painted to resemble wolves," Lazarus was saying. "The battle fires blaze and the drums beat on and on. The man next to me...he's older than me."

"Do you know him?" Atonais asked.

"No."

"Does he know you?"

"No. He's from the next village over. His hands shake on his blade." Lazarus made an expression of fear. A bead of sweat slid down his brow.

"What is happening now?" Atonais asked.

"They're topping the ridge, and the drums...the drums are silent now."

"What do you feel?"

"I'm scared," he said. His face, contorted by fear, looked younger than Flora had ever seen it. "I want to run." He took several ragged breaths and continued. "Spines, helmets, feathers, rust. Their blades are long and curved, like ours, but their eye sockets...have no eyes in them, only a strange blue fire. They don't move like we do. They shuffle...sway. But all together, like a...school of dark fish, and all I can see is the fire of their eyes."

The expression on his face was utter terror. The machine in his hands was whirring now, its bulbs brightening. Flora wanted desperately to stop it, to bring him out of that horrible memory. But it just kept going.

"What frightens you the most?"

"Their silence," Lazarus said. "I...I can't move..." His breaths grew quick, labored. "Their mouths are unhinging like snakes'."

The bulbs glowed brighter. Another bead of sweat slipped down Lazarus's nose. "There is noise now," Lazarus said. "Shouts, rusty sickles hacking, flesh rending, shields shattering, helmets puncturing. Screams. We are not ready. I—I—I am not ready. Not for...not for this."

Flora's hands bunched into fists. She wanted to shake him awake and tell him that it wasn't real, that it was just a memory, but Atonais put a finger to his mouth. *Shh! Wait!*

"One of them is in front of me," Lazarus said, and his voice was raw with horror. "Its mouth is open as though it is screaming, but there is no noise—no noise—and now it is—"

Lazarus made a choked, gargling sound. He grabbed his bandaged throat. Then he collapsed on the bed, not moving.

"Lazarus!" Flora shouted. "Atonais, what are you—"

"Wait!" Atonais said. "Watch!"

Before her eyes, Lazarus began to stir. His hands fumbled on the bed, searching for something. Then he touched his throat again, his jaw, his face. He sat up and opened his eyes, blinked a few times, then shook his head as though to wake himself up.

"Amazing!" Atonais said, taking a particularly bright bulb from the machine. "The memory is captured right in here! I was hoping someone had called you by your name during the battle, but we can search other memories later. Well done, Lazarus!"

"Are you all right?" Flora asked.

Lazarus nodded. "Now I am, yes."

"That was awfully strange, though," Atonais said. "What happened there at the end?"

"That was when I died." He pulled the bandages from his throat and revealed the deep scar that ran all the way around his neck. "When my head was cut off by a drog's blade."

Flora remembered the way he had searched with his hands on the blankets. Looking for his head. She shuddered. She thought of how he bandaged his neck every night, how he sometimes absently touched it when he was afraid.

"Amazing! What was it like?" Atonais gasped.

Lazarus looked up at Atonais, his eyes suddenly filled with rage. "You want to know how it feels to have your spine severed?" he asked quietly. "You want to know how it feels to have your head fall one way and your body another?" He stood and looked Atonais in the eye. Atonais shrank back. "Suffice it to say that it is neither fun nor *amazing* to be beheaded."

"But you're a survivor!" Atonais said. "You can tell us—"

"I am *not* a survivor." Lazarus scowled. "I didn't survive. And I'm no closer to remembering my name. I knew this was a mistake."

"Lazarus!" Flora said.

"I'm sorry, Flora. I need to be alone," Lazarus said. He pulled on a cloak and went out into the night.

Flora did not follow him.

"Well, that was rougher than I'd expected," Atonais said. "But maybe next time—"

"Shut up," Flora said, almost shaking with anger. "Just shut up. You can't just do that to people, you know? Make them relive the worst parts of their lives and expect them to be all right afterward. Next time, have a plan. Better yet, have some compassion."

And without another word, Flora went to her place on the cot, curled up under her blanket, and tried to force herself to sleep.

It could have been worse, Lazarus thought as he stood in the rain, trying to focus on the wet and cold instead of blue fire eyes and screaming. . . . *It could have been so much worse.* Gods, it had all been so real. It had been as though he were there again, on the front lines. Still, he thought, it was not his worst memory. That one had come later, when he had risen from the dead for the first time. That dark cellar. All the blood. Ana . . .

That was one memory that he would never revisit, no matter how dire the situation grew.

Lazarus took a deep breath and steadied himself. Then he began securing the caravan for the night. He circled it and checked all the wheels, made sure everything was in order to travel at greater speeds. He took care of the horses. When he went around to the back, he saw that a small pot sat on the back porch, and there, soaking up the rain, was a plant: a tiny vine that must have just been placed, as it had not yet begun to climb the porch. It was blooming, white flowers reaching up to the moonlight. Flowers that bloomed at night. And only one person could have put them there.

He sat and stared at the moonvines for a long time, putting everything out of his mind but their beauty, their simplicity, the thoughtfulness that had brought them to him. And despite the ghostly pain that still circled his neck beneath his bandages, Lazarus felt just a little bit better.

CHAPTER SIXTEEN

THE WEIR BLOOMED UP AND OUT OF THE HORIZON like a thunderhead. As they neared it, it seemed to Flora that Atonais grew uneasier by the moment. He tried to channel his nervousness into invention and had created things like striga-fighting lights and surprisingly handy lightning-powered lanterns for the front of the caravan. But still, his static rose all around them, and whenever Flora and Lazarus touched something metal, they felt the sizzle of lightning.

"Will he be all right?" she asked.

"He'll be fine."

"Will *we* be all right?" she asked.

"I should hope so," Lazarus said. But even he had recently taken to wearing gloves around the caravan.

"You know, you're *so* good at making people feel

better," Flora said. "You've got a real talent for it. I just feel all my unease drifting away."

"I try," said Lazarus.

As they drew near, their lantern light illuminated the trees and Flora could see a few signs tacked to them, all made of dark, nearly rotten wood, and most barely legible.

"Weir: The Woods of Eternal Sleep," Flora read. She gave Lazarus a skeptical look. He shrugged.

The tiny window behind the driver's seat slid open and Atonais peered out.

"What?" Atonais said from the inside of the caravan. "What was that?!"

"Um . . . nothing," Flora said, exchanging a look with Lazarus.

Atonais laughed nervously. Flora touched the hilt of her dagger and drew back in pain as another spark snapped at her fingertips.

"Will you calm down? You keep making me shock myself!" She closed the tiny window.

"I can't help it," Atonais said, opening it again and peeping out, the yellow jewel between his brows glittering in a way that made him seem even more nervous.

A twig snapped somewhere in the forest. He glanced in the direction of the sound and, sticking his finger through the window to point, screamed, "Oh, gods, what is *that*?!"

Grazing in the field just outside the Weir was a reddish stag, its velvet hanging in bloody rags from its antlers.

"Look at it!" Atonais cried. "Did it...did it attack someone? Did something attack it?"

"It's a Fal-deer," Flora said, trying to make her voice sound as soothing as possible. "Fal-deer do that when the weather gets cold, rather than when it gets warm. Just calm down."

"How do you know that?" Atonais asked, eyes wide and frightened.

"Just because I worked in a palace doesn't mean that I don't know things," she said, annoyed. "And if you don't calm down, you're going to shock us to death."

"Speak for yourself," quipped Lazarus, his eyes on the road.

"Fine, you'll shock *me* to death," Flora said. "So stop it."

"This is a terrifying place. You could...you could just wrap something around your sword hilts. Cover the metal, and the lightning won't hurt you."

"How about you make me something?" Flora said in a desperate attempt at putting Atonais's mind somewhere else. "Something so I won't get shocked by your lightning. Lightning-proof gauntlets, how about that?"

"All right," Atonais said. "I can do that." He shut the window and began clattering around in the caravan, looking for something to do.

"Good idea," said Lazarus.

"I do have them on occasion." Flora smiled.

Entering the Weir was like diving into murky water. It enveloped them suddenly and completely. Inside, the canopy overhead was thick and dark with only thin trickles of moonlight filtering down to the forest floor. The tree trunks were streaks of black on either side of the path. The entire forest floor was covered with a carpet of velvety dead leaves and white mushrooms. The path twisted this way and that, and soon they could not see the entrance through which they had come. The smell of earth was everywhere, mixed with something darker, more sinister, that Flora could not name.

But besides all the eeriness, all the damp and murk of the forest, what struck Flora the most was its silence. Atonais had made it sound as though it was running amok with monsters. She had half expected there to be screaming maidens running every which way and howling beasts chasing them. Still, the silence pervaded. It had the feeling of a cemetery, long abandoned and forgotten, its gravestones obscured with moss. Still, something urged her onward into the Weir, made her want to go deep into that darkness and seek out its heart.

Though they could hear no creatures moving about, the Weir's inhabitants announced their presence in other ways. There were clawed tracks in the mud beside a pool, deep claw marks in the trees' bark, saplings bent into arches and fastened into shape with vines. Here and there white bones gleamed among the decaying foliage, marked through with tooth marks. The only living creature she saw for some time was a bird, a shrike, in the act of impaling a mouse on a bush with large, shadowy thorns. Once, Lazarus said, "Shh!" and looked out into the trees. Flora put her hand on her sword. Then he shrugged and they kept moving.

After they had been traveling through the Weir for around two hours, Atonais opened the window behind the driver's seat and presented them with a set of all-leather gauntlets that were coated in something that gave them almost a sheen. "Entirely lightning-proof," he said to Flora. "You're welcome."

"Atonais!" Lazarus said. "If—if you're finished with the gauntlets, I need you to go back inside and focus on lightning-proofing all the hilts of our weapons. Can you do that?"

"Of course!" said Atonais, and he went back into the caravan and closed the door behind him.

Flora started to ask what all that was about, when Lazarus pointed to a shape lurking behind a tree just off the path. It was something a bit like a fox, but longer and slimmer and darker than night, and it had what looked like a very old arm bone in its mouth—the bones of the attached wrist and hand were still visible. It grew larger, blacker, stronger for a moment, its legs lengthening so that they were spindly, longer than the legs of any fox. Then it caught sight of the caravan and it dissolved, right into the ground, leaving the skeletal arm on the leaves. Flora's stomach lurched.

"Be respectful of the dead here," Lazarus said. "And do not allow the spirits to get to you. That's the real danger of this place: the sadness."

Flora tried, but the woods seemed alive with shadows, making the darkness boil and simmer like heat. Once or twice, Flora saw mossy skulls grinning up at her from the forest floor, still wearing ages-old helmets from before the Necromancer's War.

"What happened here?" she asked Lazarus as they traveled.

"There was a great battle long ago, even before I was born," Lazarus said. "The blood soaked into the earth and was drunk up by the roots. Evil spirits are drawn to bloodshed, and they have gathered here for centuries." Then he shrugged. "They've never bothered me before."

As they moved deeper into the Weir, strange plants

began to appear. At first, Flora thought there was an odd poetry to it, finding beautiful scenery in such a place. But she had never seen plants like these. They were tall, spindly mushrooms, bright blue, glowing in the dim forest light . . . and they seemed sinister. A heavy, dark scent rose from them, reminding Flora of funeral wreaths and grave dirt. Soon, they came to a place where the ground was simply covered with these mushrooms and there were no old bones to be seen. The whole forest floor glowed with their feathery light, and against the black vertical lines of the tree trunks and the thin gray light that filtered through the canopy the sight was both eerie and beautiful, as though they were traveling through a forest at the bottom of the sea.

When things began stirring in the trees and owls began to hoot, they knew that night had come into its full glory. There were howls in the forest, howls from wolves and other, bigger-sounding things. The shadows that darted between the trees grew bolder, more acrobatic. In the light of the blue mushrooms, the shadows twisted and writhed like flames. Flora saw Lazarus following them with his eyes, brows furrowed. They got closer and closer to the caravan until Lazarus turned Atonais's lighting system on and the road flared into light. The shadows scattered, fell back, and stayed at a safe distance.

Outside the lightning lanterns' glow, Flora saw

something lurching in the darkness. It was a huge, shapeless creature, bent down but still head and shoulders higher than the young trees around it. Its face and head were hidden under an ancient, ratty cloak, and as they drew nearer, it gave a piteous wailing as though its very heart were breaking in two. It approached the road, moving as though gelatinous, and before it birds and rabbits scattered in fear.

"Away, humans!" it sobbed. "I must cross! Stop still, and do not turn to face me!"

Obediently, Lazarus stopped the caravan. "Close your eyes, Flora," he said. "Atonais! Shut the windows and do not look out until we are moving again!"

Flora heard a scrambling inside the caravan, and the shutters behind her latched shut one by one. The sobbing grew louder and the creature began to move toward the road.

Lazarus sat stock-still.

"What is that?" Flora whispered, pressing closer to him.

"It is the Bugyl Noz," Lazarus said. "It is an ancient creature cursed with ugliness. The last of its kind in the world and the source of the sadness that hangs over this forest. It wails to warn people of its approach, as it is supposed to be so ugly that a glimpse of its face can kill.

If it gives us its blessing, the darkness will not weigh so heavily on us."

The sobbing grew louder, and Flora could feel its footsteps shaking the earth. It stopped behind them, its shadow darkening the night. In this shadow, all her feelings of horror, shame, sadness seemed to lengthen and deepen, and Flora knew what Lazarus meant about the darkness being heavy.

"Why have you come here, humans?" it sobbed, and Flora clenched her eyes shut. "This forest is for the lost and the things that prey on them. It is not for you."

"I am the Ankou," said Lazarus. "And this is my assistant. We request your blessing through these woods."

"My blessing," it scoffed. "Why should two as young and handsome as you ask for the blessing of one such as me, cursed with eternal ugliness, and thus eternal loneliness? Are you afraid of my sadness marring your beauty?"

Its voice was so weary, so full of endless, hopeless sadness. The eternal sorrow of being alone in the dark. And Flora understood. It seemed like that voice had been the echo after each beat of her heart when she'd first woken in Valacia. She understood the Bugyl Noz. And she knew what to do.

"We, too, are the last of our kinds," said Flora. "And

we're lonely, too. But we don't want to be forever." Careful to keep her eyes shut, Flora reached into her pocket and pulled out the pincushion. She pulled three gold pins and held them out in her palm.

"Here," she said. "Take these."

The sobbing stopped. She held her breath, kept her eyes carefully closed, her hand reaching out into the darkness. Then she felt a large hand take the pins from her palm.

"Thank you, human," it said, "for your pain."

Flora felt its shadow leave them. The unbearable sadness lightened, and when she opened her eyes, she looked after it, but could only hear it lumbering off through the forest on the other side of the road.

"Well done," Lazarus said. He reached out and wiped away a tear she hadn't felt on her cheek with his black-gloved hand. "You are so..." He stopped. For one breath-quickening moment, his hand lingered there, the fingertips of his gloves resting lightly on her cheek. Then he seemed to remember himself and pulled away.

"If we want to find the royal family, or get rid of this curse, every moment counts," he said. Then he urged the horses onward and the caravan rocked back into motion, feeling lighter than before. And though she tried not to think about it, she could still feel where Lazarus had touched her face.

They went on for a long time until dew began to form on the grass, and they knew that sunrise was imminent. Lazarus stopped them in a place where there was little underbrush, no flowers, and no shadow, and he fastened feedbags onto the horses' harnesses.

"We're stopping here?" Atonais said, his face against the small window that separated the driver's seat and the caravan interior.

"No choice," Lazarus said. "Dawn is coming, and the horses need rest."

"We can't—we can't just *stop* here."

"Don't worry," Lazarus said. "The spirits are repelled by lightning. Your lightning will hold them back, I am sure."

Atonais cursed and closed the window. Moments later, he got out of the caravan with a handful of metal wire and began stringing it from tree to tree around the caravan, completely enclosing it in a makeshift wire fence.

"What are you—" Flora started.

But Atonais shot ten streaks of lightning out of his hands and sent the streaks dancing over the wires. He held the lightning current in place for a few moments, then he slumped and took a step back. "Don't touch it!" he said when Flora moved toward the wire. "Not without the gauntlets.

I have run lightning through it. This fence should shock anything that tries to get into the area while we are asleep."

Then Atonais's eyes lost focus and he swayed on his feet. "I think I overdid it with all of the inventions lately," he said weakly. "I'll be in the caravan." And he climbed back inside and disappeared.

"Only one thing left," Lazarus said when he had a weak fire started. He took from his pocket a stack of yellowed parchment squares, each with a different, strange symbol written on them in ink.

"Spirit money?" Flora said. "You've never done that before."

"Just to let the spirits know that that we mean no disrespect."

"You're sure we're not in danger?" Flora asked. "Or were you just saying that to appease Atonais?"

Lazarus knelt down before the fire and tossed them in, one by one, muttering something that Flora could not understand. He watched them until the last parchment piece had burned to a cinder.

"It's just better to be safe," he said.

They went on like this for days. Traveling deeper into the thickening Weir and sleeping under the protection of the lightning fence and spirit money at night. The ground beneath them grew wet and swampy—hence, *Weir*, Flora supposed—and will-o'-the-wisps could be seen floating among the trees, beckoning them off the path so they could be devoured.

Flora did not ask Lazarus about the drog tissue but saw its spread in how he urged the horses to go faster than usual, in how often he stared into the dark forest, seeing nothing. One morning, she saw, with a pang of shock, that it had spread across the right half of his stomach and chest. He acted as though it was nothing, but she saw how quickly he buttoned his shirt.

That night, at dinner, they stopped in a cave in a land-bank. It was wet and cold, and a heavy fog rolled in that made them shiver with frost and unease. Flora sat outside the caravan, far from the mouth of the cave, across which Atonais had strung his lightning fence, and watched as Lazarus tried over and over to start a fire. The whetstone sparked, but there was no smoke, no catching, no blaze. No warmth or light to keep the night at bay.

"It's all right, Lazarus," Flora said. "We have a stove. We could go in and—"

Lazarus kept striking and striking with the whetstone. Striking and striking, and every spark died as the air around them grew colder and wetter with fog. Flora watched Lazarus's back as he tried again and again to start the fire. Again and again and again, with the stone. Faster and faster, still there was no spark.

Flora put her hand on his shoulder. "Do you want me to call Atonais to light it for you?"

"I will be a monster soon, Flora," he said, staring down at the ground. He moved his hair from his neck, and she saw that the black drog tissue had crept its way up his neck and was peeking out of his bandages. "I may not change today or tomorrow. Not this week or even this month," he said. "It's spreading. It's spreading, and I'm not fast enough. We can't possibly travel fast enough to stop it. And I can't remember my name—why can I not remember?"

"You'll remember," Flora said. "You'll remember. It will be all right. Come on, let's go inside and you can try again with the memory machine."

"You have to kill me," Lazarus said, taking her by the shoulders. "When—*if* I turn, you have to kill me, Flora."

"No," she said. His eyes were those of a madman, bloodshot and dark-circled. "I agreed to help you find your death, not to kill you."

"Please," he said. "When I am a drog, I can finally be destroyed. And you are faster than I am now. I trained you. I know. Maybe that is the way it is meant to be. Maybe that is what the prophecy meant—"

"Don't be stupid," Flora said, shocked to hear the worry in her own voice.

"Promise me, Flora," he said. "If you've ever been grateful to me, if you've ever considered me your . . . your friend, promise me this."

The thought of killing him, of killing Lazarus, made her sick to her stomach. Knowing that he would die at the end of their quest was bad enough. She couldn't possibly think of doing it herself, and in that moment, she hated him for asking her to.

"I *can't*, Lazarus," she said, pushing his hands from her shoulders. "Don't make me promise that."

Lazarus turned and stared into the firewood that he hadn't been able to ignite. He glanced out at the mouth of the cave, at the light streaking down through the trees.

"I'm sorry," he said, and his voice seemed flat and weighed down. He didn't say anything else. He climbed into the caravan, shut the door behind him, and did not stir again.

Lazarus woke and checked himself in the mirror. It was impossible now to keep the drog tissue covered by the bandages and it peeked out from under them, dark and ominous. He didn't let himself think about it. Instead, he dressed, bathed, and went out into the main room of the caravan to wake Flora and Atonais.

Atonais was still asleep in the chair across from the cot, a line of drool sliding down his chin. He looked pale and weary, even in sleep. *Perhaps I have underestimated the power of the Weir,* Lazarus thought. *It certainly seems to be making everyone more tired than they should be.* He did not wake Atonais.

He moved to shake Flora awake, but he found nothing but a pile of blankets. Lazarus scrambled outside and looked around and behind the caravan, and on top of it, where she liked to sit sometimes. Then he saw her, curled in a ball at the mouth of the cave, asleep in front of the lightning fence, and he breathed a sigh of relief. *I will have to apologize to her,* he thought. *Asking her to kill me . . . what was I thinking?*

Then he saw them beyond the fence. Seven or eight shapes, almost humanlike, but somehow not, and made completely of shadow. Shadow people. They were bent, watching Flora sleep, or at least, they would have been if they had eyes. But there was nothing, nothing but dark shadow matter. Lazarus reached into the pocket of his cloak . . . yes, he still had a bit of salt. He took the salt in his hand and moved toward them.

"Get back," he whispered. "You know who I am."

They stepped back, but they did not retreat. They stood outside the lightning fence, silent, waiting.

Lazarus threw the salt onto them. They clutched their faces in pain, sizzling, and the shadow people blended into the shadows of the Weir and simply were not there anymore.

Lazarus stood over Flora for a few moments. It was strange. Never in his many voyages through the Weir had shadow people come so close. "Flora," he said, shaking her shoulder. "Flora. Wake up."

She groaned, and her eyelids flickered open. He saw her focus on the black veins of drog tissue that had spread onto his jaw. Then her eyes grew wide.

There was a wet stain of blood between her legs. Her bloods had come.

"Great," she said. "Just what I need right now. I'll be back in a moment." She got up and shuffled to the caravan with her legs close together.

Lazarus looked out into the Weir again, after the shadow people who had bent over her as she slept. That was why the spirit money had not appeased them. They had smelled blood.

He and Atonais couldn't wait inside the cave for Flora's bloods to pass. That could take a whole week, and there was not a week to spare. Not at the rate the drog tissue was spreading. They couldn't travel during the day, not in a forest as dark as the Weir. No, they had to leave—soon. There were more shadow people in the Weir...thousands more...

"Good morning—er, evening," Atonais said, stepping out of the caravan. "Flora booted me out so she could take a bath. I didn't get a chance to power any magic energy into the water-heating device, though, so I hope she enjoys cold water." Then Atonais saw Lazarus's expression. "Is something wrong?"

"Remember what I said about the Weir being safe?" Lazarus asked. "Well, the situation has changed. We need to move through this forest as quickly as we can, despite anything that may want to do us harm. We will all need to be alert and ready to act at all times. Do you understand?"

Atonais nodded, his face pale.

"Power some energy into the lightning lanterns," Lazarus said. "We are going to need them."

CHAPTER SEVENTEEN

A S THEY ROLLED ON THROUGH THE FOREST, FLORA sat on the cot inside the caravan, breathing in incense smoke. Cramps had come, intense and painful, and she lay on the cot, trying unsuccessfully to ignore them. Atonais looked out the window while Lazarus drove onward. The caravan bumped violently through the forest, and every now and then, Flora could hear the crack of Lazarus's little-used whip as he urged Nik and Tal forward. The horses foamed at the mouth and whinnied, but they kept at a gallop through the forest. She thought she heard a howl. The moon wasn't full, was it?

Out the window, she could see the dark trees and blue mushrooms flash by, and among them were wisps of darkness, moving quickly, ever present, trailing behind them.

Atonais paced in the back of the caravan, looking out

through the back window above Lazarus's bed. He paced and paced, looked out the window, paced again. "Why did I agree to this?" he kept asking himself. "Why did I agree to this?"

Outside, far behind them, the shadows swarmed steadily thicker. Dark motion filled the forest close to the ground and covered the blue mushrooms. Shadows fell from the trees and moved like humans but faster, twisted, on all four legs. The forest was soundless, save for the thin, terrifying swoosh of insubstantial flesh moving through the night.

Eventually, the shadows would catch up. Lazarus had told her how they had gathered to watch her sleep. What would have happened had the lightning fence not been there? Flora shuddered and reached for another stick of the incense meant to cover the scent of her blood. She touched the censer and drew back with a yelp as a spark crackled on the metal.

Atonais was holding on to one of Lazarus's bedposts, staring out the window at the looming black shadows overtaking the field of blue mushrooms. "They'll catch up soon," he was saying. "They'll catch up soon, and I can't keep up." He turned to Flora with desperation in his ever-moving eyes. "I can't do it, Flora. I just can't do it."

"You can't do what?" Flora asked, a nervous flutter in her chest.

"I've been using lightning constantly," Atonais said. "Over and over. It's not an endless resource, Flora! At this rate, I'll run out and be too exhausted to lift a finger. And then what happens to us?"

Flora didn't know. She racked her brain for answers but found none. Dawn would come soon, and with it, Lazarus, their first line of defense and their driver, would be gone. The forest was dark enough during the day for the shadows to overtake them, and with Atonais running out of magic, it would be up to her to fight them off.

A cramp rolled through her and she groaned. She, a mortal, couldn't fight hundreds of shadow creatures by herself in her normal condition, much less now, when her insides seemed like they were turning inside out.

In the forest, black shapes shot from tree to tree, opening their shadowy jaws to grin at Flora through the window. Flora heard the horses wheeze and grunt as they pulled the caravan impossibly fast, impossibly forward.

Then the caravan screeched to a halt and Flora and Atonais were thrown forward.

"They've cut us off!" Lazarus said. Flora heard his boots hit the ground as he jumped down from the caravan. She heard Lazarus's falx slide out of its sheath.

Flora looked out the window. Shadow people were coming from all sides. They had formed a black circle around the caravan. Lazarus stood in front of the caravan, in front of the horses, with his falx in his hand.

She held her breath. They were coming from all sides, and Lazarus stood in the middle, waiting. Then they fell upon him with shadowy claws and teeth. His blade flashed in the blue mushrooms' light. He whirled, he slashed, and none of them passed him. But there were too many to defeat. They ripped and tore at him even as he healed. And there were too many, far too many for even him to fight alone.

"Help him!" Flora cried to Atonais. "Flash the lights, like with the striga!"

But Atonais was on the floor, breaths coming in gasps. "I can't!" he cried. "It's too much! I'm at the end of it!" Then he put his head in his hands and shook silently.

Outside, Lazarus cried out in pain.

Flora threw the covers off her lap. She pulled her sword from the barrel, took off one of her gauntlets and filled her pockets with salt, and struggled to the door, still bent from cramps.

"Wh-what are you doing?" Atonais spluttered. "You can't go out there! They'll kill you!"

Flora pushed him away. She opened the door and did her best to push her pain to the back of her mind. She went out into the fray with her sword drawn. There was a wall of moving darkness all around the caravan, and Lazarus was running to and fro, fighting the shadows away as they reached out to the caravan. Still more of them were coming, a black wave darker than the dark woods.

"Flora!" Lazarus shouted. One of the shadows slashed at his face, leaving a mark that vanished as quickly as it appeared. "Get back into the caravan!"

"No!" She sliced through one of them, and it was silent as it disintegrated into nothingness.

The direction of the wave shifted as the shadow people came for Flora. Their bodies whirled like black mist, then appeared, solid, in front of her. They reached out from all sides, and Flora threw salt at one before slicing two more in half. They struggled, bisected in the air for a moment, then they seemed to burn away, fraying at the edges, curling into ash like burning flags.

She slashed at another two and lurched forward, teeth gritted in pain, as a third whipped three burning claws down her back. Everywhere she turned, she faced a high black wall of claws and teeth. But she held her sword in one hand and a dagger in the other, and she stood with her legs bent and her teeth bared, ready to face the onslaught. Then Lazarus was beside her, his back to her own burning, wounded one. His face was covered with bloody lacerations knitting themselves back together as he stood behind her, blade drawn, facing the deadly shadows.

"This was stupid, Flora," he said as the blood climbed back up his face and into his disappearing wounds. His eyes were on the shadows that surrounded them now, preparing to descend upon them, rip them to shreds, drink their blood.

"I had to help you," Flora said, grimacing as another cramp squeezed at her insides.

"We have one chance," Lazarus said. "When I count to three, take all the salt from your pockets and throw it into the air, then attack. Front, sides. Maybe—maybe—"

One shadow stretched out a long hand, reaching for her face. Reaching . . . reaching.

"One," Lazarus said.

Its wide mouth stretched itself into a smile.

"Two."

The shadow drew one burning claw down her face, leaving a line of blood. The shadows rose on all sides, rose high and dark and frightening, cresting like a wave waiting to crash.

"Three!"

In unison, Flora and Lazarus threw the salt high into the air and pulled their weapons just as the dark wave broke over them. They whirled, slashed, back-to-back, blades shining as they tore through the shadows. Everything was a world of darkness, pain, searing screams, sizzling shadow flesh, and Lazarus's back, never leaving her own. The claws tore at her clothes, at her hair, her arms, her face. Burning pain all around, and then—

Blinding light, searing heat—earsplitting, brain-breaking. The ground shook as though the very world was cracking in two. Flora realized what it was: a huge, sustained lightning bolt. The shadows screamed, stretched, and ripped into pieces in the light and heat. Nik and Tal reared and whinnied.

And it was over—all the light, all the heat—and there were just the shreds of the shadows drifting like ashes to the ground.

Flora and Lazarus turned and saw Atonais there in front of the caravan. His arms were outstretched and his hair was standing on end. The tips of his fingers were charred black. He swayed once, then his eyes rolled back, and he collapsed to the ground like a hollow thing that had been broken. When Lazarus and Flora ran forward to lift him from the ground, his heart still beat strongly, but his body was weak, exhausted from the tremendous energy he had released.

"Was it enough?" he asked. But before Flora could answer him, Atonais closed his eyes and sank into unconsciousness on the ground.

CHAPTER EIGHTEEN

ATONAIS WAS UNCONSCIOUS FOR AN ENTIRE DAY after the lightning strike, but the shadows did not approach again, and when Flora's bloods dried four nights later, the shadows no longer danced between the trees or lingered at the edge of the clearing. When he did wake, it was as though he had undergone a minor transformation. Atonais no longer shuddered and sparked and looked out the window at the snap of a branch. When he volunteered to keep watch during the day, they let him.

The Weir changed around them as they traveled. The alder and oak trees were replaced by evergreens, the shadows grew fewer and the air grew thinner and colder and harder to breathe. Broad-backed trolls rumbled, slow and stupid, among the trees in these higher altitudes, but they seemed to know the Black Caravan, and they did not come near it. There were hot springs in the mountains, and as they bathed Flora's wounds in the warm water, small white monkeys sat in springs nearby and watched them.

While the others healed and grew stronger, and the land changed, Lazarus's condition worsened. The drog tissue spread across his chest, down his stomach, onto his back and up his neck, and with it came a dreadful fever. When his shivering became too much, Flora and Atonais banished him to the interior of the caravan. There, he tried to distract himself by baking black-currant scones, but of course no one wanted to eat baked goods that always had a subtle scent of decaying flesh, so he ended up having to feed them to the horses. He read, drew, played sad songs on the violin. Sometimes when the others were out, he even used the memory machine by himself. Still, he could never remember his name, not even when he and Atonais went through the memory globes together. So still, slowly, the tissue spread.

Lazarus began to count his nights as being either good or bad. On his good nights, he was almost his usual self. On his bad nights, though, the pain of his functioning organs trying to work with his rotting organs grew to be too much, and Lazarus retched and shook until he went into his chamber to die. On those nights, Atonais took the reins as Flora sat with Lazarus's head in her lap, or held his hair back as he vomited into a basin. No one knew why some nights were good and others bad, but Lazarus's health seemed to wax and wane like the moon.

He slept more often than he had in centuries, using his "alive" time on bad days to rest. With rest came dreams. Some of them were good dreams, like walking through a garden in bloom during that time of day when everything was gold around the edges. Some were embarrassing dreams, like a few of the ones he'd begun to have about Flora. Those were the dreams, though, that had begun to shift into nightmares, full of blood and viscera. Things that shuddered him when he woke, sweating, praying for it all to be over.

After one such dream, he woke in a cold sweat. His body felt raw inside. He threw on his clothes and didn't bother checking his reflection in the mirror before he walked out into the caravan's main room. He saw, just for a flickering moment, the first part of the dream: the two of them in his bed in the sunlight, her beneath him, arching her back as he kissed his way down the pale flat of her stomach. Then, the dream changed. He was standing over her body, her organs spilled, her blood soaking into the floorboards, dripping from hands that had become claws, a mouth filled with fangs.

Lazarus's stomach threatened to turn itself inside out. He ran to the door and opened it. He retched and retched until Flora gently gathered his hair and held it back.

Lazarus pulled away. He wiped his mouth and shut his mind to the flashes of the dream that lunged out of the darkness. "Sorry," he said, turning toward her. "I . . . haven't been feeling as well as I normally—"

He stopped. Flora's eyes were wide. "What?" he asked.

"Lazarus," she said, her voice the deliberate calm of someone who was about to give bad news. He moved past her to the mirror.

There, he saw that his face—his young, unchanging face—was now drastically, hideously different. His neck and the lower left side of his face were entirely covered in spidery black drog tissue, but that wasn't all. It was rough, like a burn, but rather than raised, it seemed as if his skin were being eaten into, toward the bone. He was rotting alive, he realized. There was no hiding it now.

He was not all right.

He would not be all right.

Flora's eyes were still wide and frightened.

"Well," he said, forcing a shaky smile. "My looks have finally gone. I'll have to rely on personality from here, gods help me."

But Flora didn't smile. She just took his hand and held it in her own.

They reached the end of the Weir on one of Lazarus's good days, and when Lazarus demanded to drive, Flora hadn't the heart to stop him. They traveled through the cool, quiet night, and the greenery had all but disappeared as they ascended into the crags. If Flora focused, she could hear water running somewhere in the distance. Inside the caravan, Atonais was halfway through a book about unicorns and his reading had distracted him enough to let dinner burn to a crisp.

"Good thing that I don't have to eat," Lazarus said to Flora. "Even when he does manage to cook something, it always tastes like lightning."

"He improves every day, I think," said Flora. She tried to keep her voice positive, but even though it was a good day for Lazarus, she could not help asking herself how much longer he had.

But Lazarus wasn't listening. His eyes were on the cliffs, darting to and fro.

"What is it?" Flora asked.

"I don't want to worry you," Lazarus said. "However, there was a group of monsters that lived on this mountain."

Flora groaned and pulled out her blade. "Of course there was."

"They weren't necessarily evil, but they could be . . . troublesome. Some worshipped them as gods long ago," Lazarus said. "Look sharp. They were just before the bridge."

The rocky mountain passage grew narrower, just wide enough for the caravan to pass. Flora kept an eye upward, on the shadows in the crags. She had read stories of monsters hiding in such areas, reaching down with their great, clawed hands and snatching up travelers as though they were picking berries.

But no great hands plucked her from the caravan. Instead, they left the passage, and Flora soon heard the roar of the river that cut through the mountains at the bottom of the gorge just ahead. In the moonlight, Flora saw two great stone formations, like drab cushionless thrones on either side of the bridge. And perhaps that's what they had been, because Flora could see smooth, worn places where great arms had once rested.

"The forest guardians used to be here," Lazarus said. "Looks like I've outlived them, too."

Flora quietly slid her sword back into its sheath.

Lazarus spurred Nik and Tal onward. As they crossed the old, high bridge, the river thundering below them, Flora prayed that it would hold. But it did, and when Atonais came out to sit beside her, they saw that on the other side, the ground was no longer grass and moss and stone, but sand. A heavy wooden gate, twice the height of the caravan, waited slightly ajar, as if it were inviting them into the desert. On it was the emblem of a black eye that stood out in stark contrast against the brightening sky: the emblem of the king of Parth.

Lazarus stopped the caravan in front of the door and turned to them. "This is it," he said. "If we're caught, I can't guarantee our—" He broke off into a fit of coughing, doubled over, his face buried in a handkerchief.

Flora saw blood redden it for a moment—a frightening amount of blood. Then the blood drained out of the handkerchief and it was white again.

It's gotten to his lungs now, Flora thought. She glanced at Atonais. He nodded gravely.

"We're fine, Lazarus," she said, putting her hand on Lazarus's shoulder. "Let's go. The royal family are probably waiting there for me, drinking tea with the king."

She had expected Atonais to say something, too. About how he was eager to see Parth's scientific progress in action, perhaps, or something about the Temple of Fates. But he didn't say a word for the rest of the night. For once on this trip, Atonais Kell was completely silent.

When Lazarus rebuilt the next evening and vomited his grave dirt into his pot, he didn't look at himself in the mirror for fear of how fast the drog tissue was spreading. He just washed up, threw his clothes on, and headed into the main room of the caravan, toward the smell of freshly brewed coffee, and nearly tripped over Atonais.

"Gods!" Lazarus said. "You can't just sit in the middle of the floor like that!"

"I'm making preparations," Atonais said, holding up the memory machine. "Another day, another memory session."

Lazarus glanced at Flora's cot, but the covers had been thrown back and she was nowhere to be seen.

"I asked her to check the perimeter," Atonais said as Lazarus was opening his mouth to ask. "We don't know what's lurking in these cliffs, after all. Here, drink this coffee."

"You should have waited for me," said Lazarus, putting the cup down. "She doesn't know what kinds of things are in the desert beyond the ridge! She could be killed! She could—"

"You've trained her, and she will be fine," said Atonais, his voice strangely firm. "Now, please, focus on yourself right now. We're no closer to finding your name, and at the rate this tissue is spreading, we'll be lucky to make it to the Temple of Fates at all."

"If losing my name is even what is really causing all of this," Lazarus said. "I'm telling you, this is a curse from Ana."

"Why have you never allowed me to see any memories of her?" Atonais asked.

Lazarus blinked.

"Because it's too painful, right? Too personal?" Atonais said. "Well, don't you think that kind of memory is exactly what we need to explore in order to get to the source of this curse? To really make progress?"

"What are you asking for?" Lazarus said.

"I need you to let me see what happened the night you got your curse."

"Atonais—" Lazarus started.

"Keep it from Flora all you want," Atonais said. "But as a physician of magic, I can't just sit by and let you rot when I know that I haven't done all that I could. Now, I've got one bulb left. So stop being so damn secretive and let's see it once and for all."

He was right, Lazarus knew. And as Lazarus saw the slow creep of the drog tissue up his chest, he knew that there was no other way around it. He had to let Atonais see.

"All right," Lazarus said.

Atonais nodded gravely and handed Lazarus the

bulb. They set up the machine and Atonais, too, placed his hands on the bulb.

"Show me."

And, gritting his teeth against it, Lazarus dove back into the memory, back to the source of his immortality. Back to that cellar so long ago.

He lived it all again: his death, his wrenching from the afterlife, his resurrection. Ana's death. And when the memory was over, Lazarus sat, shaking, on the edge of his bed, trying to catch his breath.

Atonais paced, holding his hands to his head. "This is bad. This is very bad." He turned to Lazarus. "Flora doesn't know, does she?"

"Of course not," Lazarus said. "She's a Kaer-Isian. How could I tell her about that?"

Atonais looked at him, and Lazarus knew that he had come to the same realization. "You know what's causing it, don't you?"

And Lazarus did know. Perhaps he had known for longer than he'd let himself realize. But how could he have avoided it? How could he have avoided any of it? Especially since she, since Flora, was part of the prophecy?

Lazarus felt smothered. "I have to go," he said, throwing on his cloak and hat. "I need to think."

"But it's almost dawn," Atonais said. "What will you—"

"I need to think," Lazarus repeated, pulling Ana's picture off the wall and putting it in his pocket. "Stay here and wait for Flora."

He pushed the door open and went out into the night, his head buzzing with *what if*s and *how*s and *why*s. He walked through scrub brush and ducked under boulders until he felt the desert sand sink under his boots. Before him lay the vast expanse of the desert, an ocean of dunes, a field of nothing. Empty, waiting.

Lazarus sat down on the sand and looked out at the nothingness for a moment. Then he pulled Ana's picture from his pocket and looked at it. Something had changed. Not about the picture. She was still Ana, the witch girl, his only friend in the days before the war, the cause of his curse. Her black eyes stared up at him with all the intensity they had always held, an intensity that he recognized now for the madness that it had been. They had often been like that in those final days before his death. He'd pleaded for her to calm down, to just listen. Once, in angry tears, she had struck him across the face, and his only response had been to apologize to her, to try to calm her down so they would be the same again.

For the first time in three hundred years, he felt a deep, confusing anger rising within.

"I don't deserve this, Ana," he said. "I never deserved any of it. After all I did for you, after all you did to me . . . Why didn't I leave? Why didn't I save myself?"

Nearby, he heard the cry of an eagle. The sky was brightening. Dawn was coming, and nothingness with it. And this time, instead of going back to the caravan, Lazarus let himself fall to bones in the morning light, Ana's picture still in his hand.

"Atonais," Flora said, climbing into the caravan. "The perimeter is clear. There was an eagle, but . . ."

Atonais wasn't in his place in the chair. She pushed back the unicorn tapestry and opened the door to Lazarus's room. Atonais was sitting on Lazarus's bed, staring into a memory bulb. Lazarus's bones were nowhere to be seen.

"Atonais," she said. "What's going on? Where's Lazarus?"

"He went out," Atonais said dully.

"Out?" Flora repeated. "It's dawn. If he's out right now, he's nothing but bones somewhere."

"Well, at least that means he won't be going anywhere any time soon," Atonais said.

"What did you do?"

"I made him show me the night he got his curse,"

Atonais said. "I wanted to see for myself what happened to him, so I could maybe try to fix it. So I could see how he got the second curse. After that, Lazarus took Ana's picture and left. I thought he'd be back by now, but..."

"Well, we've got to find him," Flora said. "Come on! Who knows what's out there gnawing on his bones by now!"

"Flora, we need to talk," Atonais said. "And you need to see this. If you want to understand what's happening to Lazarus, you need to see this."

He extended the bulb to her, and she looked at its otherworldly light. Then, against her better judgment, Flora took it into her hands. It was warm and the light inside it pulsed and shuddered. She took a deep breath. "All right," she said to Atonais.

Atonais sent a thread of lightning into the bulb, and the memory flared into life in her hands.

CHAPTER NINETEEN

THE FIRST THING SHE FELT WAS COLD. THE FIRST thing she smelled was blood. A female voice nearby hummed what sounded like a very old song.

She was lying on a dirt floor. To her left, Lazarus lay, pale and dead, hands folded across his chest, on a bloodstone altar. His head was severed, but the blood was dry, and his head and neck had been bound together with bandages. Even as a skeleton, he had never looked quite as dead.

Standing over him was a very familiar girl with long, wavy black hair. *Ana.* She looked down at him for a moment. Then she went to a nearby counter and slumped over something. There was the sound of a mortar and pestle grinding something hard. She got up and followed Ana to the counter but did not get close to her.

Is this what it's like to see someone else's memory? Flora thought. She felt like a ghost, unable to be seen, unable to act.

She watched as Ana picked up whatever she had been grinding and carried it across the room to the fire, where a cauldron bubbled. She threw the contents of the mortar into the cauldron, and the entire concoction seemed to shine. Ana watched and waited as the potion began to change to a pure silver color. Then she took a small wooden cup, filled it with the potion, and carried it to Lazarus's body.

She put the cup to his lips and poured the potion into his mouth, little by little, until it was gone. Then she took a knife from the pocket of her dress and cut her own finger. She dripped the blood into Lazarus's mouth, then stepped back to watch.

Ana barely blinked, even when her cut finger began to bleed down the side of her dress. She only waited, so fully, so intensely that, despite herself, Flora was frightened.

Then a glow began to spread over what was visible of Lazarus's body, up his belly, across his chest, down his arms, legs. Over his face, through his hair. And then his chest began to rise and fall, rise and fall. He rose to his elbows, gasping and coughing. The familiar black soil fell from his mouth onto the bloodstone altar. *Dirt from his grave,* Flora realized for the first time.

He looked around as though he couldn't see clearly. Then he saw Ana standing there, teary-eyed in her bloody dress.

"A-Ana?" he said, and his voice sounded like the noise a spade makes when it breaks the soil. He looked confused and frightened. Ana ran to him and threw her arms around him.

"You are back! Oh gods, I did not know if it would work. But here you are!"

"I—I thought I'd *died*, Ana," he said. "A drog, it . . . I could've sworn . . . And I . . . I saw Death. There were . . . there were so many colors." He pulled her to him, and she rested her head on his shoulder. "I never thought I would see you again."

"You did die," Ana said, her hand reaching up to trace the scar around his neck. "It was real, all of it. But so is this."

Lazarus pushed her away and held her in front of him. "How . . . how did you . . ." He reached up and touched the bandages around his throat.

"I dug you up from the burying grounds," she said. "I brought you here . . . I brought you back. In fact, it was you who gave me the idea for the potion in the first place, and good thing, too."

Lazarus put his hands to his head and rubbed his temples as though perhaps he was not hearing her correctly.

Then he saw something. Flora turned and looked with him.

On the counter was a fine, shimmering powder that looked as though it had been made from the finest, brightest pearls.

"Ana, what have you done?" he gasped.

"I have brought you back," she said. "I have given you eternal life."

"I'm not supposed to be here," he said, his voice shaking. He rose from the altar awkwardly, gingerly, in his risen body. "I'm supposed to be dead. I'm *meant* to be dead."

"Is this not worth it?" Ana said, eyes bright with anger. "Is living again for me not worth it?" She lunged toward him as though she were going to scratch his eyes out. He grabbed her by the wrists and held her back. Something silver winked at her neck.

"Where is the unicorn, Ana?" he said, still holding her sharp nails away from his face. "The one we saw in the forest. I know you did something to it. Where is it?"

Ana did not say anything. She glared at him, her teeth bared, then Flora saw her eyes dart toward a nearby pantry. Lazarus saw it, too, and broke his grasp. He strode across the room.

"Wait!" said Ana, but Lazarus threw open the door, then stumbled back in horror.

There, on the floor inside the pantry, was a unicorn. Brilliantly white, so white that it made the dim cellar seem even darker by contrast. Its neck and legs were long and slender, and it had a tail like a lion. Its mane looked softer than anything Flora had ever seen.

At first, it seemed as though it were sleeping, but Flora could see that something was wrong. There was a deep gash in its throat, and as she moved closer, she saw that its horn—a horn that Flora knew should be as long as her forearm—was no more than a bloody stump. It did not move.

Flora tried not to gag. The horror . . . the atrocity . . .

"What have you done?" Lazarus breathed. "Ana, what have you done?"

"Well, I needed unicorn blood," Ana explained as though it was as understandable as picking apples to bake a pie. "Blood for life and horn for healing, with good spring water to ground it. It is the ultimate potion. The ultimate cure for death itself."

"Ana, this is the greatest evil!" He touched his chest with shaking hands. "Oh gods . . . what have you done to me?"

"Don't be angry with me!" Ana said, her voice turning tearful and fervent. "Don't you see? I did it for you! For us! You'd do the same, wouldn't you?"

Lazarus didn't answer. He slumped onto his knees beside the unicorn's corpse.

"Wouldn't you?" Ana demanded again.

Still, Lazarus was silent. The unicorn in the pantry seemed to grow duller, grayer, its dark eyes dry, growing a film. Flies began to light on it, to crawl around the bloody stump where its horn should have been. The sight of it took the air out of Flora's lungs, doubled her over, and she felt how she did when she had learned about the fall of Kaer-Ise. Like a fish gasping, flailing, dying on the shore. Lazarus's shoulders sank in defeat.

Across the cellar, Ana was as still as stone. She didn't say anything for a few moments. Then her eyes sharpened with defiance. She dried her tears and said, "All right, I understand. You want me to be whatever you are, too."

"What?" Lazarus said, turning. "Ana, no—"

She snatched the cup from the altar, dipped it into the cauldron, and pulled out a steaming cup of the blood potion. "Don't tell me what to do!" Ana said. "You think I've done something awful—as though there could be anything more awful than death parting us! You're doubting my magic or my love or both. So I'll prove it to you." She dripped some of her own blood into the potion, just as she had dripped it into Lazarus's mouth.

Lazarus came forward, hands extended, like someone approaching a frightened or angry animal. "Ana, listen to me," he said carefully. "I know you love me, and

I know your magic is strong, just...what if this potion works differently on—"

He began coughing again, spitting up more black soil.

"It is a pact," she said feverishly. "As long as the unicorn's blood flows through us, we will live. And as long as we belong to each other, our love will keep us whole!"

Ana brought the cup to her mouth and drank. She gagged once but kept drinking, slowly, until it was gone. Then she wiped the potion from her lips, waiting for the glow that had crept over Lazarus. And it happened. The glow traveled over her body even faster than it had over Lazarus's. She looked down at her hands, her arms. The glow radiated through every part of her. Even her dark hair seemed vibrant.

Flora shuddered.

"Do you feel it?" Ana asked, her eyes radiant. "This is what forever feels like!" Then her face changed. She bent, doubled over, clutching her stomach.

"Ana!" Lazarus cried. He went to her and bent down, taking her hand in his. The glow turned somehow fierce. It was not a glow anymore. It was a burning. Ana's eyes grew wide and terrified. She gagged. Then she fell to the floor.

Flora could see the strange glow beneath her blouse, pulsing up her vertebrae, extending into each rib, crawling up her back and spreading out from her center up to her head. Lazarus gathered Ana in his arms. Her eyes opened wide and all their color was gone, the irises and pupils replaced by a blank, gaping whiteness.

She cried out, a high, keening cry, and pulled herself away from him, floundering around the room like a woman in fire or lime.

"Ana!" Lazarus was shouting. "Ana, no!"

Overcome with pain, she knocked the cauldron to the floor and fell in its contents, sending the blood potion spreading over the floor. Ana stopped moving. Then her flesh began to fall away, just as Flora had seen Lazarus's do, but faster.

"No!" Lazarus cried. "No, no, no, no! Ana!"

He knelt and took her in his arms, tried to put the falling flesh back onto her face, her arms, but it was too fast, burning into ash before disappearing altogether. Soon, all that was left in Lazarus's arms was her skeleton, hands grasping, mouth open. Silent.

"No . . . no," he said. "Please . . . no . . ."

But it was no use. She did not move. Did not rebuild.

Lazarus laid her skeleton down on its back in the pool of thickening blood, then, weeping, he crumpled beside her. The last thing Flora saw was Lazarus taking something from her neck and placing it around his own.

The hourglass. And then she was torn out of the memory and back to reality.

$$\text{⧗}$$

The memory bulb flickered, and it went back to its firefly glow. There was nothing left.

Flora felt as though she had been punched in the stomach. She slid into a chair and was quiet for a long time.

"Gods," Flora said. "That was—was—"

"So now we know how he got the curse. Unicorn blood. A potion made by a witch and imbued with that wild, unpredictable magic they have," Atonais said. "I'm sorry you had to see it. He didn't want you to. He didn't want anyone to see it."

"He knew I'd always wanted to see a unicorn," said Flora. "But he should have told me. Maybe if I'd known earlier..."

"There's nothing you could have done," Atonais said. "Ana's first curse is one hell of a curse, even if it was meant to be a cure."

"But what about the second curse?" Flora asked. "What is happening to him? What has changed?"

"'As long as we belong to each other, our love will keep us whole,'" Atonais said. "I didn't think much of it when I heard it at first, but there it is: That's what laid the groundwork for the second curse, whether Ana meant to or not. We're still studying the relationship between words and magic, but she declared that and . . . it happened. That's the second curse."

Her heart had begun to quicken in her chest. "I don't understand," Flora said.

"What was keeping him undecayed, still himself and not a drog, wasn't his name at all," Atonais said. "It was *their* love. A love he had a part in. And for centuries it worked. It must have been easy to prolong a dead love when he was alone and it was all he had to think about."

Flora remembered how Lazarus had laughed when she told him about the stories in which he was a rake. *I haven't lain with anyone in three hundred years*, he had said. *I've been . . . alone.*

"But then he found you on the beach," Atonais said.

"Oh gods . . . ," said Flora. "But we never—"

"The drog tissue only appeared after you arrived," Atonais said. "After he understood that he valued you deeply. And it's been spreading ever since."

Flora thought of how he had held her close on the wall. She thought of how they had laughed together, how she had made fun of his meticulous outfits. She thought of the flowers she had brought him and the way she had held her head against his chest, listening for any change in his breathing. She thought of how utterly lost she would feel if he were gone.

"You love each other," Atonais said simply. "And it is simultaneously the best and worst thing for each of you—particularly for him."

Flora felt sick. She rose and took a basket from the floor. "I've got to fix this."

"What?" Atonais said. "How?"

"When he rebuilds I'm going to let him know that it can never happen between us," Flora said. "I'll . . . say I'm not attracted to him or something."

"I'm afraid it might be too late for that," Atonais said.

"Then I'll leave," said Flora.

The door slammed shut behind her and opened again as Atonais followed.

"You can't just leave!" Atonais said. "What about the Temple of Fates? What about the royal family?"

"None of it's worth it if Lazarus becomes a drog!" Flora shouted, squinting against the morning light.

"What about the prophecy?"

"At the worst, he'll be back where he started," she said. "He can forget about me and I can forget about him, and he can go back to normal. I can eke out a living as a mercenary or something."

"We're too far into this quest and you know it!" Atonais said. "You've got to—"

"Shut up!" Flora shouted, whirling on him. "None of it matters unless we can find Lazarus! Now help me look for him!"

Atonais nodded. He fell in behind Flora, and they began to search. Lazarus probably hadn't gone too far, Flora thought.

"There!" Atonais pointed. Under a cliff there was a small pile of black clothing with dry white bones peeking out of the sleeves and the neck, a length of bandages fluttering in the breeze. *Lazarus.*

Flora would just dart out and gather his bones and that would be it. But as they turned the corner, they heard the flapping of great wings. A shadow passed over them. Flora looked up just in time to see a great eagle twice the size of a man swooping downward, toward Lazarus's bones.

"No!" Flora shouted. "No!" She ran forward, but she was not fast enough. The eagle streaked down and took Lazarus's bones into its talons, black clothes and all, and flew away with them.

Flora fired arrow after arrow. Atonais's lightning stretched across the sky, but neither touched the eagle. The great eagle grew smaller and smaller in the cold blue sky.

"I tried," Atonais said. "I'm sorry... I'm sorry..."

Flora did not say anything. She just stood and stared after it.

"What will we do?" Atonais asked.

"We'll follow it," Flora said gravely.

Something was gleaming in the sand among the things the eagle had left: Lazarus's hourglass. Flora bent and gathered what remained, including Ana's picture and Lazarus's hat and falx. Then she put the hourglass around her neck and hurried back to the caravan.

CHAPTER TWENTY

WHEN LAZARUS REBUILT HIMSELF, HE WAS NOT IN his bed or on the sand, as he remembered. He was in a cool, dark room with a stone floor. He found his clothes, but he could not find his hat or his falx. He squinted. There was no door, no windows, just rough sandstone walls rising upward to a circle of dim light and an ornately painted ceiling high above. He was in a hole in the ground, an oubliette, it seemed like. Who had captured him, and what did they want with him?

He reached for his hourglass. It was not there.

He patted his clothes, emptied his boots, searched the floor in a mad blur of panic. All that he had of his life before the curse . . . lost.

The walls of the oubliette seemed to grow taller and taller around him, or he seemed to grow smaller. He clawed at the walls. They were uneven enough for him to get a foothold but too steep for him to scale. Still, he tried, climbing up and scraping his way down, his fingers bloodying and healing again and again and again. Finally, he slumped down on the cold floor.

His mind raced. Was Flora all right? Were she and Atonais traveling back through the Weir? What had become of the Black Caravan? He did not know. But in the end, he knew that there was only one choice.

To wait.

The horses were slick with sweat and foam. As they drank deeply from the nearly dry pool they had stopped beside, Nik coughed.

"Shhhh," Flora said. She wiped a damp rag over the horses, trying to soothe them. She had pushed them too hard, she knew, and though her heart hurt for them, there was no other way.

At least it's autumn, she thought. *This desert would be unbearable in the summer.* She pulled at the tunic that was sticking to her chest and back and told herself that the horses were glad to be free of the weight of the caravan. But she knew that they could not continue like this, especially during the day. Autumn or not, the sun and wind still burned. Could they afford to rest for an entire day and travel only at night? The thought of traveling at night frightened Flora more than she cared to admit. It was one thing to travel through the darkness with the Ankou for a partner. It was another thing entirely to charge into the darkness of a foreign land alone.

Atonais sat huddled in his makeshift disguise, a mix of clothing that Lazarus never would have put together himself, a bandage over the crystal between his brows. He was sending little threads of lightning down to the sand, making tiny swirls of molten glass at his feet. No, Flora thought, she was not alone. There was no telling what awaited them in the darkness of the night. And even if it was only more sand and scrub brush, there was danger. *What if we run out of water?* They had been lucky to find this pool, but would they be so lucky again?

"How far away are we?" she asked Atonais.

Atonais unrolled the map. His arms were wind-blistered. "You don't want to know," he said. "We keep heading onward and hope we find more pools like this. Straight. Northwest, through the desert until we see the gardens and walls. Assuming the eagle went to Zayide."

"It did," Flora said. "I remember from the princess's foreign studies books. That eagle was wearing the mark of the king of Parth, and the king lives in Zayide."

"And what do we do when we get there?" There was a challenge in his voice.

"Atonais," she said. "Not now."

"No," he said. "We've left the caravan behind; we're trekking across the desert, directly to the king of Parth, to save a man who can't die; I'm wearing a disguise because it's even more dangerous for me; and I want to know: What is your plan?"

Flora bit her lip. To be honest, she didn't have much of one. Following the eagle had seemed right, but the farther into the desert they went, the less sure she was becoming. She had intended to simply talk to the king, have him release Lazarus, and ask about Princess Betheara and her parents. She imagined them already there, sitting with the king, eating rare fruits like oranges or dates or limes. Then doubt rose up inside her, filling her head like smoke. What if they were not there? What if she could not negotiate with the king?

She had visions of scaling castle walls like the heroes in Betheara's books, of Atonais using his lightning to hold everyone at bay while they escaped. But if they did that, if they rescued Lazarus and set off back across the desert, what would happen? Would Parth declare war on Valacia? Her fears compounded in her head, and she could not think of a good answer for Atonais.

"You're right," she said. "I have no plan. And I'm an idiot. This is my fault. All of it is my fault. And who knows what's happening to him now?"

Atonais did not put his arm around her as Lazarus would have. He did not touch her. Instead, he sat quietly and adjusted his spectacles. "There is no use dwelling on it," he said. "You're only making yourself feel worse. Lazarus is your family now. Your true family, in a way the princess could never be because you aren't Lazarus's servant. You've never had a family before, so of course you're ready to act hastily to try and rescue him. It's a bit frustrating at the moment, but I understand. It's just that—"

A sharp animal cry in the night cut his sentence short. The darkness seemed to fall thicker, like velvet being pulled over their shoulders by an unseen hand.

Flora smelled something on the air: decay. An uneasy feeling grew in her chest. She slid her sword from its sheath.

"Let me," Atonais said, and he lit up his fingers with spheres of cold white lightning.

"Stay with the horses," she said, pulling a torch out of the fire for herself. "It's probably a wolf. I'll be right back."

And she left Atonais and headed out into the darkness, following the cry. The smell of decay seemed to come and go on the cold, dry breeze. She saw little in the dim light. Stones, sand, shrubs, the eyes of a big-eared fox watching her from behind a rock. And then she saw it: a spatter of blood.

The blood thickened into a trail, and as she followed it, she began to hear smacking, chewing . . . bones being broken. Her grip on her sword tightened, and as she concentrated on moving as quietly as possible, she saw what had cried out.

It was an antelope, a small one, lying in the sand. Its long, delicate throat had been messily ripped open and its body sagged strangely in the middle. She moved to the other side of the animal and rolled it over with her foot. Its chest and stomach had been completely hollowed out. Its organs simply were not there. A piece of broken rib dangled over the eviscerated body, swinging to and fro as if on a hinge. Whatever had attacked the antelope had only just left it. It was probably watching her right now.

There was a scream—ragged-throated, unnatural— and Flora turned, but not in time to block the force as something lunged at her and shoved her nearly off her feet. She steadied herself in the sand, and in the dim light, she saw her attacker hanging back, waiting to see what she would do.

It had long, spindly arms and legs, spiderlike almost, and its head, vaguely human-looking, was sharp and streamlined, built for running across the desert sand. Its skin was gone in most places, revealing decaying muscle, organs, and fat, though it held on to a few patches of pale skin here and there. Its greenish flesh seemed to have melted over one eye, and its other eye shone in the light of the torch. Its organs were covered with strands of wet, gangrenous muscle from under which white bone peeked. Its hands were elongated, its fingers fused together in crablike claws. Its mouth, its chest, its claws...all were covered in dark, steaming blood.

Its mouth opened and it screamed again. Flora could see its vocal cords vibrating in its neck. Flora stood firm, her sword out and glinting in the torchlight.

Before she could do anything, an arrow of flame flew from the darkness and pierced it through the neck. It scrabbled at the wound with its hooked hands as the fire spread wildly over it, and within minutes it was reduced to cinders.

"Don't move!" said a voice. There was a black shadow at the top of the nearest dune. A man was coming toward her. "In the name of the king of Parth, sheath your weapon!"

Flora did so, thinking, *Damn, damn, damn! Caught already?*

The man lit a torch and held it up so he could see her. He was wearing a surcoat stamped with the Black Eye of Parth. A sentinel, and he had found her.

"Valacian, I guess," he said, looking her over. "Trespassing in the kingdom of Parth. I keep saying we need to have more security around the Weir."

"You don't understand! Our friend was taken by eagles and we need to find him right away!"

"Eagles, huh? Well, let's see what the others have to say about it. No funny business."

He led her back over the dunes, with the flames and the sickening smoke from the charred monster corpse behind them. When they arrived, there were six armed sentinels on white horses waiting for them, pointing their long, copper-tipped spears at Atonais's throat.

"We're here to find someone," Flora said. "The Ankou. He was taken by a giant eagle, and we—"

"Broke the law trying to get him back," said the oldest of the guards, a man with a mustache and weak chin. "And just who are you?"

"Florelle Tannett, handmaiden to the princess of Kaer-Ise and the Ankou's assistant," Flora said. "And this is Dr. Atonais Kell. Our companion was taken by an eagle and we want him back."

Atonais nodded politely.

"Toss them back over the wall," said the oldest guard, "and let's get back to business."

"Captain," the guard who had caught Flora said. "Maybe we shouldn't. This girl was fighting a ghul when I caught her and obviously has training in combat and—"

The captain leaned down from his horse. "Did a ghul attack you, girl?"

"Yes," Flora said. "But this guard killed it before I could do it myself."

"Interesting," said the captain.

"It takes strength to fight a ghul, sir," said the younger guard. "And this one's a doctor. Perhaps we should take them with us?"

The captain considered this. "Very well," he said. "We will take them to Zayide. There the king can decide their fate."

Flora glanced at Atonais. She nodded. They allowed the guards to tie Nik and Tal to their own horses, then the guards led them out into the desert night, toward the west, toward the judgment of King Ulalume.

CHAPTER
TWENTY-ONE

IN THE OUBLIETTE, LAZARUS'S NIGHTMARES GREW bloodier. He felt less and alarmingly less of his body every day. And in the oubliette there was nothing to do except feel the decay advance ever onward. Sometimes his organs seemed to grind and bleed into one another. Sometimes he felt nothing at all. But the smell was everywhere. He felt filthy, rotten, awful.

One night, a group of armored and masked guards shackled him and took him, barefooted, to one of apparently many indoor hot springs to bathe himself. "The king insists that you clean yourself before your examination," said one.

Lazarus was not as filthy as he would have been if his body did not regenerate every day, but he welcomed the idea of a bath and said nothing as they led him down the long, underground hall to a series of small wooden doors.

The room beyond the final door was tall, and the ceiling was vaulted like the ceilings of temples. The stone was dim and plain, and only the floor had any color. It was tiled with blue squares of iridescent stone. He was led past a privacy screen, and he stood before the modest, circular bathing pool, the waters of which flowed from a statue of a woman holding an urn. The bottom of the pool was tiled like the floors, all white this time, and as he bent and dipped a hand in the water (it was pleasantly warm) his drog tissue contrasted sharply against it.

"Take off your clothes," one of the guards said. "Don't bother folding them, just leave them there. Clothes will be brought for you."

"And the ones I'm wearing now?" Lazarus asked. He could only imagine the clothes that would be brought for him, and when he thought of how hideous they'd probably be, he almost smiled, knowing there was enough of him left to feel vanity.

"Do not worry about them," said the guard, and jerked his spear at him.

Lazarus undressed and stepped into the water. Slowly, he lowered himself in and began to wash his hair and face and body.

He heard one guard speak to the other in Parthan. "What is he?" the guard asked. Parthan hadn't changed much over the past three hundred years, and Lazarus understood it fairly easily.

"I don't know, but I wouldn't go near him if the king wasn't paying me," the other said. "I have on two pairs of gloves today."

"What if we catch it?" the guard whispered. "We're down here, underground. Do sicknesses carry faster underground? What if it's a curse?"

"There are no such things as curses in Parth," said the other. "You know this. As for him, he's just a distraction, that is all. Just one more thing to keep us away from our families."

"I will try to be more considerate as I decay," Lazarus said in Parthan.

The guards were silent after that.

Lazarus bathed as well as he could. He focused on the warmth of the hot spring against the parts of himself that he could still feel, on the water's green clarity, on the strange blue liquid soap he had been given rather than the hard bar soap that he was used to. He did not focus on the fact that one of his arms was now almost completely covered in drog tissue, or that it snaked around his torso to his shoulder blades and down the back of his leg, or that the tissue on his arm had begun to do what the tissue on his face had done: collapse inward as though his skin were being eaten away. He did not focus on the smell of his own flesh decaying or the time that was being lost.

Before his fingers began to wrinkle, a Parthan in a full suit of drab blue and a face mask—a physician, probably—opened the door unceremoniously. "We are ready," he said, handing clothes to Lazarus.

Lazarus changed into them. The shirt fit well enough, though it seemed flimsy and light compared to his well-made black clothes. The pants were easily two inches too short.

"What will you do to me?" Lazarus asked the physician in Parthan.

The physician did not respond.

The guards put their spear tips to his back. "Come along now," they said.

Without warning, a fire seemed to burn within Lazarus. He stumbled. His sight turned red as though blood had dripped into his eyes. He felt an inexplicable hatred, a burning, bone-deep hatred for the guard and the physician. He wanted to tear their chests open, tie their own entrails around them, smear their blood over himself. The desire howled through his head like a storm, just as it did in his worst nightmares. But this time, he was awake.

Then his hands began to raise of their own accord.

His body began to shake.

It seemed that he was standing on the edge of a great cliff, with darkness yawning inescapable beyond it: the darkness of inhumanity. He was waiting to jump, and if he did not jump, he knew that he would fall, would lose control of himself, and then . . . blood spattering . . . bones breaking . . . warm blood down his throat. . . .

"Shackle me!" he shouted. The guards stood and stared stupidly. "Quickly! Please! Shackle me!"

They fumbled with his hands and eventually pulled them behind his back. The flames rose in his chest, smoke filled his brain, and he strained against the shackles.

"*I will kill you,*" he growled in a voice that was not his own. "*I will smear your blood over the walls . . . I will rip out your teeth, burst your eyes . . .*"

"Come, to the hospital," he heard as though far away. "Hold him tightly. Keep his head steady in case he tries to bite."

There were hands on his head, on his shoulders. Lazarus held himself back, fighting the monster within, until his heart stopped pounding against his ribs and he was able to take long, deep breaths again. The red slowly faded from his eyes, and he began to walk more upright. "I am sorry," he gasped. "I don't know what happened."

But he did know what had happened. He knew too

well what had happened. He was changing. The rot had
finally caught up to him.

After three tense, sunburned days of riding, the sentinels brought Flora and Atonais to the gates of Zayide.
The walls were high and gleaming in the desert sun, and
it was nearly impossible to see the top. The guards ahead
of them blew their horns and the carved gates opened
without even the slightest creak.

Despite herself, Flora had to catch her breath.

The city was made of white stone and copper, all of it.
Spires jutted among domes and flat roofs that seemed to
be stacked on top of one another. Poplar trees spiraled up
between the buildings. There were all manner of contraptions running the length of the walls, pulling up water and
earth. There were copper pipes everywhere. Some gleamed
new and shiny, others darkened, greened, as they climbed
up the sides of the buildings like vines. At the top of the
tallest buildings, needles pointed up at the blue expanse
of sky, drawing lightning down to make glass. Everything
was connected; every house and building was connected
through the endless copper chains and gears and wires.
And everything was in efficient, fluid motion.

Flora could hear the water that flowed along the walls in green copper aqueducts to fountains all over the city. Each fountain was shaped like a woman with braided hair, bending low and pouring a continuous flow of bright, clear water from her urn. Flora saw white flowers and coins laid at the feet of each fountain they passed.

The real beauty, however, was the palace itself. It was a gargantuan pyramid of white stone. The sloping sides were comprised of layer after layer of terraces, walls, columns and arches, and they stair-stepped to a flat-topped roof. At the top of each "step" of terraces, there was a jungle—a garden. There were enormous trees, at least seventy-five feet in height. Fruits and fronds and flowers of all colors and sizes spilled over the sides, swaying, dropping petals. The smell was glorious.

Dividing the pyramid almost in two was a tall, broad row of steps that led all the way to the top of the palace. Above the door hung a great green copper disk set with twenty-four different symbols. It was a clock, much bigger and grander than any clock Flora had ever seen, and like everything else in Zayide, completely mechanical.

"Think of the intricate irrigation system it would take to support such gardens," Atonais whispered to her. His voice shook with wonder. "And look, up at the top of that building. Platforms for watching the stars! For measuring the movements of the moon! And look at that...that...I don't even know what that device is. And did you notice the gears on the backs of the doors? The entire city is mechanized! Here is a place where science is truly appreciated."

"Even in Kaer-Ise, with all our tidal mills, we never used water like this," Flora said. "I don't understand. Where is all their water coming from?"

"There must be an underground source," he said. "A subterranean river or a spring. Whatever they're using, though, they're easily a century beyond our capabilities in Davasca, even with our mages." He stopped. "And it is copper. All...copper."

"Where do they get all of it?" Flora wondered.

Atonais pointed to the west side of the city, over which the sun had begun to set, past a line of spindly poplars, where a cloud of smoke or steam rose high. When Flora breathed in, she smelled copper on the breeze: bloody, metallic, dry.

There was a scuttling noise above them, and when they looked up, they saw a giant eagle staring down at them with apple-size yellow eyes. The sun gleamed on its beak, and from around its neck, the Black Eye of Ulalume glared down at them from a large nest at the top of a low tower. The eagle turned away, apparently disinterested, and began to preen itself.

"Look," Atonais whispered. At each corner of the city was a nest, and on each nest sat another of the king's eagles, looking out over the desert sands and the mines, and inward over the gardens.

"Come," said the captain, "the king will see you," and on they moved through the city, down the main road, flanked by guards.

It was then that Flora noticed there was no hustle and bustle, no rumble of sandals over the white stone streets and sidewalks. There were no peals of laughter or children chasing chickens. There was nothing but the sounds of the fountains nearby and the copper mines in the distance. But the city did not feel empty. All around, Flora felt eyes upon her, curious, probing.

If it was not empty, though, where were the people? The windows were shuttered. A few times, she saw people who peered down at her from slits in the curtains only to vanish when she tried to get a good look at them. Twice, she saw people who quickly fetched water from the fountains, but other than that, the city was as silent as a grave. It felt wrong. It felt eerie. It felt . . . ill.

The feeling shadowed her heart and kept her quiet all the way to the steps of the palace. There, Nik and

Tal were taken from them, and the guards put spears to Flora's and Atonais's backs and made them climb the many steps to the ornate rose-gold inlaid doors of King Ulalume's palace.

The doors were opened to them, and they stepped onto a copper floor as smooth and reflective as a mirror. They walked into a long throne room, their shoes loud on the metal beneath their feet. Its high, domed ceiling was supported by eight pillars and was painted like the evening sky. Gemstone stars and an ivory moon glared down at them as the guards marched them to a platform at the far side of the room.

The back wall was covered by a blue velvet curtain, and in front of the curtain was an ornate rose-gold throne inscribed all over with eye symbols. The king was not there. Instead, a woman paced to and fro on the platform before the throne, her eyes cast down at the rug beneath her feet. She was tall and slender, and she wore layers of the finest blue and green brocades. Her blue silk breeches tapered down to her ankles, and her feet were covered in shoes that seemed to be made of the same rose gold as the throne behind her. She did not seem to notice or care about their arrival.

"Look!" Atonais said. "I can't believe what I'm see-ing! An automaton!"

Seated on a cushioned chair behind the woman was

what could only be described as a mechanical man. It was made of polished copper and reminded Flora of a kettle given vaguely human form. It had a smooth, round head with glass globes for eyes, a metal grid for a mouth (could it speak?), and each rounded joint moved without the slightest squeak. It had a scroll before it and a quill and ink, and was writing intently with its intricately constructed fingers. Flora could not tell whether or not it was properly alive. Then she noticed something that made her gasp before she could stop herself.

All around, strewn on the floor, were gigantic lizards, each the size of a man, some curled, some stretched, some lounging as though they owned the place. Their snouts were long and arrow-shaped, and Flora could see sharp teeth protruding from their closed reptilian lips. The lizards seemed to be asleep for now, but what if they woke up? Would they be fed to the lizards? She gulped.

"A thousand dead now," the woman was saying. "A thousand, and the physicians still don't know anything. It is driving me mad."

On the floor before her, one of the lizards climbed onto its hind legs and put its head on the platform to regard her with big eyes like a dog at its master's table. "The automaton is coming with your dinner in a moment," the woman said to it.

The mechanical scribe caught sight of them then and

stopped to regard them with its strange glass eyes. "On this day, the sentinels have brought before the king two foreigners caught in the desert," the automaton scribe intoned in a voice that sounded like metal scraping against itself.

Before the king? Flora blanched. That meant that the woman was none other than King Ulalume of Parth.

She furrowed elegant eyebrows at them. Flora stood as straight as she could, aware of how filthy and wretched she must look.

King Ulalume was striking from far away, but even more beautiful up close. Her lips were painted a heart's bloodred that was vibrant against her dark skin. There were rose-gold rings on every finger, including her thumbs. Her light brown eyes were lined in elegant upsweeps of black and gold, and her blue-black hair was coiled in braids around her head. At her neck there glittered a fine chain, but whatever hung from it was lost in the front of her blouse. Her beauty seemed somehow pointed, dangerous, and Flora wasn't sure whether she reminded her more of a deadly flower or a jeweled sword.

"Your Majesty, please pardon our intrusion," the guards said. "But we found these two within our borders and we await your orders in dealing with them."

"I do not have the time for this," said the king. She

waved her hand to dismiss them and Flora saw that her nails had been plated with gleaming, sharpened blades. "Why did you not send them back into Valacia?"

"They said their friend was taken by the eagles. This one says that she's looking for the royal family of Kaer-Ise. And the other is a doctor."

Beside Flora, Atonais shifted and sweated in his disguise.

"I am King Ulalume Elsayeh," she said. "You may speak."

"Your Majesty," Flora said. She stood straight, her head slightly bent downward, her eyes not meeting the king's. She spoke in the clear, gracious tone that she had been taught to use when dealing with royalty. "I am Florelle Tannett, lady-in-waiting to Princess Betheara Ilurosa of Kaer-Ise and survivor of the Kaer-Isian Massacre. This is my friend, Dr. Atonais Kell. We came only out of necessity and do not seek to anger the great nation of Parth." She swallowed, and when the king did not stop her, she continued. "An eagle snatched up our friend, Laza—I mean, the Ankou, and carried him away. So we are here to bring him back to Valacia with us."

"The Ankou is in one of my oubliettes, being quarantined." King Ulalume's voice flicked and stung like a whip. "I have no intention of releasing him so that whatever he's got can spread to my people. What were you doing in Parth in the first place? My eagles would not have harmed anyone who had stayed on their own side of the wall."

"We came because we believe that the royal family of Kaer-Ise set off for Parthan shores on the night that my nation was destroyed," Flora said. "And we sought to find the truth of that, as well as to find the Temple of Fates and go there in order to heal the Ankou. Please, Your Majesty, I beg you: please release him and let us go."

The king took a step toward Flora. "My condolences," she said. "The atrocity committed against your people was unwarranted." Then the steel returned to her voice. "But while I admire your loyalty, let me tell you how things are in Parth." The king stood in front of her. "We ask nothing of anyone. We abide, even in the desert. We flourish. And its ruler will not bend like a reed at the merest request—especially the request of an outsider. As for your previous employers, any information we have on state matters is not to be given away for nothing. And as far as I am concerned, the Temple of Fates is merely a children's story." King Ulalume waved her bladed hand absently. "Take them away."

"I think that would be unwise," Atonais said.

The king turned. "Oh?" she asked with a smirk.

"Indeed," said Atonais. This time it was he who stood tall. He pulled the bandage from his head, letting the crystal that marked him as a mage glitter in the light. "Because I am a lightning mage. And I could kill you all where you stand. The entire city, in fact. I would barely have to lift a finger."

The guards took a step back, mumbling nervously. Flora's stomach flip-flopped. The atmosphere in the room grew cold and tense, and Flora knew that soon they would feel the hard-copper blades pierce their bellies.

Atonais's throat rose and fell. His hair began to lift. The air began to spark with static. Beneath their feet the copper floor began to grow warm and buzz.

But the king simply laughed. "Forgive me for not fainting, O terrible foreign mage," she said. "I certainly don't mean to doubt you. There is enough copper here to carry your lightning into every house in Parth. But if you wield such power, why haven't you already done as you threaten?"

"I would rather solve matters peacefully," he said. His pale eyes darted back and forth behind his thick lenses.

Just then, one of the side doors opened, and an automaton came into the room, pushing a wheelbarrow of raw meat. It turned it out onto the floor and the lizards fell on the pile in a toothy, bloody, writhing mess. Atonais flinched, but the king did not take her eyes from him.

"Have you ever killed a man?" she asked, crossing the blood-spattered floor to stand in front of Atonais. She reached out and touched his face with her sharp nails. "I think not. Now stop warming my floors and begone. Back to Valacia with you, before this becomes a matter of international interest, and be thankful that I do not have you executed for bringing magic into my realm."

"Please, Your Majesty," said Flora, thinking quickly. "Forgive my friend for his arrogance. We have an offer for you."

"An offer?" she said, her red mouth turning up at the corners. "What could you possibly offer me?"

Two of the lizards began to fight then, flailing and lunging, and one bit the other's tail completely off. Flora watched, horrified, as the tail lay writhing on the floor as though it were still alive.

"Oh, don't worry," the king said casually. "Everything grows back. Now, as you were saying?"

Flora shook herself and continued.

"Atonais is one of the finest doctors in Valacia," she said. "That's part of the reason that he was traveling with the Ankou and me. He was studying the Ankou's illness in hopes of helping cure it. And the Ankou is a potion-master. He can make potions that heal and that ease pain."

"And why should I be interested in this?" the king asked.

"Your people are ill, Your Majesty," she said. "Why else would there be no people in the streets of so grand a city? You said yourself there had been a thousand deaths so far. You care for your people, it is obvious. And maybe there is a chance that new eyes could help you find a new perspective to the problem of the illness."

"I am listening," the king said with a cocked eyebrow.

"If you allow it, we will attempt to find a cure," Flora said. "And if we are successful, you must set the Ankou free and you must tell me what you know of the Kaer-Isian royal family."

"And if you are unsuccessful?" the king asked.

Flora did not falter. "Then do with us what you will. But for now, please afford us this chance to help you and ourselves. You have nothing to lose."

The king rubbed her temples and watched as the lizards finished their red feast and began to slink back to their places on the floor. As she said, the tail of the lizard who had been attacked had already begun to grow back.

"Against my better judgment, I will accept your

proposal," she said. "On the chance that your . . . *doctor* . . . may be able to help. He will be treated as my guest. He will have the finest of everything." The king turned her eyes to Flora. "As for you, though, you've given me no reason to spare your life. Or are you a Kaer-Isian unicorn yourself, able to heal miraculously with a touch?"

"I am a fighter," Flora said. "And a good one. I have been trained by the Ankou and—"

"I have no need of a fighter," said the king. "My automatons are better in battle than a hundred men." She regarded Flora. "But I am in need of a handmaiden. After my mother's old handmaiden died, I have not had a court. All the former maidservants' quarters lie empty. It would be nice to have one again. Unless, of course, I should find an oubliette for you, too."

"No, Your Majesty," Flora said with a bow that felt ridiculous in her sweat-stained clothes. "It would be an honor."

"Good," said the king. "Your duties will begin tomorrow at dawn. After breakfast, you will accompany the physician and me out into the city. Then we will see what you have to offer."

The king summoned the guards to her.

"On your way out, have the automatons prepare clothing and draw baths for each of them. I'd ask one of the servants, but with so many visiting sick family in the city, there is only the cook, the valet, and me, and I still have business here. It would be much appreciated."

"Yes, Your Majesty!" said the guards.

The king furrowed her brow. "Were there not more of your number yesterday?"

"One of our men did not appear today," said the captain. "We do not know where he is."

It was obvious that this troubled the king. "Take the mage to the guest rooms," she said. "And as for my new handmaiden, take her to Ilya's old quarters. I will send an automaton to inform her of her duties tomorrow. She will not be allowed a sword. Not unless I say otherwise."

"Yes, Your Majesty," said the captain, and the guards unshackled Flora and Atonais and led them to the door.

"So I'm a handmaiden again," Flora said, mainly to herself. "It could be worse."

"Gods, we got lucky," Atonais whispered. "We got so lucky! Do you know how scared I was? A mage in Parth, and I've lived to tell the tale—so far."

"You were very brave," Flora said. "But what were you thinking, threatening the king?"

"What were *you* thinking?" Atonais returned. "Why do you keep telling people I'm a doctor? I'm not *that* kind of doctor!"

"Well, you'd better learn how to fake it, because it's the only thing that saved us," she said. "But more importantly, did you hear what she said about the Temple of Fates? That it was a children's story?"

"It exists," Atonais said. "I'm sure of it. Or else I've been dedicating the last three years to studying it for nothing."

Behind her, Flora could hear the automaton scribe, alone on the platform, writing and talking to itself with its mechanical drone.

"On this, the tenth day of the month of the Ram, the noble King Ulalume Elsayeh admitted into her palace two foreigners in the hopes that they can help in curing our people of their illness. They are to be given..."

The tenth day of the month of the Ram, Flora thought. The tenth day. How had she forgotten? And how had it come so soon?

The room she was taken to had a small, narrow bed laid with white linens. The floor was not copper here; instead it was tiled in a simple, worn blue color that reminded her of the sea. Still, it was the nicest servant's quarters she had ever seen. Through an open door, Flora could see the steaming, glass-green waters that flowed from the statue-woman's urn into her own private bathing pool. She stared into its waters unseeingly.

The tenth day of the month of the Ram. Her birthday. Today would have been her Calling. Would have. If she were back on Kaer-Ise, she would have been taken out into the forest. She would have been dressed in white and given a lute and a bridle made of gold. She would have sat in the forest, waiting, as she had been trained. Then she would have sung the old songs until the priestesses came and touched her with the ancient horn of one of the Kaer-Isian unicorns, saved from the battle flames. They would have touched her open palms, her forehead, and her chest, and then she would have risen, a recognized woman in every right. There would have been a great feast among the ladies of the court as her hair was shorn and put out into the garden where the birds could use it for nesting.

And now she was a handmaiden again, though it was very unlike being a lady-in-waiting had been back home. In Kaer-Ise, there had always been several servants bustling here and there, castle staff to talk to, to eat with, to keep her company. Here, there was no court, just cold automatons and frightening lizards. Here, she was alone, without even a sword to defend the king.

She kicked off her boots and sat on the stiff linen bed, feeling very far away from herself.

A cool breeze swept through the room, making the curtains move in the orange light of sunset. A few thin leaves and bright petals from the window drifted in to settle on the windowsill, and she smelled the heavy perfume of the garden. She went to the window and pushed back the curtain.

The garden breeze scattered thin leaves at her feet. Far across the garden, she saw Atonais feeding pigeons from the expansive balcony of his guest room. As she watched, one of the king's great lizards lunged out of the vines beneath and, with a quick snap of its steel-trap jaws, ate one of the pigeons whole.

Down on the terrace below, she saw a flash of motion. Someone was walking in the garden. She thought for one delirious moment that it was Lazarus, that he had freed himself somehow, but she saw the glitter of the figure's hands and knew that it was the king.

The king walked slowly through the garden with two giant lizards at her heels. Her pointed shoulders were stooped and her head was down. She stopped beside another woman-shaped fountain and one of her lizards gazed up at her in a devoted, almost doglike way. The king scratched it on the head gently with her bladed nails, but her eyes were on the statue of the woman with the urn. The lizard put its foot on the king's leg. She took a final look at the fountain and walked onward. Flora saw her reach into an overhanging tree and pull an orange from the branch. She did not peel it but merely passed it from hand to hand for a moment before putting it in her pocket. She went to a bench at the edge of the terrace and sat on it, her back to Flora, looking out over the quiet city with the lizards curled on the ground beside her.

Suddenly, she bent, her head in her hands.

Flora wondered for a moment what she was doing, then she realized that Ulalume Elsayeh, the fierce king of Parth, was crying.

CHAPTER
TWENTY-TWO

FLORA WOKE BEFORE DAWN, AS HAD BEEN HER CUS-
tom back on Kaer-Ise, and put on the breezy blue-
green tunic and loose pants that had been provided
for her—a servant's uniform, presumably. After scan-
ning the list of instructions the automaton scribe had
slipped under her door, she ordered an automaton to
take her to the kitchens to retrieve the king's breakfast.
It was strange, being led by such a silent, metallic, life-
less being. It was even more strange, as a servant, to be
served. She wondered privately what would happen if all
servants were one day replaced by such things, but before
she could wonder too much, the automaton stopped in
front of a door; gave her a curt, mechanical bow; and
puttered on down the hall and out of sight.

A rich, spicy smell was emanating from behind

a closed wooden door. But when Flora couldn't find a knob, she rang a little copper bell and a rather confused-looking chef opened a slot in the door and peered out.

"You're the handmaiden?" he asked.

"Er, yes," said Flora. "I'm here to get the king's breakfast."

The chef nodded and disappeared. A moment later, the door was pushed open and Flora's arms were laden with two trays filled with plates, cups, saucers, a pot of tea, and a heavy covered platter.

"Here," said the cook, putting a napkin-wrapped parcel in her tunic pocket. "For you. Now go. The east wing and turn left. Fifth door. And hurry! The king is probably up by now."

Obediently, Flora headed down the corridor to the east wing, counting doors as she went.

When she arrived at the small, blue-tiled room where the king took her breakfast, Atonais was already there, dressed in a light gray tunic and blue pants that were clearly of fine quality, his mage crystal showing plainly. The king was dressed in crisp white linen with a fur vest, and she was listening intently to Atonais.

"I was the shame of my family," Atonais was telling the king. "It's very, very rare for a lightning mage to be born. Like lightning strikes. But we're not celebrated in the magical community like fire mages, water mages, earth mages. Their elements have practical elements, everyone says, but lightning—"

"We use a form of lightning to power the automatons," the king said. "Most of our power here comes from magnetism—lightning as you call it—or steam. I'd think you'd be very valuable, indeed."

"Oh no," Atonais said. "Not outside of my studies. An *accident*, they called me. My spectacles were often stolen and broken, and my family looked the other way. So I stayed in, making little things with bits of metal and glass and seeing what I could send my lightning into."

"So you are an inventor or a mage?" the king asked.

"Both," Atonais said. "Magic will always be part of me, but inventing allows me to make things that I can use—things that *everyone* can use. Why not make life better for everyone?"

"I completely agree," said the king. "Perhaps we are not as different as I thought." She turned then and saw Flora. "Ah, good morning, handmaiden. I trust you slept well?"

"Good morning, Your Majesty," Flora said. "I'm sorry I missed dressing you. I wasn't sure what you wanted me to—"

"I am more than capable of dressing myself," she said. "You needn't worry about that."

"Do you need any help, Flora?" Atonais said, beginning to rise from his seat at the king's table.

"She is an experienced handmaiden," said the king. "Just put the trays down, please."

Flora did so. "Is there anything you would like of me, Your Majesty?"

"Nothing at this time," said the king. "But stay. And do eat whatever the cook gave you before it gets cold."

Flora bowed and hung back by the door, doing her best to eat her breakfast (flat bread and a pear) as unobtrusively as possible while watching to see if tea needed to be poured or cushions needed to be fluffed. Atonais was doing his best not to be awkward about Flora serving him, too, but was doing a terrible job.

The king, however, seemed unbothered. Flora noticed that she was not wearing any metal today, save for the rings and nails. The lizards were at her feet again, sleeping in one of the broad sunbeams that filtered through the windows.

Flora's mind buzzed with worries. Still, she dared not ask the king about Lazarus, not before they had even tried to cure the sickness.

"You are uncomfortable in my clothes, eh?" said the king, and Flora realized that she had been fidgeting with her pointed shoes.

"I am sorry, Your Majesty," she said, and she could feel herself blushing. "I feel almost as though I am disguised as a Parthan. And I wonder if I am paying you respect by wearing them."

"Notice that I did not give you rose-gold rings," the king said calmly. "Only clothes. And I did *give* them to you. There is a difference. Do you understand? Besides, this is a wonderful color for you. Much better than all that black and gray you were wearing."

When they were done with breakfast, the king rose and said, "Come, Flora. Come, Atonais. We will go out into the city. What we will do today will not be easy. Not for you or for me. But you have agreed to it, and so you must see what you are up against."

Flora followed Atonais and the king out into the foyer. A pair of automatons opened the doors of the palace, and the three of them stepped out into light so bright it made them squint at first. The king produced from her pocket a small bottle of light green lotion and three white cloth face masks. "Put the lotion on," she said to them. "It will vanish immediately, but it will protect you from the sun. Then put the masks on. My physicians are still unsure of whether or not the illness travels through the air, and we do not want to take risks."

Flora and Atonais exchanged worried looks, but did as they were told.

"Well," said the king. "Let us begin."

She led them down the long stairs, all the way, five stories down, and out the gates into the city as the eagles watched from their perches. It was as quiet as it had been when they arrived. Bone quiet. Breath quiet. In place of the normal hustle and bustle of a castle town, Flora heard only their own footsteps, the ever-present grinding of gears and flowing of water, and the sounds of dry garden leaves being blown over drier streets as the fountain women watched. The king walked toward the nearest house, a large one with two automatons posted outside the door, and stood in front of it, making sure her mask was securely fastened. The king looked at Flora and after a moment, Flora rapped on the door. No one answered.

Flora rapped again and said, "Your king wishes to pay you a visit. Open your doors!"

"I am coming, Your Majesty!" came a weak croak from behind the door.

They waited for a few moments. Flora could hear the sound of someone dragging something—perhaps a leg or a cane. Then the door opened and the thick, stale smell of sickness was nearly overwhelming.

Before them stood a woman of about the king's age.

Her hair was in a messy, stringy, unwashed bun at the nape of her neck, and she wore a simple, earth-colored linen dress that almost had more stains than clean patches. But she did not seem poor. The curtains that were drawn over the windows were made of fine, embroidered linen and there was a bowl on her dusty table that was full of fruit just about to go bad. Still, she was very thin. Her face was sunken to the bones, and her eye sockets were sharp and defined as the rim of a crystal glass. Her skin was covered in lesions and milky-red blisters. She, too, wore rose-gold rings.

"Your Majesty," the woman said. "I'm afraid I am worse than when you last saw me. I've grown weak. I'd hate to imagine what our grandmothers would think of my state."

"Our grandmothers would be proud of you for fighting," said the king.

The woman saw Flora and Atonais then, and her eyes widened in alarm.

"These are visitors from Valacia," the king said to the woman. "The girl is my new handmaiden, Flora, and the other is a physician, Dr. Kell. I have employed him to help end this sickness."

Flora and Atonais bowed slightly to the woman. She swallowed and looked down to the floor. "Forgive me," she said. She did not meet the king's eyes. "I mean your party no disrespect, but if I bow, I may not stand up again."

The king put a hand on the woman's shoulder and said, "There is nothing to forgive."

The woman met the king's gaze, and Flora wondered if any of Beth's subjects had ever looked at her with such genuine admiration.

Then there was an awful gurgling sound in the woman's belly. Her bloodshot eyes widened in alarm.

"What is happening?" Atonais came forward, but the automatons pushed him out of the way.

"Get her to the washroom!" the king shouted, and the automatons sprang into action, taking the woman in their arms and quickly carrying her to a back room and out of sight. There was a splattering, coughing sound and the trickle of running water. A door across from the back room opened, and two sunken-eyed children peered out at them.

"She is so much worse than last time." The king whispered so low that only Flora heard.

"Pardon me, Your Majesty," Flora said. "How do you know her?"

"When my grandmother became Parth's first female king, Cyrdi's mother was a servant in the palace. She and

I played together. She was the first child to bathe in my grandmother's fountains."

"Your grandmother?" Flora asked.

"It is she who is depicted on all of the fountains, pouring water," the king said. "Ularia the Designer, she is called, an architect as well as a king. She designed the entire aqueduct system and the automatons. She was the one who found the reservoir that feeds Zayide when the river dried up. She was a great woman," said the king. "I once hoped to be greater."

The washroom door opened, and the copper automatons carried the woman out in their arms. She was still breathing—wheezing—and her stomach made that strange gurgling sound. Her eyes were not open, but her chest heaved.

"Take a sample of blood from her," the king told the nearest automaton. "And leave her be."

The automatons nodded and pushed open the door from which the children had watched them. They disappeared behind it.

"Goodness," Atonais breathed.

"It is this way all over Zayide," the king said to Atonais. "Those who are infected vomit and vomit until there is no water left in them. Boils grow on their skin, bursting and giving them pain at all times. They are weak, and no matter what food they eat from the gardens, they are starving. Their legs have no muscle anymore, and they hobble with canes. If they fall and there are no guards around, often..." The king faltered. "They lie there until they die of thirst or hunger, or the sun cooks them alive."

"What do you do for those who fall ill in the palace?" Atonais asked.

"No one in the palace has fallen ill," said the king. "Except the occasional guard. So that suggests that it is something out here, something among the people."

Atonais furrowed his brow. The jewel on his forehead glimmered in the dim light. Flora waited for him to say something profound, to tell the king just what was wrong, but no such thing happened. "May we continue?" he said instead. "I must see more."

The king looked back at the closed door beyond which Cyrdi had begun, once again, to retch. "There is plenty more to see," she said.

And there was. They went to dozens of houses, and in each one they were met with a similar picture: People retching, crawling with lesions and blisters. Some writhed on the floor, some sat in chairs, their breath rattling in their throats as though they were at death's very door. But always, each house was clean, each household was provided with care by automatons and supplied with plenty of food and clean, clear water. By the time the sun set on the beautiful, empty streets, Atonais had no answers for the king.

"Do you have any ideas?" Flora whispered when the king was out of earshot, gathering vials of blood from two masked guards.

"I don't know, I don't know," he muttered, and his voice teetered on the precipice between nervousness and panic. "I'm an inventor before I'm anything else. And *magical* illnesses make up the body of my medical knowledge. Their elements are out of balance, but I don't know what that means. We could really use Lazarus and all his old-fashioned potions and herbs."

The king came back to them then. In her hands was a basket full of abnormally dark blood in vials. Suddenly, a flock of sheep exploded from around a corner. Flora and Atonais and the king stepped back, and the guards stood before them, as sheep streamed past with a spotted dog on their heels. Two shepherds came after them; one was well, or seemed to be, despite the lesions beginning on his arms. The other leaned on the first, his legs plainly weak, his arms thin and covered in bandages. Still, they trudged after the sheep, whistling to the spotted dog who weaved behind the sheep, nipping and driving.

"Have any animals gotten the sickness?" Atonais asked.

"Yes," said the king. "But they do not die as fast as their masters."

The sick shepherd gurgled something and the two shepherds knelt before the king. The one with lesions on his arms said, "Your Majesty, we have three fewer sheep today. We do not know how. We do not know where they could have gone . . . unless the eagles—"

"My eagles are specially trained," said the king. "And my automatons feed them twice a day. But I will send someone to look for your sheep. Now, go on. Make sure that your friend is comfortable."

The shepherd rose and helped his friend to do the same. They hobbled along until they turned another corner and went out of sight, sheep and all.

There was a sound of bells tolling seven times as the mechanical clock chimed the hour. Flames jumped up into the globes of streetlamps that hung overhead, and a flickering red light was thrown down on their shoulders before the streets had even begun to darken.

The king looked at Atonais, her face grave. "Are these from today enough?" she asked, holding them out to him. "If not, we have plenty more samples back at the palace."

"Yes," Atonais said. He pocketed the vials of blood. "I will do what I can with these."

They went back through Zayide along the main road,

and as the sky darkened, the streetlamps glowed brighter. The ill watched them pass from windows, and the eagles watched from their posts at the city's corners. Wind blew through the poplars, smelling of metal and fruits and flowers, and in the distance, Flora could hear sheep bleating. Over it all hung the heaviness of the sickness, weighing it all down.

Atonais walked swiftly ahead of them, between the guards. The king, meanwhile, fell back, her eyes on the houses. Flora slowed to walk beside her. "Are you all right, Your Majesty?"

"It is bad enough that I didn't send you away, but to request help from the outside—my grandmother would never have..." The king rubbed her temples. "Your mage doctor had better find a cure. Quickly."

Flora did not hear any malice in the king's voice. Only a sense of doom.

They stopped in front of one of the palace's great carved and lacquered doors. "The mage may take the blood to the physicians," the king said to the guards at the door. "Leave him there. Allow him to work with them. Perhaps he will be able to help. I, meanwhile, am going to my chamber."

The guards pushed the doors open, and two automatons escorted Atonais down a corridor. He gave Flora a helpless glance over his shoulder as he was whisked away. The king, meanwhile, headed down another corridor, and pushed open an iron gate that led into the garden. Only when Flora stepped off the entry rug and her footsteps rang out in the hallway did the king even realize she was being followed.

"Oh," the king said, absently waving a bladed hand at her. "You are dismissed for now. If I need you, I will send an automaton for you." Without another word, the king strode off into the garden, disappearing into the greenery.

Flora stood there for a moment, breathing in the heavy, fruit-flavored air. In the bushes, a few of the king's lizards watched her. One of them flicked a long, forked tongue out at her, then it slunk under the bush and was gone.

I could go back to my room right now, Flora thought. *I could go and try to find Lazarus right now. I should* try to find Lazarus right now. But she had seen the king's eyes when she dismissed her. The king was at the end of her rope, and it was Flora's duty as her handmaiden to comfort her.

Flora wound through the many circuitous paths of the garden, passing potted forests hanging low with fruit, butterfly-crowded blooms as big as her hand, even a plant in the act of eating a medium-size lizard. She was almost ready to turn back when, on a whim, she took a path down by a vast pool with water lilies bigger than she was. On the other side, standing beneath a fountain of Ularia the Designer, was the king.

"I thought I dismissed you," said the king, wiping her eyes as Flora approached.

"I'm sorry, Your Majesty," said Flora. "A good handmaiden doesn't leave when her mistress is in distress."

"Pff," said the king. "Distress. My distress is minimal compared to the rest of my people. It's nothing. Go back to your quarters."

"It's not nothing, Your Majesty," said Flora. "It isn't good to grieve alone. You must conquer your grief. Please let me help you."

"Why would I want help from you, handmaiden?" snapped the king. "You wear your own grief like a cloak. It covers everything you do. Do not lecture me on conquering something that has conquered you!"

Her words hit Flora in the heart like an arrow.

The king motioned at her to send her away, but Flora stayed, too dumbstruck to move. Angry words rose, scalding in her chest, and before she could stop herself, she heard her own shaking voice.

"How dare you?" she whispered.

The king turned to Flora, her eyes wide in disbelief and outrage.

What am I doing? What am I doing? Flora thought, but she couldn't stop the anger and hurt flowing up and out of her.

"My people were murdered!" she cried. "My home was destroyed! I will never see anyone I knew ever again!"

The king stared at her, and Flora wished she could be angry, wrathful even, but Flora's eyes were filling with tears despite herself.

"Do you know what happened the night of the massacre? Do you know what happened to *me*? What the Skaar-dan soldiers did?" Rage howled through her. Her chest felt as though it had been burned hollow. "If I were back in Kaer-Ise, I'd be shamed for what They did to me, but now there's no one left to shame me. Still, my grief has not 'conquered' me. If it had, I wouldn't be here. I fight against my grief every day and will continue to, maybe until I die. And if I'm not giving in to grief, how can you think of doing so? Your people aren't gone! They're still here and they're depending on you! So you've got to fight it, Your Majesty, because you still can."

The king's hard demeanor softened. Her expression changed to one of realization and pity. Her bladed hand, which she'd raised to stop Flora, fell to her side. Then the king did something Flora did not expect: She came to Flora and embraced her.

"From the deepest part of my heart," she said, "there is no shame for you here."

Flora returned the king's embrace, and for a long time, the two of them just stood there, weeping, holding each other in the garden, beneath the statue of the first female king of Parth. When finally the hurt and rage subsided, Flora and King Ulalume sat down by the fountain and looked up at the serene face of the king's grandmother, pouring eternally from her fountain of plenty. For a moment, the divisions between them—culture, class, nationality—all were gone, in a way that they had never been gone even between Flora and Beth, and the two of them were just women, sitting by a fountain, each understanding the other better than before.

"Do you know why I am a king and not a queen?" she said after a moment.

Flora shook her head.

"Respect. Queens don't get the same amount of respect as kings do from other royals. From other men," the king said bitterly. "Just because a king is a man, he is seen as strong, sure, a force to be reckoned with. My grandmother wanted that, and in taking the title of king, she took it. She took the respect that was owed her and proved herself worthy of it ten times over. I only wonder...what would she think of me now?"

"She would understand how hard you're trying," said

Flora. "She would know that you are trying your best to save your people. And you will. We will. I promise."

"If only I could vanquish the sickness myself," said the king.

From the lip of a great lily, a frog jumped into the pool and disappeared.

"Maybe you will, Your Majesty," said Flora.

The king said nothing. She simply looked down at her reflection, fixed the black kohl around her eyes, and bade Flora good night.

Lazarus lay on his back in the physicians' chamber, focusing on the pressure of his chest expanding as he breathed. He was not in pain, not after the physicians had fed him a certain potion that tasted of cumin. He felt pressure—and now, that pressure was confined to the right half of his chest. Only one lung was still working, they'd told him after they strapped him to the table.

A serene-looking corpse hung suspended in an enormous glass box filled with honey. From what he could gather, the corpse honey was supposedly a strong cure-all. He watched a physician scoop a cup of the honey into a container and walk away with it.

The physicians, guarded behind their masks and gloves

and lenses and smocks, stood before a cabinet of blood-filled vials—blood taken from the sick. Lazarus was aware, in a general sense, of the sickness and of the physicians' many failed attempts to cure it. The physicians were curious about him, too, but it was the sickness that took up most of their time. Today, he lay on the table as they strained the blood of the ill and mixed it with herbs and honey from the "mellified man," as the physicians called the honeyed corpse.

Lazarus heard footsteps, three sets of them, crossing the tile floor. "What is he doing in here without a mask?" a physician said. "Get a mask on him quick! Has he been bathed?"

"I have a mask in my pocket!" said a familiar voice. "Great gods! What is he lying like that for?"

"Atonais!" Lazarus said.

He heard Atonais come forward only to be stopped by the physicians. "Leave him. We do not know what is wrong with him. We cannot find the source of his illness," one said. "And we cannot run the risk of it getting out into the city—"

"Yes, I understand, but this is a magical illness. He is my patient. May I speak to him alone?"

Tension hung heavy in the air as the physicians considered it. Then one of the male physicians spoke. "We will allow it, but only because we need to replenish our stock from the herb room. But put on the mask and lenses. We won't have you carrying whatever he has out to the people."

"Thank you," Atonais said. Lazarus heard the door close. Atonais approached, obediently masked. "You certainly have a way of making me end up in places where my life is in danger, don't you?" Atonais smiled behind the mask. "The king isn't so bad, though."

"I thought when I woke in that oubliette that I'd never see you or Flora again."

"No such luck with that one," Atonais said. "Can't have the Ankou getting carried away by an eagle. Not on my watch." Lazarus saw his eyes pass over his rotting arms, legs, chest, face. "Gods, it's . . ."

"It's not as bad as it looks," Lazarus lied. He didn't want to tell Atonais about the rages he flew into or about the deep gouges he had slashed into the walls of the oubliette. But somehow, Atonais knew.

"It's started, hasn't it?" he said. "You've begun to change."

"They've given me a potion that makes the rages go away while I'm out of the oubliette. I have requested to be chained anyway. So I am. Or I am strapped down. Or thrown in that hole in the ground to feel myself rot." Lazarus took a deep breath. "But perhaps this is better. Perhaps I can stay in the dungeon until I can be killed."

"Flora is here, too," Atonais said. "I showed her the memory. So she'd know what you're up against. So we could try to help."

The memory. The one thing he'd been avoiding talking with Flora about. In a way, he was glad he hadn't been there when she'd learned about it. He could only imagine her horror, her disgust, possibly even her anger at the death of the unicorn—its life sacrificed for his. He had not wanted to see himself become lesser in her eyes, to reveal Ana and her madness and the whole ugly debacle, not to Flora. Now she knew all of it.

"How did she take it?" Lazarus asked, his heart thudding in his half-numb chest.

"Well, she thought of abandoning the quest altogether."

"That bad, huh?" Lazarus said, trying not to imagine how he must have looked to her. "Can't say that I blame her. Not after the rot. Not after the unicorn."

"She thought leaving was the best way to *save* you," Atonais said. "And when that eagle swooped down and carried you away, we set out for Zayide to find you, no matter the cost. It's only due to her quick thinking that we're both still alive."

"What about the Kaer-Isian royals? And the temple?" Lazarus asked. "I've tried asking, but the physicians don't like to talk to me. We must find them for her."

"We aren't certain about that. The king knows something, but she's not telling us, and she won't tell us—or let you go—until we cure whatever's ailing the people of Parth."

"*You* will cure it?" Lazarus said. "What will you do?"

It was then that the door opened and the physicians returned, arms full of herbs ready to be made into potions. Atonais put his hand on Lazarus's shoulder, the one that was not covered with drog tissue, and said, "The best I can."

And then Atonais's hand was gone.

As Lazarus waited for the guards to come and take him away, he listened as the physicians told Atonais of the state that the people were in. But everything Atonais suggested, the physicians had already tried. They could only agree on one thing.

"The blood is thick," said a physician. "Thick and almost fizzy."

Lazarus turned his head and watched as Atonais held the blood vials into the light. The color seemed fine. But when he turned the vials upside down it was true: The blood did not flow properly. He had seen something like this before, long, long ago.

"Atonais," Lazarus said. Atonais and the physicians turned to him. "May I see the blood?"

Atonais looked to the other physicians. They nodded. Lazarus's hands were unshackled, and he flexed his wrists and fingers before taking the vials.

Lazarus held up the vials, swirling the contents of each, watching the blood flow. He uncorked the last vial and, with a dropper, took one drop. He opened his mouth to place the drop of blood on his tongue and there was a collective gasp.

"Lazarus! That is ridiculously unsanitary." Atonais's voice rose. "That blood is infected!"

"What's it going to do, kill me?" Lazarus said.

The other physicians exchanged scandalized glances as Atonais gave him the go-ahead.

Lazarus grimaced as he tasted a drop of blood from the vial. The coppery, metallic taste gave way to something sour and foreign. He tasted blood from the other two vials, and the same taste lingered. It was barely noticeable in one, stronger in the next, and even stronger in the last one. He nodded.

"Well?" Atonais said. "Have you found something?"

Lazarus did not answer right away. Inside, the part

of him that took over when he lost consciousness, when the hate reared up inside him, seemed to stir at the taste of the blood. He tried to ignore it. And, thankfully, it seemed to subside.

"There's something in their blood," Lazarus said. "Something is making their blood foul as well as thick. Poison that emanates through the skin of a magical being. Something reptilian, probably, but definitely something magic."

"We've tested the blood over and over," said one Parthan physician. "And we've never found anything we could identify."

"The biggest lizards in Parth are the ones the king owns," another physician said.

"But their skin," the first physician said with uncertainty. "I've heard that if you lick one—a baby one, of course, not a big one—you'll hallucinate. I heard that teenagers were doing it for fun a few years back. What if—"

"What if everyone in Parth is out licking lizards?" the other physician said impatiently. "That's preposterous. Even if it were true, people aren't hallucinating; they're dying. Besides, we tested it against all the known venoms and poisons in Parth, including the secretions of those blasted lizards. You must be mistaken."

"If there is one thing I understand better than

anyone," Lazarus said, "it is the many, many ways there are to die. I've seen something like this before when a wyrm was poisoning an orchard in the north of Valacia. Entire batches of cider had to be thrown out. This is poison from the scales of a magical reptile and you must find and slay it. But be careful. Whatever is causing the sickness will be even more deadly itself."

CHAPTER TWENTY-THREE

P OISON, YOU SAY?" ASKED THE KING THE NEXT morning as she led them into the city.

"Yes," said Atonais. "Some kind of reptilian thing that exudes poison through its skin is what the Ankou says. The only matter now is finding it."

"Then we haven't a moment to lose," said the king. She was carrying a sword today, and Flora, too, had been permitted to carry one. She wasn't sure what she felt more like now: a handmaiden or a warrior. All she knew for certain was that Atonais had seen Lazarus.

"How is he?" Flora whispered to Atonais. "Where was he? Was he all right?"

"He hasn't changed yet. Don't worry," said Atonais. "He's still got his wits about him, as much as usual, anyway."

Flora thought of Lazarus chained to a wall or held in a cell, slowly rotting. Was he afraid? Was he lonely? "I wish I could have seen him," Flora said. "If he'd even want that now."

Atonais opened his mouth to answer, but he was cut short by a piteous wailing. They followed the king to the door of the house they had visited yesterday. Even outside, Flora tasted the thick, hot air of sickness. When they opened the door, a sick man knelt on the floor beside the body of Cyrdi, the woman from before. She was somehow thinner, her lesions deeper, her chest pigeoned inward, and on her face she wore the waxy pallor of death. The man beside her did not even raise his head when the king opened the door. Flies began to gather, and she could hear weak wailings as Cyrdi's children cried from behind a closed door in the back of the house, kept shut by the automatons.

King Ulalume's face was expressionless. She did not even blink. She just stared down at the man and his dead wife and said nothing. Then she bowed her head and walked quietly out of the house. Flora followed her.

The king took her canteen and hurled it down on the ground. She stood with her foot on the canteen until the water turned the sand to mud.

"Your Majesty?"

They turned to see a little sick boy standing at the corner between two houses.

"Do you need some more water?" he said, and Flora saw that in his bandaged hands he held a worn wooden bucket.

"Thank you," said the king. "But no. Run along to the fountain." She waved him away and her bladed nails glinted in the sunlight. Her eyes were blank as she watched the boy walk to the fountain and dip his bucket into the water that flowed from the statue's urn.

"Wait," Atonais said with a strange expression on his face. He ran to the fountain and took the bucket from the boy's hands. The boy fell back, confused.

"What are you doing?" snapped the king. "Let the child carry water for his family."

"The water." Atonais turned to face the king. "Lazarus mentioned a wyrm who had contaminated an orchard. What if something is contaminating the water?"

"My grandmother built the marvel of all fountains," said the king. "Two of them, made to filter clean water forever, uninterrupted. It's hard to believe that her design could be flawed."

"Two reservoirs?" Atonais asked. "Why two?"

"The first, the great underground Lake of Auber, was made to filter water for the city. A second, smaller aquifer unattached to the first is closer to the palace, and filters water for its inhabitants and the gardens." The king frowned. "And, once more, both people in the palace and out of it have gotten sick, though admittedly fewer in the palace."

"But the ones who have gotten sick—they're guards," Atonais said. "And I'd bet anything that they're guards who have duty out in the city, aren't they?"

"Yes," the king said, "they all have been. But there cannot be a problem with my grandmother's design. There simply can't."

"If everything is in place, then it will do no harm to go to the source and make sure once more. Just to see," Atonais said. "Please, can you take us to the Lake of Auber?"

The king's eyes followed the back of the boy with his bucket. Flora saw a pinprick of doubt appear in her expression.

"Follow me," she said, and she led them past the fountain and into the Copper District on the west side of the city.

The doors that separated the cavern from the city were locked with three ancient locks. Unlike the pristine doors of the palace, the copper doors to the cavern were so blue-green with patina that they were almost black. Onto each door a familiar face had been sculpted: the serene face of Ularia the Designer.

The king reached into the front of her blouse and pulled the chain from around her neck. On it were four very old-looking keys: three dark copper, like the locks and the doors, and one a narrow, gleaming rose-gold that looked even older than the others. She took the three copper keys into her hand and unlocked the doors, then put the keys back in her blouse.

The doors groaned open, and Flora was met with a blast of cold, dank air that settled on her skin and made her shiver. The king took a small object from her pocket, clicked it, and used it to set flame to a torch that hung in a sconce on the wall. She offered Atonais another torch, but he shook his head and simply created an egg-size ball of lightning in his hand.

In the light, the cavern did not appear any less frightening or cold. Though there was a clear, well-carved path, in many places stone teeth jutted up from the floor of the cave, and slimy things crawled between them. The smell was wet and deep like mildew, acrid like lime, and all around them was the sound of dripping. Water dripped like saliva from the stone teeth that snarled down from the ceiling into small pools, and, farther along, Flora could hear the sound of a large amount of water groaning its way through the cavern. Flora imagined herself in the belly of a colossal dead whale.

But the king did not seem bothered in the slightest. She moved quickly and confidently, undaunted. Flora and Atonais followed the flickering halo of her torch and the sound of running water until she left the path and went to stand next to an enormous copper pipe, bluish green in color and wider around than even a troll's arms could reach. It snaked out from the darkness like a massive green serpent before branching upward into a veritable forest of copper pipes and rising out of sight. The king tapped the pipe with her metallic nails.

"This is the pipe that carries water to the city," she said. She pointed into the darkness beyond. "The filtering systems are back that way. Come."

They followed her off the path and moved along, their hands on the pipe, until it disappeared into a white stone dam. There was a door in the dam, and Flora and Atonais followed the king through it.

Inside were several chambers where the water was purified through a system of tanks filled with gravel. From there, the water flowed into the pipe and out to the city. The king inspected, explaining to Atonais (with, Flora could tell, great pride) how this thing worked and how that over there had been implemented shortly before her grandmother's death. It all seemed very technical and boring to Flora, but what she got from the conversation was that yes, the filtering system was in order and that they should move on. The king went through another door, out into the cavern again, and Flora and Atonais followed.

They walked down another, smaller path next to what the king called settling tanks. Apparently, the water flowed slowly through the tanks and was infused with several potions that the physicians had determined were beneficial for the people. Atonais chirped things like, "Fascinating!" and "Ingenious!"

They passed mixing basins and came to another dam that smelled putrid and was filled with big vats of potions. They went through it and out again, and passed systems of filters and pumps. All were in fine working condition; still, Atonais wanted to see the reservoir itself, the Lake of Auber.

Flora glanced behind them but found nothing. Only darkness that followed at her heels and made her feel cramped and smothered and afraid. Her hand hovered close to her sword. She knew in the speed of her step and the bend of her knees: Somewhere in the darkness, something waited. Something sinister.

"These are the screens," the king was telling Atonais. "There are eight of them to catch any debris that may be present in the water before it goes into the first purifier. Then the water flows through the potion chambers, the mixing tanks, and the settling tanks. You see, my grandmother thought of everything."

"It certainly does seem sound," Atonais said. "Perhaps Lazarus was wrong?"

"No," Flora whispered. "There's something here."

The king raised her torch and pointed upward at the stone teeth. Tiny bats hung here and there, shrinking away from the light.

"There are all sorts of things in this cavern," the king said. "That does not mean that we are in danger. Do not let the lack of light get to you."

Still, the feeling remained.

Flora glanced behind herself again. Only darkness and the flowing of water through the various tanks and chambers. She followed the king's torchlight until they came to a stop at the shore of a vast expanse of deep black water, smooth as glass. There were trees there, tall, gray-barked cypresses whose dead branches hung over the water as though bent in mourning. The ground was covered with sparse, feathery leaves, and where a thin mist hung over the water, knobs of the gray-green cypresses grew toward the ceiling. The feeling was eerie, and Flora hoped that they would not linger.

"The Lake of Auber," King Ulalume said. At the

center of the lake was a tiny island, filled with those knobby gray trees, and on the island a figure stood on a pedestal. It was a green copper statue: Ularia the Designer, standing with her head down and her arms open.

"She is buried out there, on the island in the middle of the lake," the king said with reverence. "The first female king of Parth."

Flora stepped up to the water's edge, her hand on her sword. She looked in and saw only her own reflection peering up at her. Still, the feeling of a malevolent presence in the cave had grown. It hung over her head, lurked behind her back, twined around her ankles. Something was very, very wrong.

"What is that smell?" asked Atonais suddenly.

And Flora smelled it, too: the scent of decaying flesh. It was not the festering, rotten, evil smell of the ghul, nor was it the unnatural smell of Lazarus's drog tissue.

"Look," the king said, and Flora saw that her hand, too, was close to her sword. She followed the king's line of sight, and there in the shadows lay a white thing, marked all over with dark stains. It lay completely still amid the mist and the knees of the cypresses.

"It looks like a dead sheep," said Atonais.

"How did a sheep wander down here?" Flora asked.

"There is a pool beside the grazing grounds that is

also fed from this lake," said the king. "Perhaps there is an opening and the sheep wandered in and starved."

Flora remembered the shepherds they had met in the city. Another sheep had gone missing, they said. How many sheep had wandered in here and gotten stranded? And if others had wandered in, where were their corpses?

Swords drawn, they moved along the shore, the smell of decay strengthening, until they approached the white thing. It was indeed a sheep, or, rather, the front half of one, decaying and covered with insects. Its hindquarters had been torn away, and its wool was scattered in pieces all around the cypresses. It did not appear to have been dead for long.

"Something attacked it," Flora said.

"Its hind legs could have been eaten by cave lizards after it starved," said the king. "And what killed it is of little concern to me. What I want to know is whether or not this has anything to do with the sickness."

"The other corpses," Flora said. "Could they be poisoning the water as they decay?"

"It is possible," said the king. "But the purification system—"

"What is that over there?" Atonais pointed to where something gleamed between knobs of cypress.

Flora squinted and then took a step back. It was a

man's arm and shoulder, still clutching a gleaming, hard-copper sword.

"My missing guard." The king's grip tightened on her sword hilt. "The one my men are still searching for. How did he end up here?"

Atonais edged toward the water, an unstoppered bottle in hand.

"Atonais!" Flora hissed.

"I have to get a sample of the water," he said. "I must do what I came to do." He bent and let the bottle fill.

Two rows of blue lights appeared under the surface, opening like eyelids. And out of the black water something rose and reared in the dim light. Three-headed, snakelike, spiny, with three mouths full of long, dagger-size teeth.

They scrambled back as it swayed before them like a cobra on four sturdy, crocodilian legs, eerie in its own blue light, its head nearly touching the ceiling. It opened its mouths in an earsplitting shriek of challenge, and the king cursed as she dropped her torch. Then the only light was from the monster itself.

It swam straight for them, its thin, sharp spines cutting a V into the water. Blood beat through Flora's body telling her to run before it was too late. But there were trees all around, knobs, stumps. She could not hope to escape.

The monster shrieked again and reared back one of its heads. It struck, mouth open, fangs extended. The king's sword clanged against its teeth as she raised it above her head. It drew back, rearing with two heads this time. As it lunged at her, the king sliced downward, through its neck.

It struck at Flora with another head, all teeth and swift motion. Flora, too, cut the head from its neck and dodged as the third head snapped at her legs. The two severed heads fell to the shore. Dead. The monster fell back, its remaining head looking bewildered, frightened.

"Just the third head now," Flora said. "Do you want it or—"

But the king raised her hand, her eyes narrowed. The stumps of the creature's necks began to throb, to pulse in the thin blue light. There was a sound of suction as air entered the slit throats. "No," the king gasped. "No, no, no . . ."

From each stump burst two more heads, writhing and blinking in the blue light as though they had just been born.

It lunged again and again, two heads at once, black mouths open, needle fangs dripping. It whipped its black tail, and the king was knocked off her feet. It struck at Flora with two heads, but she rolled, avoiding the snaps of jaws to her left and right as she parried attacks from its tail and claws.

The king scratched one head in the eye with her bladed nails, but its ruined eye filled with fluid and mended itself almost immediately. Flora hacked at the monster's chest, at its legs, but every wound she made closed nearly as quickly as it had been made.

The king screamed as three heads bore down upon her. Flora ran forward and slashed at its chest, slashing and slashing, though she knew it would do no good. She plunged her sword deep into its chest.

Atonais shouted something, but she could not hear over the monster's shrieks. Lightning sizzled all around her. It blinded her for a moment, and then the creature screamed and shrank back. Her sword vibrated with the lightning, but her gauntlets kept her safe, and when she wrenched her blade from the monster's chest, the wound left was open, charred, and it did not close. Atonais sent another lightning bolt from the bank.

The force from the blast sent Flora tumbling on the stony shore. There was a sickening snap and her arm bent behind her. The pain sent sparks dancing in front of her eyes, and she could barely breathe, could barely see.

The creature advanced on her. She gasped and rolled onto her stomach to crawl away. It was over her, its mouth open wide, its blue lights ablaze. It arched its neck, venom dripping from its fangs. Flora held her arm over her face. But then one of its great, snarling, open-mouthed heads fell to the ground at Flora's feet.

"Quick," the king panted. "Follow me."

They darted into the trees to hide in the wide roots and knees of the gray cypresses, lungs heaving. Flora held her arm to her chest. It felt as though it were on fire from the inside. She breathed in and out through her teeth.

"Let me see it," the king said. She took Flora's arm into her hands. Flora tried hard not to cry out. Already it was swelling. "It is surely broken." The king took off her cloak and fastened it into a sort of sling that tied behind Flora's head.

"I'm sorry, Your Majesty, I—"

"Shh!" said the king.

There was a blur of motion as Atonais leapt into a grove of cypresses opposite them. From behind a gray trunk, he sent lightning bolt after lightning bolt at the creature. It snarled and flinched from the light. And as they watched, it backed up. . . .

"No, no, no," Flora breathed, but it was too late. The creature had backed into the only route out of the cavern, trapped by the humming, pulsing lightning. Atonais could not hold it off forever. He would run out of strength, collapse like he had in the Weir, and then what would happen?

"We need a way to kill it," the king said. "We need a way to make the wounds permanent!"

Flora remembered then: the one wound that had not closed on its own. She had struck it when Atonais had thrown his first lightning bolt. It had cauterized. Something about cauterization kept the wounds from healing.

"The lightning," Flora said. "It keeps it from healing itself! We have to find a way to cauterize the wounds we make!"

"That's it," said the king, her eyes suddenly afire. "Quick. I need your blade and your gauntlets."

"I can't hold it off much longer!" Atonais shouted.

Flora held out her arms and the king took her gauntlets, fastening them on her own arms. They traded swords, and Flora made sure that the king's hilt and pommel were covered with leather. She took the king's hard-copper blade in her good hand.

Holding the sword firmly in the gauntlets, the king walked calmly toward the creature, who shrieked at the mouth of the cavern.

"What are you doing?" Atonais shouted between lightning bolts.

"I am the king! I will be the one to kill it! On three,

send your lightning into this sword!" The king raised her sword overhead. "One!" she shouted.

Behind the trees, Flora held her arm in the sling and watched. The creature's eyes were on the king. It moved slightly away from the mouth of the cavern.

"Two!"

"Your Majesty, it might not work!" Atonais shouted. "The gauntlets weren't made for direct—"

"THREE!" the king bellowed.

Atonais directed the bolt into her blade. Flora could hear the lightning as the sword sang under the gauntlets. The creature struck, and when two heads attacked the king at once, she cut off one, then the other.

There was a sizzling, searing, smoking, and this time the heads did not grow back. The creature flailed, confused. But the glow was fading fast from the sword. The king jumped back, dodging a strike.

"Again!" Flora shouted from behind the trees. "Again, Atonais!"

Once more, Atonais's lightning lit up the sword, and they heard it sing. The king ran at the creature, slicing deep into its chest. Again and again she swung, leapt, jumped, blocked. Dark blue blood spurted in every direction before the veins and arteries were cauterized, burned shut by the lightning blade. Soon, there were only two heads left.

But the monster was wary. It kept its remaining eyes on the king, puffing itself up. Flora saw it twist its tail, preparing to swing out at the king as it had with her.

Flora ran from behind the trees. She screamed up at the monster. Its heads turned in her direction for just a moment, and the king slashed through both the remaining necks, sending its heads thudding to the ground. "That's for my city," the king said. The monster collapsed into a shuddering pile, and its blue lights went out.

"Thank you," she said to Flora, straightening her shoulders, all her poise coming back. "It would have taken us much longer to figure this out without you two."

"But you did it," said Flora.

"Do you think you can get what you need from this?" the king asked Atonais.

Atonais came forward with more glass vials. He gathered a bit of the creature's saliva as well as a vial of the substance that covered its scales. "This should definitely be enough to make an antidote."

"Excellent." The king shrugged into her cloak and adjusted her hair. "My physicians can mend broken bones in mere days, but I suggest Flora stay in the infirmary until her arm is healed."

"Yes, Your Majesty," said Atonais. "But remember, we've done our part, as promised."

"I have not forgotten your requests," she said, "and I

will be true to my word as well. Come, let's head back to the palace. There is still work to be done."

The king relit her torch, and they began the long, long walk back along the tanks and chambers. When she turned, Flora saw the king's eyes linger on the island at the center of the lake, where her grandmother, Ularia the Designer, slept in peace. Then she held her head high and took her place at the head of the group.

CHAPTER
TWENTY-FOUR

LAZARUS SAT, WRISTS SHACKLED, AT THE BOTTOM OF the oubliette. The rages ebbed and flowed. The pain came and went, and he vomited often. He could feel himself slipping. Had the demon Moloch lied to him? Or, perhaps, this was what the prophecy had foretold all along, for what was death if not the loss of oneself?

Then he heard a sound, footsteps so familiar they made him catch his breath.

"Lazarus!" said a voice, and he looked up to see Flora peering down into the oubliette at him. Her fiery hair curled around her face, and despite everything, his rotting heart sped just as it had when they almost kissed by the fire that night.

"I've come to get you out! There is so much to tell you." She beamed down at him. "We fought a cave monster,

Atonais and the king and I, and we won. It broke my arm, but they fixed it in the physicians' chamber."

"Was it a wyvern?" Lazarus asked.

"Something like one," Flora said. "Atonais thinks one of the king's lizards, a small one, got into the water tanks somehow and one of the potions they use to filter the water caused some sort of reaction and it grew to be a monster. But whatever it is, now the physicians are creating a medicine to cure the people. You're free. We're free. Come, I'll call the guards in and we'll get you out."

His heart gave a painful squeeze. He looked at his arm: more rot now than whole flesh. He felt his cheek, his exposed teeth. He was a horror.

"Did you hear me, Lazarus? You're free!" Her voice was insistent. "King Ulalume has ordered it. She'll finally tell me what she knows about Beth. Then we can go—"

"To the Temple of Fates?" He moved out of the shadow and raised his arms so that she could see the extent of his decay. Above him, he heard Flora catch her breath. "Look at me, Flora," he said softly. "It's too late."

"Lazarus," she whispered. "I'm so sorry. This is my fault."

"Neither of us knew this would happen," he said. "I should have guarded myself more. But now it's happened, and there's no use blaming anyone." He scrambled for something else to say, anything else. "Did you bring the caravan with you? Are the horses all right?"

"The caravan is waiting just inside the gate to Weir. We had to abandon it to travel quickly. And the horses are in the king's stable. They're doing well."

"Good," said Lazarus. "That's one less loose end to tie up."

"We still have time," Flora said, but her voice had the quaver of uncertainty to it.

"Do you see these?" Lazarus jerked his head toward the deep gashes in the walls of the oubliette. "I made them, Flora. I'm turning, and not just my body. My mind, too. I'm becoming something else. Something horrifying. That's why I have these." He showed her the shackles that bound him. "There will be nothing left at all in a few days but a rotted body full of hate and rage. And we have no idea where to go."

It was the truth, all of it. He had been stupid to think that there ever could be a happy ending to his story. Maybe there was one for Flora, still. "You and Atonais go. Choose a third to go with you. Get your princess back, get your people back. But leave me here. It's better for everyone."

"I crossed a desert, Lazarus," Flora said. "I bargained with a king. I fought a monster, broke my arm, and got knocked senseless, all for you. All to rescue you so we could go to the Temple of Fates. And now that I'm here to let you out of the oubliette, you tell me that you're just going to lie there alone in a hole and become a monster? No one truly wants to be alone. Believe me."

"I don't *want* to, Flora, but it's got to be this way," he said. "I can't run the risk of turning and hurting you or Atonais or anybody else."

Flora looked down at him for a long time. After a moment, she said, "If you turn, I will kill you, just as you asked."

"Flora . . . I never should have asked that of you. Just forget about—"

"I don't want to do it," she said. "But if you come with us, if you see this through, like we planned, and you still turn, I will end it for you. I promise. Just please, please do this. If you won't do it for you, then do it for me."

Her voice caught what was left of his heart and twisted in it like a knife. All he could think was how beautiful she was in the torchlight. He knew then that there was no escaping. She would be the end of him, one way or another.

Slowly, Lazarus rose to his feet and stretched as well as his shackled wrists would allow. "All right," he said. "I'll come."

Flora smiled a sad, wan smile. Then her face disappeared from the circle of light above the oubliette, and he heard her whistle. The floor of the oubliette began to rise beneath him, and soon there was no oubliette at all, just level ground beneath his feet. He braced himself for the jolt of horror that would go through her, the disgust that would pass over her face when she saw him up close. Flora said nothing. Her gray eyes flickered over his body, over the decay that ravaged it.

"I know," he said. "I'm a monster."

But she didn't flinch like the guards behind her did. Instead, she came forward and put her arms around him.

"You'll never be a monster to me."

He closed his eyes and breathed in the smell of her. And, just for a moment, everything felt beautiful.

From around her neck, she pulled the hourglass on the chain. It gleamed in the low light of the torches as she put it around his neck. Then she reached into her pocket and pulled out a square of paper. "Here," she said, her voice losing all its buoyancy. "You left this, too."

Ana's portrait.

Lazarus took the picture, though he knew that it would never help him again. He put it in the pocket of his terrible quarantine clothes.

"Come on," Flora said, forcing a smile. "The king is waiting. And we can't have her seeing you underdressed."

"I'd rather die," said Lazarus. But neither of them laughed.

When Flora led Lazarus into the throne room, the king and Atonais were waiting. A table had been set before the throne, with seating for four. Lazarus's chains rattled as he adjusted the black half-mask he had been given. Flora hoped fervently that she wouldn't have to use the sword that hung at her belt. Not on him. Not yet. She knew that he felt awful, monstrous behind the mask, but she told him that he looked fine with his old hat and the new Parthan clothes (clothes that Flora had demanded be black).

"Don't worry," she said. "With the mask, no one can tell."

"Liar," he said softly.

It hurt her to see him like this. Where he had once been so handsome, so sure, he had become lank and spare. In place of the grace he once moved with was a feebleness she had never seen before. And though he had been given a potion to kill the pain and nausea, his rotted limbs were hard to move, and he limped as they crossed the copper floor. He stumbled once, but Flora gave him her arm and he righted himself again, well enough to stand before the table and give the king the customary bow.

The king rose and waited patiently until Flora helped Lazarus to his seat. Flora saw the guards standing almost out of sight behind the pillars, waiting in case Lazarus turned or went into a rage. She hoped Lazarus hadn't noticed them.

"Thank you for your presence, Ankou," King Ulalume said. "And thank you for your help. It may have taken me much longer to figure out the source of the illness. Without you, Flora, and you, Atonais, I may never have killed it."

Flora watched as Ulalume extended her gold-ringed hand to Lazarus. "Though you have every reason to, I hope that you do not bear me ill will. I could not let your condition spread to my people. I did not know what to do with you. So now I offer you my deepest apologies."

"I barely know what to do with myself, Your Majesty," he said, and he put his black-gloved hand in hers. "And I don't bear you any ill will."

"That is a start, I suppose," said the king.

From a copper carafe, Ulalume poured coffee for each of them—coffee that was not as thick or strong as Lazarus's, but as Flora watched him smile behind his mask, she knew that it was a gesture that did not go unappreciated. He took a cup, as did the king and Atonais and Flora, and, though Lazarus had to tilt his head at a certain angle to keep the coffee from leaking out of his decayed cheek, they drank.

"The physicians are working on a cure for my people's illness," said Ulalume. "The poison samples were absolutely invaluable."

"What will be done about the poison?" Flora asked.

"I've formulated a plan for filtering it out of the lake." Atonais's hair sparked with excitement. "As it turns out, the poison can be filtered—completely filtered!—from the water with a large amount of lightning, cotton, and quite a lot of conductive metal made into a sort of net over the whole thing. Until then, the people will have to use the palace's water supply. Once it gets going, it should be quite a simple procedure."

"And we thank you," said the king. "But I have summoned you here for one purpose: to make good on my promise. Now I will tell you all that you have asked of me."

Atonais fell silent, and Lazarus put his coffee cup down quietly on the saucer. When the king spoke again, her voice was heavy.

"Months ago, I watched from my tallest tower as Kaer-Ise burned. I saw the glow over the horizon, and I knew what had happened . . . and I thanked any gods that there have ever been that my forefathers cut ties with the outside world."

The king rubbed her temples. Flora's heart felt taut as a bowstring.

"The escape ship carrying the royal family of Kaer-Ise sank after colliding with a reef off the northern coast, close to Yuraleth, a week after the massacre. My viziers watched the wreck from the shore but did not offer aid."

Then the king spoke the words Flora had been dreading, waking and dreaming, for months.

"There were no survivors."

It was too much. Too much. Her breath was coming in spurts. She had to leave. Flora pushed herself away from the table and stood, sending her coffee clattering.

"Flora!" said Lazarus, but she barely heard him. She imagined Betheara floating, cold and dead in the water, hair lank around her.

"No," she gasped. "Not after all we've done to get here." Flora folded herself down, shaking, her head in her hands. Princess Betheara was dead. She had died far from their home, crying out for help among the raging waters and being denied. Flora imagined her drowning—had she panicked? Had she reached upward for a hand that would not extend to help her?

She heard someone push a chair back. Arms wrapped

around her, and she smelled spices and decay. Lazarus held her close, his chains rattling softly. But it was the king she spoke to next.

"You knew?!" Flora spat. "You had already let them drown, and you let me play the servant for you! You pretended to be my friend! Damn you, why didn't you at least have the decency to *tell* me?"

"I didn't know you," the king said somberly. "And I could not give such information to strangers. Not when Parth was also vulnerable. I am sorry, Flora. I am so sorry. But this is why I am prepared to do something for you that violates centuries of decrees by my ancestors. I am going to open the Temple of Fates for you."

Silence fell over the hall.

"You said the Temple of Fates was just a story," Flora said.

"That is what the nation of Parth wants the world to believe," said the king. "The Temple of Fates is as real as you or I am. After the Necromancer won the Artifact and the Necromancer's War was fought, my many-times-great-grandfather made the decision to seal the temple, to let it pass into legend, so that no evil men could ever lay their hands on the Artifact again."

"The Necromancer touched the Artifact?" Atonais gasped. "That explains everything, how he was able to raise the dead, and so many of them. Gods, if I'd only brought my notes!"

Flora saw Lazarus put his hand to his throat, over the scar on his neck. She reached out and squeezed his hand.

"As the king of Parth, I have a certain responsibility," said Ulalume. "I am the temple's guardian, as were my ancestors before me." From around her neck, the king pulled the key she did not use in the cavern: the rose-gold key. *The hidden golden key.* "I understand your need for a miracle. And after what you have done for Zayide, I can grant you this, knowing that the Necromancer's evil is not within you."

Flora and Lazarus exchanged glances. This was it. This was what they had worked so hard for. A cure for his curse. Kaer-Ise and her people, alive and well again. Miracles.

"I will be honest with you," said the king. "No one has passed through the last door for over three hundred years. It rejected my soldiers when I sent them in hopes of ridding Zayide of the sickness, and they could go no farther. It may reject you, too." She paused. "But if it does not . . . if you pass the temple's challenges, if you live through its tests and achieve the Artifact, perhaps your miracle will come. Is that what you wish?"

"Please," Flora said. "It's our last chance."

The king nodded. "Gather all that you need," she said. "I will go down to the physicians' chamber and check their progress. If they have succeeded, I will instruct them to administer the cure, even in my absence. Meet me on the upper balcony, and we will leave straight away."

CHAPTER
TWENTY-FIVE

WHEN LAZARUS ARRIVED ON THE UPPER BAL-
cony, the sky was dark and clear and the moon
was haloed and full. A cool wind played over the swaying
poplars, and the smell of flowers and fruit was everywhere. Around him, automatons bustled, beeping
and clanging, while the king—already dressed in what
Lazarus assumed were traveling clothes—oversaw everything. All that seemed to be packed for them was a few
skins of water, food, and a few hard-copper weapons.

"King Ulalume," Flora said. "The horses will need
water. Is there more for them downstairs?"

"We don't have time for horses," King Ulalume said.
"Not if we're going to get the Ankou to the temple before
he changes."

Five shapes flickered past the moon, throwing

fast-moving shadows over the balcony: the eagles. They swooped downward, their enormous wings making soft *beat, beat* sounds against the night air. The king took a few steps back, and they landed on the railings of the balcony, sending small clouds of dust shimmering into the air.

Two of them were not like the others. Three of them had saddles and harnesses, but the largest, calmest two of the eagles had had their talons outfitted with leather gloves. In those leather gloves, they held what looked like big cloth-covered rings. As Lazarus opened his mouth to ask the purpose of the rings and gloves, the door opened and four servants entered, carrying an iron-and-copper cage. And Lazarus knew exactly the monster who was intended to ride inside it.

"We felt that this would be the best option for you," the king said. "So that if you do turn, you can be contained. I am sorry, but we didn't see another way."

"I understand," he said, feeling more wretched than ever.

"It's nearly sunrise," Atonais said. "If we're going to fly, we need to go now."

"He is right," said the king. "Quick, we must leave." And the king climbed up onto one of the saddled eagles, swinging her leg over it as though it were a horse.

"What if one of us falls?" Atonais asked.

"Your eagle will catch you," the king said. "Don't worry. They're very well-trained."

Lazarus touched the cool metal of the cage with the hand that could still feel. It seemed strong enough to hold him. Even if it crashed to the dunes below, it wouldn't likely break. There was a curtain that could be drawn around it, to shield his companions from the sight of his transformation, no doubt. He expanded the curtain so that it covered the entire cage.

"Come on," Flora said. "It's almost morning."

With a final look back at the ground, Lazarus climbed into the cage. As he closed his eyes, he felt the cage lurch upward, and all around him, the beating of wings filled his mind as the curse came to claim him.

They flew through the night and into the morning, with the high, cold wind at their backs. Flora's legs ached from riding, though the eagles' flight was smooth and graceful. They needed no direction. They merely followed the king's eagle as it flew westward. In only a few hours' time, the city of Zayide was completely out of sight—even the tallest, gleaming tower. The desert stretched out in front of them like a map too long for the table it had been spread on, and the misty, wavering horizon seemed ever farther.

Flora looked down at the still desert hundreds of dizzying feet below, watching the eagles' shadows, broad and swift, flash over the dunes. They reminded her, just for a moment, of whales she had once seen pass beneath the king's ship during a day on the ocean. King Ulalume, Atonais, Flora, then Lazarus's eagles, lagging behind, carrying the shrouded iron cage. Lazarus would be all bones by now. She wished that he could be alive and awake to experience the thrill of flight.

They stopped in the afternoon and had a quick meal in the shade of Lazarus's cage while the eagles rested. When the eagles were refreshed, they put darkened spectacles over their eyes and climbed back onto their birds. Then they were away again. The sun beat down on them, despite the wind at their backs. Had it not been for the skin potion that the king had provided for them, Flora and Atonais would have burned to a crisp by the endless sun and wind.

When the sun set, the horizon was no longer hazy. It was a great, high wall of darkness. At first, Flora thought there was a mountain range looming ahead, but it looked as though it were moving. And, Flora realized, it was. It was a wall, not of stone, but of sand and wind, swirling, flying toward them, threatening to slam into them and knock them from the sky. She could hear its dry roar as it approached.

The king shouted back to them, "Sandstorm! Aim for the moon. Drive your eagles high!"

Flora pulled the reins. Her hair fell back from her face as the eagle climbed. Behind her, Lazarus's eagles struggled, trying to follow her higher. Then there was a roaring, murderous shout. The eagles squawked and looked down at the shrouded cage they carried. *Lazarus must have rebuilt*, Flora thought. *He must have rebuilt and gone into one of his rages.* The eagles were frightened. The cage swung, shook, threatened to fall, and the wall of sand and wind swept ever toward them.

There was another murderous yowl from beneath the shroud, and suddenly a decayed arm tore an enormous jagged gash in it. Lazarus's hand clutched the bars of the cage—but it wasn't Lazarus's hand, it belonged to something else. Horror and panic flashed through her.

No, she thought. *Please, gods, no...*

There was a roaring within the cage, a terrible, inhuman voice that was Lazarus's and not Lazarus's at the same time, and through the hole in the shroud, she could see one gleaming, decayed eye, bluish and glowing in the gloom.

"Lazarus!" she cried. "Fight it! Please!"

The creature who was not Lazarus yowled again, a sound of pure hatred that froze her blood in her veins. The eagles squawked and began to veer off wildly.

"Come on, girl!" Flora cried to the eagles. "Follow! Higher! Higher! Follow, please!" And it seemed to work, because the eagles did follow her. But as the storm rumbled beneath them, they could not raise the cage out of the swirling sand.

There was no help for it—Lazarus's eagles simply couldn't fly any higher, and the wind and sand slammed through the cage, cutting into the shroud and Lazarus beneath it. They kept flying, Lazarus's eagles dragging the cage through the sandstorm, and, hours later, when it was over and the night wind went back to normal, there was barely any shroud left at all.

She held her breath as the last of it blew back, and she could see what was inside the cage.

"Lazarus?" But when it raised its head, she could see that the thing inside wasn't Lazarus. This was something different. The thing threw itself against the bars, gnashing its teeth, reaching out with what seemed more like claws than hands. Its mouth opened wide—unnaturally so—and its eyes gleamed with an unholy, blue-white fire that shook her to her core. It screamed and gnashed and flailed.

She could not take her eyes from the horror that Lazarus had become. "No!" she begged. "Don't turn yet! Come back!"

Flora began to pray to any and all the gods. To Emir of Kaer-Ise, who didn't exist, and to Lazarus's God of the Unknown. It didn't matter as long as someone listened. *Please, please don't let him turn. I don't know what I'd do without him. Please . . . please, if there is anything good left in the world, let us get to the temple . . . please.*

And someone must have listened, because the thing that wasn't Lazarus grabbed fistfuls of hair and shook its head back and forth, like a dog slinging water off itself. Then it crumpled to the floor of the cage and lay so still that Flora thought that it was dead for a moment.

Then Lazarus stirred. She knew it was Lazarus—something about the way he moved—and warm relief flooded through her. Flora flew her eagle downward, close to Lazarus's cage. He looked out through the bars—his eyes were his own again, tired and dark—and said, "I'm so sorry, Flora."

"I'm so glad you're all right," Flora said. "I thought I'd lost you."

"You almost did," he said, pushing himself against the back bars of the cage, far from Flora. "I felt myself slipping away, becoming nothing . . ."

"You haven't turned yet," she said, forcing strength and positivity into her voice. "Just hang on, all right? It can't be long now."

Flora looked at Lazarus, slumped and shivering in his cage. She only hoped they were fast enough.

CHAPTER
TWENTY-SIX

T HEY TOUCHED DOWN IN FRONT OF THE CLIFFS
when the moon was almost overhead and their
shadows were barely visible beneath them. The temple
was carved into the cliff face itself, made of copper-pink
stone the color of the rings that Parthan women wore,
and for a moment, all Flora could do was look up at it
and feel the strange, supernatural thrum that pulled at
them to come inside. The temple was massive, higher
even than the highest tower in Zayide. If Flora stared at
it hard enough, she could see the many spires and stairs
and columns carved into the rock. There were curved
eaves and water-catching urns that reached up out of the
rock. Six columns with flowering tops bloomed upward
into solid rock, and a set of wide, low steps led to a set of
doors with two sleeping faces on it.

There was no handle or knob. There did not seem to be a keyhole, but King Ulalume pulled the rose-gold key from her blouse, took it off her neck, and held it in her tightly clenched fist.

Flora held Lazarus's arm as he limped up the steps. She could feel the sickness rolling off him in waves now. *How can he face the challenges?* she thought. *How can he possibly hope to get through?* Then she shook herself. *I just have to get him to the temple,* she thought without knowing why. *Just get him inside and it will be all right.*

The king and Atonais had stopped at the wide stone doors. The faces carved on them were separated by a ray of moonlight falling through a hole in the carved roof above them. The king held the key into the moonbeam, letting the light make it almost pink-silver. Then the keyhole was simply there between the two faces. Gently, reverently, King Ulalume put her key in and turned it.

There was an echoing click, and a deep, earthen-metallic noise that sounded like the gears of Zayide's great clock grinding. Then the doors' faces opened their stone eyes and smiled, and with a rumble of stone, the doors parted and opened inward to reveal a square of looming, dusty darkness.

"Quickly," the king said. "Before it changes its mind!"

"Your Majesty—" Flora said.

"Go, now!" the king said. "And may you receive the miracle you need!" She gently pushed them forward, and as they plunged inside, the heavy doors closed behind them.

The darkness was sudden and enveloping, but it did not make them cower. Instead, it seemed to fill their lungs and thrum there like the pulse of the temple. Atonais did not or could not make lightning, because he did not light the way. They went down the wide hall that they somehow knew was there until they came to a circular room where a trough of many-colored flames danced upward, throwing their light up the walls and eaves.

"This entire place is *vibrating* with energy," Atonais said. "But it is an energy I don't recognize. I can't make even a simple spark here. It won't let me."

That is correct, Atonais Kell, said a voice that sounded like grinding stones. *The Temple of Fates has its rules.*

Flora and the others turned and looked around, but, she realized, this voice did not echo. It was inside her head—in all of their heads. The voice from her vision.

Why have you come to the Temple of Fates? the voice boomed, vibrating through Flora's bones.

"To be tested," Lazarus said finally.

Those who seek to enter the temple need no powers, no weapons, for all will be provided. They need only their true names.

They exchanged glances.

"I am Florelle Tannett," she said. "Former handmaiden to the princess of Kaer-Ise. And assistant to the Ankou of Valacia."

Atonais gulped. "I am Atonais Kell, Order of Lightning, Second Class."

The voice boomed through them again, resonant as thunder. *What is your name, son of the grave? I cannot sense it in you.*

"I have chosen a name for myself. I—I can't remember the rest."

Speak it, the voice said. *For you must have a name to go forward.*

"I am Lazarus," he said, drawing himself up to his full height. "The Ankou of Valacia."

There was a feeling in the temple, as though it were smiling, perhaps. *Lazarus*, the voice said. *A fine name. But before you may continue, you must be restored.*

Suddenly, Lazarus bent, clutching his stomach. All over, his rot began to heal. Flora watched, hardly daring to believe as the flesh of his cheek grew back over his teeth, over the exposed tendons of his neck. One by one, all his rotten places smoothed, and he stood and flexed his once-rotted arm, gasping as he saw that it, too, was as it had been. Flora nearly wept to see him whole again, standing straight and tall in his broad black hat.

You will remain as you are for as long as you remain within these walls—for time does not pass here—and you may not be permitted forward without being whole.

"Thank you," Lazarus gasped, feeling his face.

"Hey," Atonais whispered to Flora. "That wasn't there before, was it?"

She followed his gaze and saw an enormous stone door with a high, leaf-shaped arch. As she peered up at it, she saw three intricate designs, almost like sigils, appear as though they were being carved soundlessly into the stone: a palm with ten small stars on it, a bolt of lightning striking a mountain peak, and an hourglass. The three of them.

Within three chambers you will be mortally tested. In each chamber, I will choose which of you will move onward, until there is only one of you left. And it is this one who will be permitted to the final chamber to receive my boon. Only one.

"O-only one?" Atonais breathed. "But my research..."

Only one of you may have a wish granted.

Atonais was worried and pale. Beside them, Lazarus was quiet. *Only one. What if I receive my wish and undo the destruction of Kaer-Ise? What happens to Atonais and his inventions?* Flora's stomach lurched. *What about Lazarus? How will he ever find his death?*

If any of you die, your bodies will become part of me, the temple said.

"We won't be able to retrieve the body of someone who is killed?" Lazarus asked.

No. It is required. It is also required that you leave your weapons here.

Flora, Lazarus, and Atonais dropped their weapons

on the ground. Lazarus turned to Atonais, the only one of them not there for a miracle. "You can turn back now if you want," Lazarus said. "We would understand."

"No," Atonais said, his hands shaking. "I've come this far. I must see this through." He took a deep, bolstering breath. "For science."

Lazarus turned to Flora next. "No matter which of us is chosen, please know that you deserve this."

"So you do," she said. "No matter who is chosen."

He held out his hand to her, and she took it.

Are you ready? the temple boomed in their minds.

"We are," Lazarus said gravely. There was a thrum of approval. And as they moved forward, the door opened for them and they moved through it into darkness.

It seemed to Flora that the entire temple groaned as they passed through the doorway, as though the temple were growing the room they were entering around them as they walked. She heard gears turning, a sound like thousands of locks clicking, and the room sprang into life around them.

"A jungle?" Atonais mused.

The chamber they'd entered did look like one. It had a high, vaulted ceiling, and the entire room was covered in leafless green-and-black vines that draped down almost to their heads. They seemed to root at the base of the walls, climbed up to the vault of the ceiling, and disappeared into an enormous cluster of delicate, transparent flowers. There was a path that wound around several small carved pools, clear and deep. No lilies bloomed on them and no fish swam in them. The whole room was damp and smelled of metal and something sour and alien. On the ground were dark shapes—Flora squinted in the dim light to see them: skeletons, dozens of them. Skeletons still armed with shields and swords leaning against vines, slumping into the pools. What had killed them?

"What do we do?" Flora heard herself ask. There was no echo in this room.

Atonais snapped his fingers and a bright spark appeared. "Whatever it expects from us, the temple's allowed me to use my lightning here," said Atonais. "So there's that."

Flora moved to dip a toe into one of the pools, just to see. But as her boot was about to break the surface of the water, Lazarus pulled her back. He touched the surface of the pool with his fingertip and drew back with a yelp. Frantically, he rubbed his finger against his tunic and covered it with his cloak. When he withdrew his finger, Flora saw bone sticking out from the burned flesh of his fingertip.

"Acid," said Lazarus as the flesh grew back. "We'll have to be careful."

There was a crunch as Atonais accidentally stepped right in the middle of a fallen skeleton. "I beg your pardon," he told it. But it merely crumbled to dust under his boot.

They weaved around the pools, tripping over vines and stepping around the skeletons. The room remained as silent as a tomb. They went to a door on the other side of the room that was so far away from the sconces that it was nearly completely shrouded in darkness and ran their hands over it, but there was no way to open it.

"I wonder why there are no pools of water close to the light?" she muttered.

Lazarus shrugged. "Atonais, give us some light," he said.

Atonais put his hands together, and when he parted them, a sphere of lightning glowed in his hands.

Then there was a feeling as though she were being grabbed by the wrists. Suddenly, Flora found herself flying across the room and held down to the ground by an invisible force. When she recovered from her panic, she realized her gauntlets and belt were holding her to the wall, dangerously close to one of the acidic pools. From all over, swords and shields and daggers flew toward the walls and the ceiling, only to be held there by the black vines.

Frantically, she searched for Lazarus and Atonais. Lazarus, too, had been dragged across the room and was slumped under one of the sconces, barely safe from the flying blades. A sword was lodged in the wall no more than a handsbreadth from his face. He struggled but could not free himself.

Atonais seemed completely unaffected and stood in the middle of the room with a look of growing realization on his face.

"What happened?" Lazarus shouted. He wiggled his wrists, but his gauntlets were held fast to the vines just as Flora's were.

"Magnetism!" Atonais said excitedly. "The vines are made of a metal that attracts other metals. It's hard to explain." He pointed down to the ground where other weapons were still on the floor. "But see? It only attracts certain metals and not all of them. These must be made of a different metal."

"Wonderful," Lazarus said.

"I wonder how this is possible?" Atonais was saying.

"Don't just stand there," Flora shouted up at him from her place on the floor. "Help us!"

Atonais ran forward to help Flora, and as he did, his

robes pushed one of the skeletons into a nearby pool. There was a splash and sizzle as it disappeared into the liquid, leaving it bright, sickly blue.

Then, all around the room, the other pools began to bubble. The acid began to rise, forming itself into blobs with heads and arms. They pulled themselves out of the pools, making gurgling, croaking sounds. Coming for them. "Oh no," Atonais murmured.

"Go faster!" Flora cried as Atonais's fingers fumbled over the straps of her gauntlets. When she had one arm free, she reached down and unfastened her belt. Then she wrenched her arm out of her other gauntlet and leapt out of the way as one of the acid creatures reached for her ankle. She took a sword in hand, thanking Emir that it was silver rather than iron.

More acid creatures slithered forward, toward Lazarus, but they reached the edge of the candle's halo of light and did not come closer to him.

"Behind you!" Lazarus shouted.

Flora spun and swung down with her sword. The sword passed through the acid creature like water, sending it in a sizzling spray, and the place where her blade had touched it was black. As it gathered itself back together, Flora darted to the side.

"Flora, help Atonais!" Lazarus shouted. Beside Atonais on the ground, a skeleton lay half inside, half outside the circle of light. Flora saw Atonais reach for it with his foot. Then there was a deep burning on her leg. One of the creatures had brushed against her.

She screamed and jolted away, trying not to focus on the burning, because across the pool from her, four of the creatures surrounded Atonais. He sent a lightning bolt into the nearest of them, and the lightning passed through it. It grew larger—waist-level now.

She needed something bigger, blunter than her sword. Flora plucked a silver shield and dagger from one of the skeletons on the ground. She jumped over the acid pool and slammed the shield down on the nearest monster, splashing it away from Atonais in a sizzling spray. The other monsters absorbed the scattered droplets, and Flora and Atonais jumped to a safer spot. Atonais picked up a shield of his own and stood, his back against Flora's, his spectacles sliding down his nose.

Atonais craned his neck to check on Lazarus, who still struggled on the wall. "Hold on!" Atonais said. "Let me try something!" He put out his hand and sent a pulse of lightning toward Lazarus. The vines released their hold on him, and the many weapons that had embedded themselves in them clattered to the ground.

Lazarus flexed his wrists and picked up a blade. With the other hand, he touched the skull of the skeleton at his feet, and when it crumbled, Flora saw him gather a handful of the bone dust. He hurled it onto the creatures, and they gurgled and moved back just enough for Lazarus to leap over the monsters and join Atonais and Flora.

"Bone dust," Lazarus said. "It turns them blue and makes them slower!"

Flora, too, grabbed a handful of bone dust and flung it at them. They fell back, blue in the places where the bone dust had hit them. "We must make a pathway to the candle!" she said.

"And what then?" Lazarus said. "Shortly, there will be no more light."

The candles were burning rapidly. The wax was dripping. The circles of light grew smaller, the room dimmer.

Atonais was lost in thought. "There is a way out... There is a way out... but what is it?"

The creatures began combining, congealing and growing larger like dew drops sliding together on morning grass, sliding toward them.

"We have to smash them," Flora said, standing on one side of Atonais. "It takes them a long time to get back together. Then we pour bone dust over them?" She glanced at Atonais.

"I don't know, I don't know!" he said. "I can't use my lightning, it just makes them bigger, and if I hit those black vines..."

"Whatever we do, we've got to do it fast," Lazarus said.

"At this rate, the light will be gone soon." He looked over his shoulder at Flora. "Are you ready?"

Flora nodded, and they each ran, smashing and splashing the acid creatures as they did. They fought hard, throwing their entire weight into their shield swings. Acid burned holes into Lazarus's boots, his cloak, his shirt, his skin. Flora swung the old silver shield, and she screamed as her arm was flecked with acid.

The room became darker as one of the candles snuffed itself out.

"Everyone, down!" Atonais said suddenly. He put his hand into the air and sent a concentrated pulse of lightning into the black vines on one side of the room. Weapons and helmets flew across the room at them, and Lazarus and Flora dove to the ground and covered their heads. The acid creatures, however, could not dodge the weapons, and they were flung backward. They splashed away from Lazarus and Flora and up against the vine-covered walls.

Before they congealed, Flora saw something. The monsters' splashings that had flown against the vines had left them gleaming and metallic: iron and copper. She looked up at the flowers, really looked at them, and saw that they were made of glass, like the globes in streetlamps and on the memory machine. "Atonais, look!" she shouted.

Atonais turned and his eyes grew wide. Flora watched them flicker to the place in the center of the floor, just beneath the cluster of flowers. "I understand now!" he said.

Another candle went out, and the darkness of the room was almost opaque.

Flora glanced to the door: They had a clear path.

Atonais saw it, too. He picked up a shield and dashed toward the center of the room where the wires were their densest, splashing monsters as he went.

"Atonais!" Flora screamed.

Lazarus saw the acid burn holes deep into his legs and robes, but Atonais did not stop running.

"To the door!" Atonais shouted. "Go now!"

They sprinted. The monsters, liquid and flowing, closed in on them. Flora and Lazarus sprinted around them, dove under their splatterings, ran to the door, and stood with their backs to it, their stolen shields facing outward.

In the center of the room, the monsters advanced on Atonais, ready to crash themselves over him, to eat away his flesh, to burn him to bone. They reared up in a great, cresting wave of acid.

Atonais looked up.

Then Atonais slammed his hands down on the knot of green copper wires.

His hair rose as though in a wind, and his body was racked as lightning poured out of him, through his hands, into the vines, and up into the curled white flowers. The green wire ceiling was suddenly aflame. A shower of sparks rained down like the night sky was breaking.

The flowers unfurled and bloomed into white, dazzling light, and as the monsters—all of them—gurgled and burned to nothing in the falling flames, the sound of gears and locks was heard above it all. Only then did Atonais fall to his knees in exhaustion and collapse. And as she and Lazarus went out through the door, Flora was sure she saw a smile on his lips.

CHAPTER TWENTY-SEVEN

THE DOOR TO THE SECOND CHAMBER SHUT BEHIND them, and they found themselves in the dark once again. Lazarus could feel it, alive and shifting all around them. He heard Flora give a hiss of pain through clenched teeth.

"Are you all right?" he asked.

"I'm fine," she said. But Lazarus could see the places where the acid had burned through her leggings and deep into her legs.

"Do you think Atonais will be all right?" Flora asked.

"He mastered the challenge," Lazarus said. "He'll be waiting for us when we come out, I bet. Are you sure you're all right?"

"I'm sure," she said unconvincingly. "I'm sure."

Then the room went black entirely, and once more they heard the sound of gears turning and stones grinding against one another. Lazarus thought he heard the soft *shing* of blades. He tried to calm his mind and not wonder what design the room would fall into next—which of them would be tested.

They didn't have to wait long. The ground rumbled, then steadied under their feet, and the blackness gave way to a wall with two doors and a torch burning between them. One door was tall and black and arched like a temple window. The other was rounded and ornate, painted a soft violet color. Carved above the black door was an hourglass, symbolizing him, he knew, and above the other was the symbol that the temple had adopted for Flora, the hand with ten stars. Lazarus shivered.

"It wants us to split up," Flora said. "I don't like this."

"I don't either," said Lazarus. "But we've come this far. We have to."

"On three," Flora said. "One...two...three."

Together they took a deep breath, then they moved forward and plunged through their doors.

Past Lazarus's was a long, dark room with a narrow path running down the middle. Dim light streamed foggily up from either side of the path, and Lazarus could see that the ceiling was long and arched, like the rib cage of a great stone snake. A thick gray dust seemed to appear from the air itself, and it covered everything. Lazarus found himself making small clouds rise when he so much as shifted his weight. The air was suddenly very dry and smelled of mildew and metal and dust.

"Well, this is a bit insulting," Lazarus said softly, his voice echoing in the silence.

"What?" came a voice from the other side of the wall, to his left.

"Flora?" Lazarus said. "You can hear me?"

"Yes," she said. "But there must be something wrong. Inside my door is just a gate with some kind of green burning torch at the top of it. I can only go a few feet. I can't open it."

"Try going back and come through my door," Lazarus said.

"I've tried that," Flora said. "The door is locked. I'm stuck in here. What's in your room?"

There were no vines here, nothing to hold on to, nothing to use. There was only the closed door behind him, the dark path before him, and Flora's voice somewhere beyond the wall. Then, far at the end of the path, he could make out a faint green glow.

"Wait a moment," Lazarus said. "I think I understand.

There's a green light on my side, too, at the end of a long path. I think I am supposed to go to that green light, and maybe, when I do, it will open your gate."

"Are you sure?" Flora said. "It's getting cramped in here."

"There's only one way to know," Lazarus said. He adjusted his hat and took a few steps down the path, leaving dark tracks in the thick dust.

Suddenly, he heard a sound and dodged something flying and sharp and metallic just in time. Another sound, another metallic thing flying at his throat. He dodged again and stood still. Then he took a few more steps forward, slowly, peering into the darkness. He could see slots in the walls that were, no doubt, filled with things that would fly out to kill him.

"What was that?" Flora said.

"Blades," Lazarus said. "If I go down this path, blades will fly out at me. If I move slowly, though, I think I can dodge them."

There was a grinding sound from the other side of the wall, a sound of stones sliding against one another.

"Oh no!" Flora said. "Oh gods!"

"What?" Lazarus said. "What's happening?"

"The walls!" Flora shouted. "The walls are closing in! They're getting closer! I'll be crushed!"

"Hold on!" Lazarus said. "I'm going to get you out of there!"

And Lazarus did the only thing he could think to do: He began to run.

He kicked off down the path, the sound of his boots echoing off the walls. The dust rose behind him in clouds, and from the walls, death came for him with claws bared.

"Hurry, Lazarus!" Flora shouted.

Blades pierced his arms, his legs, his chest as he ran. He saw his blood fly out from him and come back as his black clothes ripped and tore. Pain flared all over his body.

The air was full of more blades than he'd ever seen in his life. Dirks. Sabers. Sickles, falxes swung by unseen arms. He ducked under them, spun, and kept running. The pain made him feel like he was on fire. Still, he could not stop. When scythes swung from the ceilings, he jumped between them. When spikes rose from the floor, he leapt over them. When they dropped from the ceiling and pinned his cloak to the ground, he shrugged out of it and kept running.

Then a swinging blade hit him with the force of a battering ram. He flew backward and slid on the narrow path. Pain hit him so hard everything went white. He felt his spine in two pieces, felt his intestines spill into the dust. The blade had almost cut him in half. He dangled over the edge of the path, looking down into deep, black nothing. And all around him rose that horrible grinding sound of Flora's walls pressing in on her.

"Lazarus!" she shouted. "Hurry, please!"

Lazarus gagged from the pain. *Just a few yards more*, he thought as his body knitted itself back together. *A few blades more.*

He took a deep, chest-hurting breath of dusty air, and ran. The blades flew, but he ran faster and felt them fall from his healing body. He ran until all he could hear was the sound of his breathing and Flora's screams.

And then the blades stopped flying. He was at the gate, the iron-bar gate with the green light, a torch burning with a green flame. Now that he was closer, Lazarus could see that the door had no knob, no knocker, no way of opening it, unlike the others before it. There was only a lever. Lazarus scrabbled for it, pulling it downward with all his weight. A small alcove opened in the wall.

"Lazarus!" Flora shouted.

Lazarus's mouth was dry. He ignored the wounds knitting themselves back together and focused on solving the problem. At the foot of the alcove there was a rectangle of wood built into the wall, like a shelf or desk. And just beneath that was a cushioned bench.

"It wants me to kneel," he said, frantically feeling around the alcove. "But why? For what purpose?"

Then he felt it. A rope hung down out of the darkness. When he squinted upward, he could see the long, straight gleam of metal. A blade. A blade wide enough and sharp enough from the looks of it to cut through bone in a single downward blow. And it was designed to fall straight down and into the desk, right through where a kneeling person's neck would be. *I have to behead myself*, he realized.

"Lazarus, hurry!" Flora shouted.

Lazarus knelt in the alcove, his breath coming fast and sharp, his hands shaking.

Stop it, he told himself. *You'll live. You always do.* But the memory roared into his mind: Those drogs with their blue-fire eyes. The feeling of the blade slicing through him, bringing the darkness. His head falling one way and his body another. He had lived, but that moment, the moment of his death, had stayed with him longer than even his name.

"Lazarus, please!" Flora screamed.

Gritting his teeth, Lazarus reached for the rope and pulled. His last thought before the blade fell was *Please don't let me be too late*.

The walls were advancing on her. They were only shoulder-width apart. Flora braced herself against the walls, trying to push them apart with her legs. She felt as though she were suffocating. Her pulse ticked in her neck. Where was Lazarus? The walls moved closer and closer, pushing her knees toward her chin. Flora closed her eyes.

Then there was a metallic click. The walls creaked to a stop. The green torch at the top of the gate blew itself out and the gate swung open.

Gingerly, Flora stepped into the darkness beyond. The room whirred and clanked, then took shape before her. The room was long and low like a root cellar, lit by torches that hung along the walls, and in their flickering light, Flora crept the length of it, wary of blades that might fly from the ceiling like they had in Lazarus's room. No blades came, however, and she was able to move all the way to the end of the room, where the door to escape seemed to be comprised of a floor-to-ceiling tangle of black, wrought-iron bars and pipes that led to who knew what.

"Lazarus?" she tried.

There was no answer.

To her right, on the wall that separated her room from Lazarus's room, there was an iron grate with a lever next to it. Flora pulled the lever, and a long window stretching from where Flora stood all the way to the end of the room opened.

Flora peered through, not sure what to expect. Lazarus was kneeling inside an alcove. His head and shoulders weren't visible, but his legs and torso were ripped to shreds, bleeding from a score of healing wounds, some which were so deep they looked all but impossible. He was slumped as though dead, and for a moment Flora panicked, but then he began to stir. He fumbled around for something in front of him. There was a groan. A few moments later, he emerged from the alcove, looking pale and shaken as he fastened the bandages around his neck.

"Lazarus!" she shouted.

He turned and saw her and relief flooded over his face, restoring his color. "Oh, thank the gods," he said, coming to the window and embracing her. "I thought I might be too late."

"Don't worry about me," she said. She took him by the shoulders and looked into his eyes. "Are you all right?"

"Eh," he said. "I'll live."

Then she saw the door that rose behind him. It was an extension of her door: high and black and elaborate as a pipe organ, and it stretched all the way across the back wall. Up near the top, glass bulbs filled with red lightning spelled out the word *exchange*.

Lazarus followed her gaze. "That wasn't there before. It must have come on after I opened the door for you."

"So now I have to do something on my side," Flora said. She stood back and scanned the wall of pipes and bars. "But what?"

He leaned through the window. "Look up there," he said, pointing. "Does that look like a tank of some sort?"

High up toward the ceiling, there was what looked like a pane of glass, dark and shining. On the left side of the door, amid the pipes, was a pull-out basin, thin and slanted. The basin angled downward into a pipe. The pipe wound all the way to the tank.

"I think I have to fill the tank somehow using this basin," Flora said. "But there's no water or anything."

"Try some of this infernal dust," Lazarus said, brushing himself off.

Flora put a handful of dust into the basin, but when it hit the metal, it simply disappeared as though it had never been there at all. She furrowed her brows. Then, after a moment, she spat into it. Her saliva, too, disappeared as soon as it hit the basin.

"Seems to be picky," Lazarus said. "What if—" He made a disgusted face. "Ew, I hope you don't have to piss into it."

Flora shook her head. "There isn't a risk to that. It has to be something else."

She scrutinized the door and the basin. What could be an equivalent to Lazarus's side of the wall? Surely her puzzle would be something only she, of the two of them, could do. Her eyes narrowed. "I think I know what it wants." She pulled out her dagger and pricked her finger, and let a drop of blood fall into the basin. Just as she thought, it did not disappear. Flora rolled up her sleeve.

"What are you doing?" Lazarus leaned through the window. "Flora, the amount of blood it would take to fill that tank—"

"The tank doesn't look that big," she said. "Besides, I'm the only one who can bleed. I have to."

Before he could say anything else, she cut deeply into her arm. Her blood ran down into the basin. It disappeared into the pipe and appeared at the bottom of the tank, pooling there, almost black. Flora angled her arm so that none of it dripped onto the floor. Up it traveled, through the pipe, into the tank. Though the flow of blood was heavy, there was still so much space left to fill. The loss wouldn't kill her—she didn't think so, anyway. But it would weaken her. And who could guess what awaited one of them through the next door?

She could feel herself becoming faint. She knew that she should lie down, but she couldn't. "Lazarus," she said. "Talk to me."

He stood at the window, watching her blood fill the tank. "I can't think of anything to say," he said finally.

"What's your favorite color?" she asked. "Besides black, I mean. I don't think we've ever talked about usual things like that."

"Um...blue, maybe?" he said. "Yellow? I don't know."

"You don't know your own favorite color?"

"Well, you eliminated black. What am I supposed to say?" He paused, his young face pale, watching the blood. "You were right about me, you know. I really do just love a theme."

The tank was over halfway full. She began to shift from leg to leg. She remembered how it felt only a short time ago when she lay upon her makeshift bed in the Black Caravan, bleeding as Lazarus's medicine coursed through her. She remembered him hovering, tending to her gently, nervously, hardly saying a word. "Do you remember back in the beginning?" she asked, smiling a little. "How distant you were?"

"I didn't know what to do with you, what to say, how you'd react. I just did what I knew how to do: be aloof. Aloofer than aloof."

"I don't think *aloofer* is a word." She winced. Almost to the top now.

"Sure it is. Aloof, aloofer, aloofest?" His eyes flickered from her face to her bloody arm to her face again. "Almost there," he said gently.

"Almost there." She nodded, dizzy. "But don't worry. You improved with time."

"It's easier when you have someone like you to talk to," said Lazarus. When he spoke again, his voice was heavy. "I'll miss you, you know. Even though we don't want to talk about it, I think we both know that no matter who goes through the final door, there probably isn't a future where we see each other again after the final room of this temple."

Flora's heart gave a sharp jolt in her chest. He was right. No matter what wish was granted, this was likely to be the last time they saw each other. She thought of herself, a handmaiden again, back on a whole, undamaged Kaer-Ise. She thought of Lazarus, dead and buried beneath a tree somewhere with moss growing between his ribs and moonvines blooming over his grave, finally having the peace he deserved. "No. I don't think so."

"Still," he said. "It has been worth it. For me, anyway."

She wanted him in the room with her. She wanted him holding her, her head against his chest, listening to the sound of his heart. Then her arm went numb. "I can't feel it anymore," she said. "Does that usually happen?"

"It—it'll be all right," Lazarus said, his eyes on her paling skin. "Just a bit more."

The blood climbed toward the top of the tank. And then, miraculously, it was full. Flora withdrew her arm and closed the wound with her thumb. She stumbled to the window and held still as Lazarus fashioned her a bandage made from a long piece of cloth ripped from the hem of his tunic. She felt faint and she could barely walk, but the blood had stopped.

Behind the tank, a message written in lightning-filled bulbs flared into murky red light.

The wall between them lowered down into the floor and disappeared. Flora stumbled forward, and Lazarus caught her. She leaned against him, catching her breath.

As he held her close, the pipes and bars began to curl back like vines until an open, arched doorway appeared before them, the words *equal exchange* burning over it. Beneath the words, the pipes twisted themselves into their symbols: the hourglass and the hand full of stars.

"Equal exchange," Flora read. "What does that mean? Which of us is going forward?"

"I don't think this is over yet," Lazarus said. "I think we were tested together, and now we're going through to the last room together. Then the temple will make its decision."

Flora stared into the dark beyond the door, wondering what shape the next room would take.

"This is it," Lazarus said. "Can you walk?"

"I can," Flora said. "But stay with me anyway."

"Of course," he said. He extended the crook of his arm to her, and she took it. Together, they crossed under the archway.

CHAPTER
TWENTY-EIGHT

AFTER THE METALLIC GRINDING AND DARKNESS receded, they found themselves on a bridge, walking toward a high, flat piece of land. As soon as they stepped off the bridge, they felt grass and soft earth beneath their feet. Tall yellow grass grew, and a warm breeze blew, smelling of straw and vineyards and faraway smoke. It was just after sunset in this room, and there were high out-croppings of stone all around, dark and rough and mossy. They were on the top of a long, cliff-like peninsula, over-looking a bottomless black gorge.

"Valacia," Lazarus breathed, stepping forward into the grass. "As it was three hundred years ago. This is the field near my village. Yes, my village was just beyond these rocks! And this field...this field is the one that the cattle grazed in!"

Lazarus bent down to pick something up from the grass. When he rose, his clothing was different. Gone was the black and the hat and all of it, and in its place was a plain, rough-spun shirt and tan breeches tucked into boots. A sickle-like falx was in his hand, like the one-handed one he used as the Ankou, only this one was new and gleamed in the light.

"I haven't seen a falx like this in at least a hundred years," Lazarus said. "I have to get mine specially made." He turned it over in his hands, letting the warm light of sunset glint along the blade.

He scanned the cliffs ahead, excitedly pointing to where this would be and that should be. He looked so young, so at home that all Flora could do was watch him and marvel.

This is the Lazarus he used to be, Flora realized with a pang of emotion she didn't recognize. *Lazarus before he was Lazarus.* She wished, despite everything, that he could be this version of himself again. Then she saw the bandages at his throat, covering the scar that had made him who he was.

There was the familiar sound of stones sliding against one another. A stone bridge assembled itself across the gorge from the Valacia cliff to another mass of land. It was a clearing bordered by forest, a clearing she knew like she knew her own body, and the smell coming from it was a heart-wrenching mixture of green grass, violets, the sea.

"Kaer-Ise," she whispered. "Betheara's clearing."

Flora drifted forward as the bridge laid stone after stone in front of her. Her clothing changed as Lazarus's had as she walked, changing from her ripped, stained tunic and leggings and boots to a gown, white and embroidered with unicorns and cresting waves. Her feet were bare and the stones were cool underfoot. But her hair remained the same, short, shaggy hair that she'd had for the past few months, and the scars on her palm remained. *No*, she thought, *magic can't remove scars like ours.* Then she stopped still on the bridge, breath caught in her throat.

In the middle of the clearing in front of her was a large white stone with something golden glinting on the ground beside it. Flora knew, even from the bridge, what it was. Dread enveloped her like a storm cloud.

"Flora, what is it?" Lazarus asked, moving toward her through the tall grass.

It was a bridle. A bridle made of purest gold, spun into threads and braided, just as her ancestors had done for centuries, into rope. The only thing in the world that could hold a unicorn. And as fireflies floated around the stone, and crickets and nightbirds sang in the trees, she knew that this was a test that she could never hope to pass.

"It's my Calling," Flora choked. She turned back toward him. "Lazarus, I can't go over there. I can't do it. There's got to be a mistake."

Lazarus came to her on the bridge and took her hands in his. "This temple doesn't make mistakes," Lazarus said. "It tests us, yes, but only in ways we can overcome, remember? You can do this. You can."

"But I'm not..." She pulled away from him, her eyes on the clearing. There was a dull ache in her heart that rose to sit in her throat. "I'm not virtuous. Not anymore. I *can't*, Lazarus."

"What does virtue mean anyway?" Lazarus asked. "You're the most virtuous person I've ever met, and I've met a lot of people. Come on. Try. For me. And if not for me, try for the princess." He let her hand fall and stepped back off the bridge into Valacia.

With her hand on the railing, she walked toward the stone and the illusion of Kaer-Ise. Soon she felt soft black earth underfoot, clover still wet from rain. Night had fallen on this side of the bridge, and fireflies rose around her, blinking into the darkness. Back across the bridge, in the sunset light, Lazarus stood among the tall grass, watching.

Flora took a deep breath and went to the alabaster stone. She took the golden bridle in her hand, and she sat as straight as she could, feeling the soft metal warming in her hands. She was supposed to sing the song, the sacred, wordless song of the maidens, but her head echoed with *impure*, *filthy*, and *impostor*. Still, she tried. She closed her eyes and, very faintly, began the song. She sang as well as she could, but something wound tight in her chest, and a lump grew in her throat, and when she reached the final aria, she broke into sobs.

"How can I do this?" She wept. "How can I ever hope to do this?"

A mist had fallen on the middle of the bridge. Lazarus stood at the edge of it, but when he tried to come to her through the mist, he stopped short. "I can't move past this fog," Lazarus said. "You have to do it without me. But you can do it! You can—"

Thunder rumbled overhead. The wind changed. It grew warmer, and it carried an unmistakable smell: decaying flesh. Across the misty bridge, she saw two shadows rise from the earth behind Lazarus, shadows with yawning mouths and blue-fire eyes.

"Lazarus!" she cried. "Look out!"

Lazarus turned just in time to block a stroke from the first drog, then ducked under a blow from the second.

There they were: the creatures from his deepest, most horrifying memories, as real as his blood, as real as his bones. But he was not some young man now, frightened by the sight of blood. He was the Ankou of Valacia, the deathless death, and he faced them down with his falx as he wished he had done three hundred years ago.

But they turned from him, moving through the tall grass toward the misty bridge. Toward Flora. And somehow Lazarus knew that the mist would not stop them as it had stopped him.

Lazarus didn't have time to think. He had to draw them away from the bridge. He ran and leapt in front of them, his falx clanging as the first blocked his strike. The second lunged for him, and he sliced half the ribs from its right side. The creature screamed and began to follow him away from the bridge.

The first drog went for him, and as Lazarus dodged again, the drog's ax sliced deep into his arm. But this time, Lazarus didn't feel the sensation of the wound knitting together. This time, the blood flowed free. Horror twisted his stomach.

They can kill me, Lazarus realized. All the fear, all the panic from three hundred years ago came roaring back to him, along with a new one that rang in his head like a bell. *And if they kill me, they will kill Flora, too.*

The drogs advanced on him, their jaws opening

wide, wider than any human mouth could stretch. Their eyes burned blue-hot.

"Keep singing!" he shouted to Flora. "Call the unicorn! It's the only way!"

Roaring, the drogs raised their axes, and as they came for him, Lazarus gritted his teeth and stood his ground, determined, for the first time in three hundred years, not to die.

On the other side of the bridge, Flora watched as Lazarus jumped and slashed, feinted and spun. Blood flowed from wounds on his arm, his shoulder, his face—wounds that weren't healing.

Desperately, Flora ran to the bridge and into the fog. When she touched it, it was a solid, invisible wall. She could go no farther. Lazarus was a brilliant fighter, but the drogs were fast, strong, fueled by eternal hatred. It was only a matter of time until they got the better of him, until they killed him and left him to be claimed by the temple.

"Damn it!" Flora shouted at the temple. "What am I supposed to do?!"

In her heart, though, she knew what she was supposed to do. The only things that killed the drogs three hundred years ago were the unicorns, called by Kaer-Isian unicorn maidens. She had to call a unicorn. There was no other way.

Beyond the bridge, Lazarus screamed as a drog sliced across his back; then he spun and knocked the drog backward.

Flora ran back to the alabaster stone and took the bridle in her hand again. She screwed her eyes shut, trying not to concentrate on the clanging of blades, the roaring of the drogs. Over all of it she sang the old songs, desperately, fervently. *Please,* she thought. *Please, please, please, just come to me. I know I'm not virtuous anymore, but please come to me. Come to me.*

She heard Lazarus scream again. But she kept singing. Tears began to well in her eyes. *How can I do it?* she thought. *How can I ever hope to do this?*

She felt a shadow pass over her, smelled the scent of smoke, sweat, and fur. Horror roiled in her belly. She didn't have to look to know who was standing behind her.

The Skaardmen. They were there. She could feel Their shadows growing. The temple had made Them real, had brought Them here, where everything depended on what They had taken from her. They had come to finish what They started.

She felt one of Them lean closer, could smell his fetid breath. She could almost feel his hand on her shoulder.

"What pretty hair you've got, Princess," said the voice that haunted her nightmares. "No, not the princess, are you? Just a handmaiden. A handmaiden with no family, no one to serve. No virtue. There's nothing of value left to take from you."

Then something lit in Flora's heart like a match. "You're wrong," Flora growled.

She felt the hand halt, inches away.

"I am a monster-slayer now, the Ankou's assistant, the survivor of Kaer-Ise, and some things can never be lost or taken. Not even here."

The golden bridle in her hand began to burn. And though her eyes were closed, she knew that something had changed. She heard Their footsteps as They faltered, took steps back. She opened her eyes and turned to look into Theirs, to know Their fear of her.

But They were gone, and in Their place was something else. Out of the trees it stepped soundlessly, its cloven hooves making no indention on the ground. It glowed with the light of a hundred moons, soft, luminous. It lowered its head and came to her. The grass, the flowers, the trees, everything seemed to grow toward it as though it were the sun itself.

Truly, it thrummed in her bones, *you are a virtuous Daughter of Emir.*

Tears welled in her eyes.

Across the bridge, the drogs had pinned Lazarus down. One of them was raising an ax.

"Go!" she commanded the unicorn. "Save him! Now!"

The unicorn turned from her, and with her head high and heart full, Flora watched as the unicorn she had called streaked away from her like lightning. It fell on the drogs like a comet, spearing them on its horn and kicking them in half with its hooves. Yowling, the drogs fell to ashes all around Lazarus.

He rose from the grass, dazed and wondering, looking around for the beast made of light that had saved him. And it was only after, when her Calling gown faded back into her normal clothes and the unicorn faded to moth dust and blew away in the disappearing fog, that Flora realized her face was wet with tears.

Lazarus was coming across the bridge, back in the ripped black clothes that suited him so well, immortal again as the wounds the drogs had left him began to heal.

"I did it!" Flora wept. "I did it, Lazarus!"

"Of course you did." He smiled. "Why would you ever doubt it? I never did."

She ran to the bridge to meet him, to wipe the blood from his face and tell him all about the unicorn and the Skaardmen and all of it. But just as she reached the bridge, the telltale ringing of stones rose over everything else.

The final door was building itself.

As Flora watched, the bridge grew a fork, branching out from the middle where Lazarus stood to the door appearing in the open air.

Flora knew that out on the bridge, Lazarus was thinking what she was: *This is it. The final door. My last chance for a miracle.* And Flora's heart felt pulled so tight that she wasn't sure which miracle she wanted anymore, if she wanted one at all. All she could do was stand and watch, silent as the stones came together into a high, arched door in the nothingness. Above it, a blank stone readied itself for the symbol that would call one of them beyond the door to achieve his or her greatest desire.

Flora held her breath, trying not to think, to hope, to dread. She looked at Lazarus. *This is the end*, she thought. Gravely, he nodded, as though he had heard her. Then, before their eyes, a symbol appeared, stark on the pale stone above the door, and Flora felt all the air leave her lungs.

It was an hourglass. An unmistakable hourglass, carved deep into the stone.

So this was how it ended. This was the end of the Ankou, the end of Kaer-Ise, the end of being the Ankou's assistant. From this moment, she would truly be alone. But Lazarus would finally be at peace after so long, and though it made her heart ache, she knew that it was what he needed. *Go*, she thought. *Go and win your death.*

But Lazarus turned from the door. Instead, he continued across the bridge to where Flora stood, weak and burned and bleeding in her ripped tunic and boots.

"What are you doing?" she asked. "You have to go. You've been chosen."

"You deserve this, too, Flora," he said. "You called a unicorn. Not just anyone can do that. It's not right."

"I'll be fine," she said, faking a smile. "I promise. I'll miss you every day. Maybe for as long as I live, but it's the only way. So what are you waiting for?"

Without another word, he leaned in and kissed her. He kissed her deeply, hungrily, a kiss that felt both like the first time and the last because it was both. And when the kiss broke, they stood with their foreheads touching, thinking of what could have been if things had just been a little different.

She pulled her pincushion from her pocket and put it in his hand. "Here," she said. "To remember me by."

"Goodbye, Flora," he said finally.

"Goodbye, Lazarus," she whispered.

Then Lazarus turned and walked up to the door that bore his symbol. He hesitated just for a moment, then he pushed the door open and went through.

CHAPTER
TWENTY-NINE

B EYOND THE DOOR, THE BETWEEN EXPANDED BEFORE Lazarus in all its beautiful, terrible vastness, that dark infinity he knew so well. But he was not stuck this time. He streaked onward toward the end, and it seemed that everything was open to him—all the worlds, everything that had ever been.

And suddenly he was somewhere else entirely: a grassy hillside in that time of day when everything is gold. And he was not alone.

Ana was both impossibly different and exactly as he remembered her all at once. Not as beautiful as he had built her in his mind. He could see an odd sharpness to her nose now, a narrowness of her eyes, a slight weakness of her chin that he would have been incapable of noticing before. But more surprising was that all the anger that had been in him was gone.

"I'm sorry for the pain I have caused you," she said, her voice clear and sad.

"It's all right," Lazarus said, and, somehow, strangely, it was. "I've forgiven you."

"I don't deserve to be forgiven," she said.

"No one *deserves* it," said Lazarus. "But I've chosen to forgive you, nonetheless."

He sat down and she sat beside him, not touching him, not looking at him, nor he at her. Everything had changed between them. Something was gone now, irretrievable and far away, but he did not miss it, nor want it again, and he could tell that she did not either.

They watched the wind move the grass on the ground and the clouds in the sky. "Is this what is beyond the Between?" asked Lazarus.

"If you want to call it that, yes," she said. "It is the place that we all go, one day or another. Even you."

"I remembered my name," he said to her. "When I passed through the Between, I remembered it. It was Radu. Radu Ionasca."

"That is not your name anymore. You've made a new truth for yourself."

He heard his own voice ring out over the hills. *Lazarus.* Three times.

"Don't you remember?" she asked. "If you say something three times, it makes it true."

"Witchery," Lazarus said.

"Maybe."

"Why didn't Ankou become my true name?" Lazarus asked. "I've introduced myself by it for centuries."

"Because it's a title," Ana said. "A title is something you wear, not who you are."

The wind blew over the hills and the long grass was swept into waves like the ocean.

"What will happen now?" Lazarus asked.

"You have a wish to make," Ana said, pushing the hair out of her eyes. She reached into her pocket and pulled out a tiny hourglass, much like the one he wore around his neck. "Are you ready for your death?"

Lazarus looked out over the fields and tried his hardest to feel at peace, tried his hardest to want the death that had eluded him for so long.

He sighed. "I can't, Ana."

Ana took a deep breath and smiled a sad sort of smile. "I know," she said. "I had hoped you'd wish to start over. Here, with me, so I could have a second chance. So I could do it right this time. But our love is gone."

"It never was love," Lazarus said. "We wanted it to be love, but it wasn't. We didn't know how to love then, so instead it became something dark, something harmful."

"Yes," she said sadly. "I know."

"I kept it up as long as I could, even so." He handed her the portrait he had drawn. "But in the end..."

"I know," she said. She took it and looked at it for a moment. Then she kissed him on the cheek. "I forgive you, too."

They sat there for a few moments more. Then Ana said, "I know the wish that is on your heart. It is a good one, a noble one. But you must understand what will happen." Ana paused. "The world will go on as always. The problems your mage friend and the king of Parth surmounted with Flora's help will be surmounted still, as Fate intended. But when you leave the temple, you will find that they will have been surmounted through different routes. The world will be different and yet the same. And only you and your mage friend will have any memory of how things were."

"And Flora?" Lazarus asked.

"She will not know you," Ana said. "Because you will have never met. Only you and your mage will remember anything about what has happened here. You will still have had a great adventure, but she will never have taken part in it."

The wind blew cold.

"I understand," said Lazarus. "But it's the right thing. For everyone."

"What about you?" Ana asked. "What will you do for yourself?"

Lazarus considered this. "I'll stay in the temple. I can't turn into a drog if time doesn't pass."

"Are you sure?" Ana asked.

Lazarus imagined life in the temple—eternal life, without daily death. He imagined wandering alone among the columns, hearing his own voice echo through the silence until he forgot how to speak. Alone for eternity. It was a harrowing thought. But he had been alone before, had always assumed that he would be alone. And the prophecy . . . It had only said that he *could* die, not that he *would*. What was death to him if Flora could be happy again?

"I'm sure," he said.

Ana looked him in the eyes, and a softness came into her voice. "This is real love, then," she said.

"Yes," Lazarus said. "This is real love."

Ana gently dropped the hourglass into his hand. "Then make your wish."

Lazarus took the hourglass and held it in his hand. Closing his eyes, he made the wish that had been in his heart since he set foot in the temple.

There was a great, thunderous rumbling of magic, world-bending magic that could alter space and time. Lazarus felt the familiar tugging at the marrow of his bones. The hill faded, then, and Ana with it. But he could still feel the breeze, and on it he heard her words.

"I will not doom you," she said. "For all of me you will not suffer more. Go and live. Live well."

And he let himself fall back into his bones, back into his body, to rebuild one last time.

When Lazarus walked through the doorway, he found himself back in the temple. He looked around for Flora for a moment, but already, he could feel her absence. She was gone, just as he'd wished. Only Atonais was there, singed and dirty but alive.

Atonais ran to meet him. "What happened? Did you receive the Artifact?" He looked behind Lazarus. "Where's Flora?" He searched Lazarus's face, read the strange expression he was wearing. "She's gone," Atonais breathed, "...isn't she?"

"I made a wish," Lazarus said, "for the Kaer-Isian Massacre to have never happened. Kaer-Ise will still be thriving, the royal family still alive, and Flora..." He sighed. "She will still be a handmaiden, serving the princess, at home with her people again. Only we will remember what really happened."

"And this is what you wanted?" Atonais said.

"I want a lot of things," Lazarus said. "But I was in a position to undo everything horrible that had happened to her and make everything right again. How could I do otherwise?"

Atonais said nothing, but Lazarus could tell by the sympathy in his eyes that he understood. Lazarus was happy, knowing that Flora was safe, that her people would live, that she would not have to face the agony that had brought her to him. But, gods, how he missed her already. He reached for his hourglass necklace and drew back with a yelp of pain.

Sometime during the trials of the temple, the hourglass had burst. All the sand had fallen from it and now it was nothing more than a few shards of broken glass in a frame. Ana, he thought. He searched his pocket, but the portrait of Ana was gone, as he somehow knew it would be.

"I'm beginning to feel it now," Atonais said, his hand to his forehead. "The change. It's like a new set of memories is growing alongside my own. If I wasn't here in the temple myself, I'd swear that everything since the massacre was only a dream."

Lazarus began to feel it, too: History retelling itself, happier, less savage. Memories he had made with Flora, fighting the mountain monsters, meeting the Bugyl Noz, going to Parth, even the trials of the temple itself, were rewriting themselves in his mind and on the fabric of space and time beyond the temple. It was as Atonais said: There were two versions of the truth, one with Flora and one without her. But no matter how the memories changed, her face did not fade from his memory. It hurt, but he was glad of it. After all they had been through, he did not want to forget.

"Lazarus," Atonais said. "I think you're bleeding."

On his fingertip where he had pricked himself was a bead of swelling, dark blood. He waited, but the bead of blood did not disappear. Slowly, Lazarus turned his hand over and let the blood fall in a single round red drop to the floor. "I am mortal now," he said, smiling a sad, hollow smile. "After all of this, I am mortal now."

"But if you wished for Flora's wish instead," Atonais muttered, "then how..."

Lazarus knew. He remembered Ana's words, *For all of me you will not suffer more.* After three hundred years, Ana had lifted her curse.

"Come," Lazarus said to Atonais. "There's nothing left for us in this place."

It was still dark outside, and the desert plants were still curled closed from the night. In the distance, the sky had just begun to lighten. The king sat half-asleep on a blanket and watched as the eagles slept, perched high on the rocks and cliffs nearby. When they went out onto the temple steps, one of the eagles raised its head and called to them.

The king shook herself awake and came to meet them. "You are alive!" the king said. "Does this mean that you made it into the last chamber? You received it?"

"Yes," Lazarus said. "But it was Flora who received the boon, not I."

The king glanced behind them at the closed doors of the temple, confused. "Who?"

A jolt of pain shot through Lazarus's heart. He opened his mouth to explain, but Atonais answered instead. "It's a long story," Atonais said. "I'll tell you all about it while I can still remember."

The king looked from Lazarus to Atonais and back to Lazarus again, confused, but in the end, she and Atonais left Lazarus alone with his thoughts.

The sky was growing brighter. Dawn was coming. Three hundred years of experience told Lazarus to run for cover, to lock himself away so that no one would see when Death came and took him apart. But not this morning. This morning, he would wait. Lazarus sat down on the steps of the temple, his eyes on the horizon.

He reached into his pocket, hoping that Flora's

pincushion hadn't disappeared as well. He took it out and held it, grateful that at least he had this to remember her by.

There was a quivering of gold, almost as though the sun were hesitant. But then it rose. It leaked over the horizon like the yolk of an egg, and it seemed to spread in streaks across the sky. And as the shifting light washed over him, Lazarus did *not* fall, he did *not* die, he did *not* go to bones. He simply watched it rise. And as he sat there with Flora's pincushion in his hand, he knew that, for the first time in a long time, everything was truly going to be all right.

EPILOGUE

THREE MILES FROM THE PORT CITY OF NORMYND, in a forest full of whispering leaves, the Black Caravan stood alone in the dim light just before dawn. It was still solid black, but all along the windows and sides of the caravan all sorts of vines grew from boxes now, curling their way up to the roof. When the sun rose in earnest, they would bloom in elaborate sprays of white and yellow and purple rarely seen outside the gardens of Parth.

Though the caravan remained one of the greatest mysteries of Valacia, the stories about the one who drove it had changed. There were still stories of the Ankou being a rake who stole young girls' souls, but new stories had begun to circulate, too—stories in which the Ankou was the source of the mended relations with Parth, in which the Ankou broke a curse placed on him by a witch, in which there were now a thousand different reasons for the Ankou to suddenly be able to travel during the daytime. The people in the various villages he passed certainly seemed less afraid of him, at any rate, and only rarely did he see a salt line in front of a doorway.

Lazarus thought this last thing was probably due to Atonais and the groundbreaking thesis he had written about their travels before he took a job in King Ulalume's court, aiding the reintroduction of magic into Parthan technology. Lazarus had not read the book, which detailed their travels without Flora, the version of history that had happened now. He wasn't ready for that yet. But Atonais had sent him a copy, inscribed, *To the greatest hero of Valacia. May you have peace. Dr. Atonais Kell, Order of Lightning, First Class, Royal Ambassador to Parth.* Lazarus wondered how Atonais's family felt about him now.

It was early springtime in the north, and since he had returned from the Temple of Fates, Lazarus had already had to cut his hair twice—something that he botched the first time and got better at the second before deciding that his usual haircut suited him best. This, he supposed, he would just have to get used to as a renewed, permanent mortal. Shaving, however, was proving to be something else entirely.

"Ouch! Damn it!" Lazarus said as he nicked himself again with his razor. He reached for the bottle of arrowroot powder beside his dresser and dabbed some onto his cut. "I don't see how anybody does this regularly."

There was a stirring outside, and Nik whinnied. Tal was fussing, too, stamping his hooves and huffing excitedly.

"Just a moment," Lazarus said. "Ever since we started traveling during the day the two of you have been intolerable. You'll have to adjust to this schedule eventually, you know. The Ankou is available at all times, day or night."

Lazarus looked into the mirror again. It would take time to get used to not wrapping his neck with bandages every day, but for some reason, his scar did not repulse him as it had before.

He threw on the sleek black clothes and broad black hat that were still his trademark and fastened his falx at his belt. He stopped for a moment to look at the new portrait that hung tacked to the wall beside his mirror. A pang of sadness rippled through his heart as it always did when he looked at it, and he chided himself for his masochism. From the crisp white parchment, a drawing of Flora looked out, rendered in charcoal and pencil, her hair curling in the light. He could never really capture how it had looked, how fiery it had been and how beautiful, but he remembered her face and her voice and her ways, and that was enough.

Outside the horses whinnied again, and Lazarus said, "All right, all right. I'm coming."

He threw open the door and stepped out into the cool morning air.

He went to the horses and stroked their manes. "Shhh," he said. "Shhh. You've already been fed. What is it?"

"Ankou?" said a voice from the forest.

He turned and squinted into the trees. There, between two birches, stood a figure wearing a tunic, breeches, and a faded blue cloak still wet from the rain that had fallen during the night. This figure in the early morning should have shocked him, but her footfalls, her movements were as familiar to Lazarus as his own. Impossibly, she was here. Even before she took off her hood, he knew her. And when she did so, her red hair fell into her eyes—very short now. His heart leapt. Flora must have been able to have her Calling after all. He started to rush to her to tell her all the things that had happened since the Temple of Fates, but then he remembered. She did not know him anymore.

"Thank goodness I've found you, Ankou," Flora said to him, coming forward. "I've been looking for you for weeks."

"What can I do for you, handmaiden?" he asked. "You're a long way from Kaer-Ise. Is everything all right there?"

"It is," she said. "Everything on Kaer-Ise is good. The princess is getting married soon, to a young man from Parth."

"I heard," Lazarus said. "Congratulations to her."

"Everyone is going wild about it in Kaer-Ise." Flora smiled. "It's royal wedding this, royal wedding that. I've been helping the princess pick out flowers and dresses and cakes." Her smile softened. "But alongside all of that, all the happiness, there is something else, something wrong. Wrong with me, I think. In all my dreams, for months now, I see monsters, fire, death. I see eagles and deserts and forests. I feel a sword in my hand. But more than anything else, I see . . . you. So I felt—I knew— that I had to come find you."

There was a painful twist in Lazarus's chest. "You must be mistaken," he said. "I sometimes appear in people's dreams, yes, but only to . . . er . . . steal their souls. But now that you have complained, I will stop it immediately so you can have peace."

She looked at him as though she were reading him, then smiled. "That's not right," she said. "You don't steal anyone's souls. You're not a rake or a ghost or a villain. You're . . . Lazarus. And I know you."

She held out her hand and opened her palm. Despite all the magic the temple had spent, the constellations of pinpricks remained.

"This is how I know it's true," she said. "All of it. The destruction of Kaer-Ise, the journey we took, Atonais, the Temple of Fates. Your curse and my part in it. I remember all of it like the clearest dream, but now that I see you, I know more than I've ever known anything that this is the truth."

"But how?" Lazarus asked. "Why? After all I did so that you could have a life without all that, why didn't you just forget like you were supposed to?"

"I think that, no matter how strong the magic, some things are meant to stay with us." She took a deep, shaking breath and continued. "And I think that, because of all of it, Kaer-Ise isn't the place for me anymore."

"What are you saying?" Lazarus asked.

"I want to live the life I had," Flora said. "I want to come back, if you'll have me."

Lazarus's chest gave a painful squeeze. "It isn't about me, Flora. This is about you. There are millions of lives you could have, millions of partners out there—men and women alike—who don't have three hundred years of bad memories to wake screaming from. Millions of people who don't fight dangerous creatures for a living, or who—"

"Who know how to shave?" Flora smirked.

"It's harder than it looks, all right?" Lazarus absently wiped the blood from his chin. "Flora, I wished for everything to be *right* for you. I wished to give you a life you deserved."

"Why can't this be it?"

"Flora, I—" Lazarus began, but before he could protest further, Flora leaned up and kissed him softly. He kissed her back, and as they let themselves fall into kissing, a feeling he hadn't realized he missed washed over him, warm and comforting. A feeling of coming home.

Maybe this could *be it*, he thought suddenly. Maybe it really was that easy. Maybe this time all that stood in their way was letting themselves be happy.

Their embrace finally broke, and when it did, they simply stood there for a moment, Flora leaning against him as they watched the horses cropping the clover in the light of the rising sun. *Yes*, Lazarus thought. *This is how mornings should begin.*

"What's the mission for today?" Flora asked.

"Kelpies this time." He pulled his black book from his pocket. "Four of them in a stream, awake and hungry with the melting snow. They're absolutely terrorizing a village a little east of here. Lots of blood. Lots of intestines floating in streams. That sort of thing."

"Do you want help?" she asked. "I'm good at this, aren't I?"

"I want everything you are willing to offer," he said. "And I will give everything I have in return. That's my bargain this time." He extended his hand to her. "Do you accept?"

"Yes," she said, putting her hand in his. "But only if you agree to come to Beth's wedding with me. Want to be my date?"

"Well, obviously," said Lazarus. "I love any chance to dress up. Won't the other handmaidens talk if you show up to a wedding with the Ankou?"

"Let them talk." Flora beamed. "I don't mind. Just make sure not to upstage the bride." She pushed back her cloak and he could see her handmaiden sword winking in its scabbard. "We should probably get started, huh?"

"Don't worry," Lazarus said. "We have all the time we want now."

"That's something I could definitely get used to," Flora said.

They stood there for a few moments more, drinking in the closeness and the coolness and the morning. And with that, the two of them set off into the forest, side by side, leaving the Black Caravan where it sat, its flowers opening toward the light of dawn.

ACKNOWLEDGMENTS

I would like to let it be known that this book, whatever you thought of it, is the book of my heart. These characters simply appeared one day in my mind when I was twelve and have lived there ever since. As I grew and learned and loved and experienced pain, they changed, grew, and deepened with me. This book is the first book I ever wrote, and I rewrote it seven times. I learned to write by writing this book. My characters learned their grief and trauma and resilience as I experienced those things in my own life. This book is for me. It is mine, more than I think anything else in the world could ever be. It is, in so many ways, the essence of who I am now, who I have become. However, it is not only to me that this book owes its existence.

Thank you first to my agent, Sara Crowe, who fell in love with my characters before anyone else in the publishing world. You have been a steadfast, determined ally and advocate, and have fought for me and Lazarus and Flora in ways that I have rarely been fought for in the past. You are wonderful and I will always owe you so much. Thank you to Hallie Tibbetts, my editor, who took on this book after the enormous acquisition of Disney Hyperion by Little, Brown Books for Young Readers. You didn't choose this book, but rather inherited it, and you took on the project with such professionalism and aplomb it often seemed like you *had* chosen it after all. Also, we're *Watership Down* buddies, and those are few and far between.

Thank you to my family, particularly my parents and Aunt Diane, who have always enthusiastically encouraged me to become a writer, not because it would one day make me rich, but because it would make me happy. Your encouragement has meant so much, and I am so fortunate to have a family that supports my dreams. I love you.

Thank you to my friends as well. To Ramsey Knighton, my best friend, who has been one of the few constants in my life. I promise to always return the favor. To Brandon Stewart, a fellow artistic soul, who is always excited about my work, no matter how weird it is—you are also weird and wonderful! To Aimee and Autumn and Jenn, and the other VCFA MAGIC IFs, thank you for reading countless versions of this book, listening to my complaints, celebrating my successes, and getting me out of publishing's various quagmires, both real and imagined. YAM.

Also to VCFA, thank you to Mark Karlins, April

Lurie, Susan Fletcher, and Louise Hawes, my four advisors throughout my MFA, and to VCFA itself for fostering such joy, wonder, and creativity.

Without all of you, the realization of this multi-decade dream would not be possible. I love you all. Thank you.

Sincerely,
Kate Pentecost

Vic Clark Photography

KATE PENTECOST

was born and raised on the Texas/Louisiana border but has lived in many different places. She holds an MFA in Writing for Children & Young Adults from Vermont College of Fine Arts. She currently lives in Houston with her dog, Stevie Nyx, and has plans to build her own Black Caravan, just for the fun of it.